Fathers
and
Brothers
and
Sons

You can find more of John Andes's work at
www.crimenovelsonline.com

Fathers
and
Brothers
and
Sons

John E. Andes

FATHERS AND BROTHERS AND SONS

iUniverse books may be ordered through booksellers or by contacting:

iUniverse
1663 Liberty Drive
Bloomington, IN 47403
www.iuniverse.com
844-349-9409

Because of the dynamic nature of the Internet, any web addresses or links contained in this book may have changed since publication and may no longer be valid. The views expressed in this work are solely those of the author and do not necessarily reflect the views of the publisher, and the publisher hereby disclaims any responsibility for them.

Any people depicted in stock imagery provided by Getty Images are models, and such images are being used for illustrative purposes only. Certain stock imagery © Getty Images.

ISBN: 978-1-6632-4422-2 (sc)
ISBN: 978-1-6632-4423-9 (e)

Print information available on the last page.

iUniverse rev. date: 08/15/2022

Dedicated to more than three hundred years
of fathers and brothers and sons.

M

J

S

D

V

W

E   W   R   T

W   P   J   N

T

I

Chapter One

Millenia ago, wolves slept near the camps of the hunters and gathers, who fed them scraps from the most recent kill. The animals were an early warning system because they growled and barked to awaken the humans if a larger beast were to come near the camp. Today in central Pennsylvania it was different. Today wolves were about to drive small forest animals away from the safety of their warrens and burrows. Initially, the noise coming from the drivers was so deep and the volume so low that it was felt more than heard. As the source of the reverberation came closer to the small quarry, the grumble had become a deep throated growl. Low hanging leaves quivered and the forest floor detritus twitched. The growling was generated by thirteen wolves. The alpha was larger than the other twelve. Never howling or barking, the wolves snarled causing the small animals to panic. Some stood stock still, shivering and peering left and right to get a glimpse of the noise. Some had since left the safety of their nests and were scurrying about … in no particular direction. The noise had become a loud growl. The pack had formed a semi-circle that was gradually shrinking and pushing the quarry toward an open area in front of a cottage that sat on the edge of a lake. The pack was driving the rabbits, chipmunks, possums, skunks, and raccoons onto a killing field. Peering down onto the open space from the surrounding trees, medium sized birds of prey sat quietly while much larger birds circled. The avian armada awaited the arrival of their feast.

Sitting at the table in the breakfast room, the old man stared at his breakfast, a large mug of coffee, a small slice of quiche, an orange, and an onion bagel. No butter or cream cheese. He made the quiche using Mary's recipe that included mushrooms, bacon, and broccoli. This substantial meal, plus a protein bar, would have to carry him from five-thirty am until lunch, most likely after one pm.

The stillness of the kitchen and peacefulness of his thoughts were shattered by an intense two-second flash of lightning and six seconds of roiling thunder. The splitting noise started far away and became a big boom somewhere near the city. The celestial intrusion into Joe's morning musing caused his head to snap and the hairs on his arms to stand. A chill ran through his body. The bright light and noise were signs of a large and aggressive summer storm. A storm that could make driving to the cottage difficult for him and slow the travel of his brood coming from out of state. Hopefully, the wind and rain would not make impassable the narrow dirt road that led to the family cottage.

During mornings like this, his mind skipped around like drops of water on a hot griddle – miscellaneous people, places, and things were somehow connected. He envisioned people simultaneously from the here and now and the past. These people then connected to others who connected to events that led his thoughts to collateral events, and so on and so on. His mind was sharp. It sought connections. As he took the first bite of the quiche, his eyes moved to an array of critical items for his ten-day trip ... two manila envelopes, bottles of twenty-five year old scotch, a box of protein bars, and his medications.

Some meds he took twice daily. Some once. Two years ago, he mentioned increasing fatigue and strange stomach uneasiness to his lifelong friend and doctor for the past thirty years. After the routine physical, the doctor sent the patient to see a specialist. That visit included an excruciatingly detailed work-up, a disconcerting diagnosis, and a prescribed regimen of medications to relieve the discomfort and delay the inevitable. Not to prevent the occurrence of it but simply to minimize the accompanying pain. Since that time, the regimen has been modified; some meds were dropped, and new ones added. Some pill dosages were increased, as was their intake frequency. Both men felt the inevitable could be stalled, at least temporarily, but the patient required a check-up every four months. Joe jokingly referred to the variety of pills as his sprinkles. He just couldn't put them on his nightly ice cream.

Since the beginning of the pill regimen, he had become tired more easily, thus requiring him to take naps. He was told this would happen. These were not long sleeps, but deep thirty-minute to one-hour recharges. His night's sleep had become episodic. Some nights he could sleep from eleven pm to five am, arising at that time as he had all his adult life. More and more of late, he awoke somewhere between one and three due to a noise outside, a strange dream, or an ache somewhere in his body. If he was unable to get back to sleep, Joe went downstairs to the study. There he sipped from a small glass of scotch, listened to classical music, and re-read one of his many books.

Again, his musing was interrupted by a flash of light outside the bay window. The flash was followed by thunder that started as a sharp crack and pealed down to earth as a basso crash. The sequence and combination of sounds startled him anew. This was more than just a normal summer storm he thought. But what could he do about it. Nothing. He shrugged, stared straight ahead, and let his thoughts drifted. He envisioned various scenarios triggered by his upcoming family time. This past week, his reveries had been based in the time when he and Mary were young. They were in bed. He could feel the texture of her deep brown hair against the pillow and the eiderdown of her flat, taut stomach before the boys began there. He was captivated by her fragrance; delicate lily of the valley enhanced by the natural oils of her skin. He did not see her face nor hear her voice. His sensations were tactile and olfactory. He snapped back from the reverie to the present as a result of another violent lightning and thunder decree.

As a part of his doctor-prescribed regimen, he had to eat four times a day. Small meals to sustain his energy. Light on the bread and heavy on the protein and vegetables. He was told never to skip a meal. A protein bar at mid-morning and a piece of cheese or fruit at mid-afternoon were important components of the meals. Food energy was critical. Plus, the food helped calm his mildly upset stomach brought about by the medication quantity and diversity he took. During the day, he tried to take brief walks through the neighborhood before the protein bar in the morning and before the cheese or fruit in the afternoon. The specialist recommended this, saying, "keep active or rust." The sojourns were part exercise and part social. The more social they were the longer they took. He was aware that he became tired after the afternoon walks. So, they were becoming shorter and he walked more slowly.

One afternoon a week, he led a discussion group at the local college. The head of the history department referred to Joe as a scholar in local history. He was committed to not letting the history of the colonial capital, Conestoga wagons, Kentucky long rifles, the Paxton Boys, the first general merchandise chain store, and first tobacconist fade away. All in all, the discussion days were filled with the past. He liked that. He felt comfortable with the past. He also enjoyed playing bridge and wine sipping Thursday evenings with longtime friends. They all seemed to have similar physical difficulties, but no one ever whined or went into detail. They simply referred to their conditions as "just getting older".

The pill bottles arrayed before him represented a wall of sentinels protecting his life. He checked their contents to be sure he had enough for a four-week stay away from his home. After that, he would have to return and have his prescriptions refilled. He placed the eight plastic bottles in a brown leather bag that once held his toiletries on trips. The brown leather bag, a gift from Mary bearing his initials, and the box of protein bars were separated from the bottles of single malt by the manila envelopes. All items were in a large paper brown, handled shopping bag. Dishes washed. He was ready to see his family. Out the back door.

1-2-1-7-1-2. ON.

As his fingers pressed the buttons on the keypad, the old man noticed that the skin on the back of his hand had become more wrinkled and the veins were clearly visible and dark. Was this flexible human organ shrinking? Had his weight loss extended to his appendages? He had lost weight in the past nine months as evidenced by the clothes that once fit handsomely but were now loose fitting. His belt had a new notch. He smiled when he imagined himself shrinking. In his youth, he was nearly six feet tall. He was five-ten at his last doctor visit. He understood that aging was a process that accelerated with age. Stop! No time for pity.

With the brown shopping bag in one hand, he turned the key to lock the back door with the other. The sharp arthritic pains in his thumb, wrist, and elbow put an exclamation point on his age and condition. He had to exit the back door and lock it in eight seconds. Standing outside by the back door and staring at the keypad, new memories flooded his mind.

Years ago, he installed the electronic door and window alarm system. This protection wasn't necessary when he and Mary were raising their children. But the demography of the city morphing into the new, and ethnically diverse, normal required the protective change. Mary repeatedly urged him to move into the new age of security. She never nagged. She was patient with her logical point of view, knowing her thoughtful, often stubborn husband would ultimately see the light. So, he contracted for an electronic monitoring system linking his residence to the police. He did this also for their cottage deep in the bowels of the next county.

Two years ago, Mary died of cancer. Joe Bickham missed her profoundly. Pictures of the couple, her alone, and the entire family at various stages of life adorned the first-floor bookshelves, end tables, and the wall of the stairwell. Some of the tabletop pictures were near crosses, wooden or brass. A special picture of her and her dog, plus a small cross resided on his bedside table. Mary's dog, Sarah, a burly all-black German Shepherd, always kept Mary in sight. They seemed to be joined at the hip. Wherever Mary went, so went Sarah. For a walk in the neighborhood, shopping, visiting friends. Sunshine. Rain. Snow. It didn't matter.

No leash was needed; Sarah would not stray or chase a squirrel, rabbit, or cat. She stayed by Mary's side … not underfoot. Her role in life was to protect Mary. Once, a stranger approached Mary asking directions and Sarah stepped between the man and the mistress. She did not growl but stared at the stranger. She was a watchful canine bodyguard. Sarah was not by Mary's side when Mary and Joe went out together. It was a family joke that those were the only times Sarah entrusted Mary's care and safety to Joe, albeit temporarily.

Sarah saddened when Mary was hospitalized. Her beloved mistress was away. The dog perked up when Mary came home … only to die within a month. Joe remembered the night. He was reading in the library. At 8:47, Sarah came down from the master bedroom where she kept watch over Mary. The dog gently placed her head on Joe's lap beneath his book. She looked into Joe's eyes as if she were trying to tell him something important. Sarah had blue-gray eyes. Wolf like … uncommon for her breed. She took a deep breath and let out a whimper as if it were her last. Those actions spoke volumes about love and death. Joe put down his book and went upstairs to confirm what Sarah had communicated. Mary had died.

After the funeral, Sarah became depressed. She slept nearly all the time except for eating and bathroom breaks in the back yard. She didn't want to go on Joe's walks. Occasionally, Joe would hear her moan as if crying out for her mistress. The dog's muzzle had turned completely white and her steps were halting. She was twelve and her hips were the focal points of pain. Three months after Mary's death, Sarah once again put her head on Joe's lap while he was reading. Once again, her eyes were her voice. She stared deeply into his eyes and touched his soul. She exhaled deeply as if to say good-bye. Then, she painfully climbed the stairs to the master bedroom, stretched out at the foot of the bed where Mary had died, and fell asleep … forever. Joe had to carry her down the stairs. Given her size and his age, this task was substantial for the old man. But willingly done out of love and respect.

Again, he was rudely rattled from his musing by another flash accompanied by rolling thunder. The thunder followed the lightning by fewer than five seconds. It was getting closer. A knot briefly appeared in his stomach. The storm seemed to be moving rapidly from beyond the east side of the city and seemed to be heading toward Joe's house on the west side. The silence that followed each splitting crack and boom allowed him a brief return to his memories.

Joe lived in the house that was built for his grandfather, Josiah M. Bickham, and expanded by his father, Joseph James Bickham, who raised four boys in the house. Joe, the third, is the remaining son. He and Mary also raised four boys in the house. Today, all four have moved on. Joe Jr. died of pneumonia. At least the doctor said it was pneumonia. Joe and Mary knew that his life choice had weakened his health and thus hastened his death. That fact did not dull the pain of loss. David was killed by a drunk driver. Now his widow and child lived in California. Joe got yearly birthday and Christmas cards, and the very rear telephone call. On some nights, he could see the young faces of Joe and David and hear their laughter. The remaining two sons, Gabriel and Michael, had their own homes distant from their father. Gabriel, a business consultant, lived in Chicago and Michael, a healthcare consultant, lived in Center City Philadelphia. The attic and what had been the boys' bedrooms in the back half of the second floor had been closed off. The activity of youthful exuberance once abundant in that half of the second floor was now a pleasant memory.

The man was alone, and his space needs were limited. He felt there was no sense in heating or cooling space that was just space. So, he closed the air ducts and boarded over the connecting doorway. There would be no more alterations to the house during Joe's lifetime. The next resident could make any changes he wanted. The man once hoped the next resident would be one of his remaining sons, but now he knew that dream would never be. Sadly, it was the end of a tradition. Life, as he had known it, was winding down.

Chapter Two

The path from the back door to the garage passed a cast-iron water pump and trough, signature items produced by his family's foundry. The trough was converted to a planter by Mary years ago. She planted two rose bushes, a red one that represented their love and a white one that represented their unity. In memory of his wife, the old man religiously tended the bushes. He pruned them each fall to ensure flowery growth the next spring, fed them with the proper chemicals, and sprayed to protect them from insect and fungal damage.

Decades ago, pumps, troughs, plow blades, and harrow discs made by the family foundry were sold almost exclusively within the two Central Pennsylvania farming counties. The Amish and Mennonites respected the high quality and fair value of these items. The foundry was the financial lifeblood of the family for more than one hundred years. Around the turn of the last century, big, national manufacturers began aggressively offering these implements to owners of small farms. The items were mass-produced and thus could be sold "on the cheap." Farmers who relied on four-legged horsepower were hesitant to buy them at first. But they could not resist a bargain. When the implements became damaged, the "Black Hatters", who owned the farms turned to the Bickham foundry for repair. Soon it became cheaper to replace them than repair them. By the end of World War II, the foundry's decline in sales was matched by diminished income from repairs. The business was dying.

A toy manufacturer that wanted to produce cast-iron cars, trucks, and cap pistols made an offer for the foundry. After much debate, the

Bickham family accepted the offer, took the money, and bought land in remote sections of the neighboring counties. The plan was for the land to be farmed by tenant families. But, as the supply of reliable tenants shrank, the farmland was sold to real estate developers. More money, but nothing earned from work; this was the way of the latter half of the twentieth century. But it was a break from family and community traditions.

Joe's Land Rover awaited. It was packed with everything needed for the opening of the summer cottage; bed linens, towels, toilet articles, beer, bottled water for the entire family, and some of the boxed food for the holiday weekend. He would stop at his favorite market to buy fresh produce and fresh cut meats. Basic household and meal preparation items, like pots and pans, remained in the cottage over the winter. Fresh food shopping would be necessary by Wednesday after Memorial Day. He turned to glance at his home and wondered how much more time he had. The morning weather was cool as the storm had pushed cooler air before it. He felt compelled to hurry. Get ahead of the weather. First stop, the train station downtown. Michael and his son, Micah, would be arriving at 8:35. Out of loving anticipation, the old man would arrive at the station thirty minutes early.

No rain at his house yet. Just lightning and thunder heading his way. The storm seemed to be holding over the eastern side of the city. It was a huge, black, and roiling mass that was not moving. He could not remember a storm this fierce this early in the season. He had better get going. His trip would be westward. Hopefully, well in advance of the potential down pour.

Chapter Three

The wolves stopped their growling and herding when they reached the edge of the clearing, while the small creatures ahead of them furiously scampered around in the open. In their frantic state they bumped into and fell over one another. Gradually, the small panic stricken animals slowed their aimless scurrying and stopped altogether. They stood quietly and panted. Their minds could not understand what was about to happen but their instincts must have told them whatever it was, it was not good. At a multiple-bark command from the alpha wolf, the other wolves stealthfully crept into the open space. They were in the canine crouched attack mode. Each driver crept forward ... pausing a few seconds until the wolf was close enough to a target that it could pounce. One-by-one they sprang upon a target and ripped open its neck. Death was not always instantaneous. The killers did not howl or bark but a cacophonous chorus of high pitched shrieks, squeals and protestations confirmed the suffering of the death experience. The wolves did not eat their kills. Their role was being the killers. Eating was to be the enjoyable duty of the vultures, buzzards, crows and ravens, which were keenly aware of what was going on beneath them. They stared down at the wolves and patiently waited for their turn in this grotesque passion play. When all the small animals were slaughtered, their screams quieted, and their bleeding carcasses strewn over the clearing, the wolves silently retreated into the woods. They went back into the forest primeval.

The Pennsylvania Railroad station was built during the era when rails ruled ... well before the interstate highway system and commuter airlines were preferred methods of public transportation and shipping goods. This station was a grand edifice manifesting the human engine that drove the country out of the Great Depression. The town's historical society raised funds for its refurbishing about three decades ago. The result was extensive cleaning, a partial facelift, and some structural strengthening for the three-story monolith that covered nearly two city blocks. The massive front windows allowed light into all three stories.

The station was returned to the grandeur older residents remembered. Since the refurbishing, the station had slowly slid back into disrepair as service on this main line of the PRR suffered mightily. All stations except commuter stations near the major cities on the line suffered the same fate. This station, like the iron horse, had lost the battle for freight and passenger traffic. Death of the station and the railroad would not come soon. The demise would agonizingly linger for, perhaps, three more decades.

The old man bought a newspaper and a bottle of water from the Hispanic woman who ran the concession stand. The liquid purchase made him smile. Profit and trash were two by-products of a readily available natural resource sold in a convenient single-use package. He knew that many municipalities had safe, if somewhat unpleasant smelling, water. The citizens there bought a great deal of bottled water, as well as in-home water purifications systems. Progress? Public water fountains went the way of the horse and buggy. They simply fell into disuse because of the potential for the spread of disease and the social badge of carrying a bottle with an au current label.

He sat on one of the large solid oak benches and opened the paper. First glance was at the obituary page. No one he knew. That's good. A smile of relief. Then to the sports section. Beyond high school, sports had become distastefully professional ... even college sports. He cared little about the trials and tribulations of young men who earned fortunes yet were unable to properly handle the pressures of wealth. He felt precious little compassion for professional athletes who lost their star power to drugs. Ugh! Now to international and national news. All the articles were taken from the wire services. He heard these items on the early TV network news as he was dressing for the day. Then to the best section – comics, daily puzzles, and games. His ever-present ballpoint pen would help him pass the time. Mary loved crossword puzzles. She would spend all day on the *Sunday New York Times* and *The Times of London*. These mental gymnastics gave her an edge when she and Joseph discussed nearly anything. As erudite as the man thought he was, he felt like a dolt when he tried to have a deep conversation with his wife.

One across: "Scream like a_____." *Banshee.* Four down: "Angel of death_____." *Samael.* Seven across: "Renaissance painter: "_____." *Raphael.* Fourteen across: "Cheers psychologist_____." *Lilith.* Twenty across: "Child actor Woods "_____." *Elijah.* Twenty-four down: "Child of God_____" *Agnes,* and so it went. Interlocking words. There was no overall clue, so each answer had to stand on its own.

Now arriving on Track Number Two, the Cincinnati Limited. Now arriving on Track Number Two, the Cincinnati Limited.

The Joe was startled by the loudspeaker. They're here. His heart quickened as he stood and walked purposefully to the double doors leading to the stairs to the platforms. He would wait there. The walk down and up the three flights would tire him too much. Anyway, Michael knew that his dad would be waiting at the top of the stairs. The ten minutes the father waited seemed like ten hours. The man smiled. He was not sure if he loved his son or his grandson more. The double doors opened and out walked a woman alone. Then two young men. Then his treasures.

"Grandpa! Grandpa!"

The 14-year-old Micah ran up to his grandfather and hugged him powerfully.

"Good golly, Micah. You have gotten bigger and stronger since Christmas."

The old man recalled a time not too long ago when he knelt to hug his grandson. Now Micah squeezed his grandpa's ribs like a bear. The two of them were nearly nose to nose.

"Michael, what have you been feeding this man-child? Looks like he'll grow as big and as strong as an oak. He's nearly there already."

"Luv ya, Dad. Micah will be taller and stronger than I am. I'm sure of that."

Father and son hugged and kissed each other's cheeks.

"Got all your bags? Good. Anybody need to visit the restroom? Good. Let's get rolling. We've a lot of work to get done the cottage ready before dinner."

Michael and Micah's bags were placed on the rear seat alongside the grandson. Grandfather and father were up front. The men headed off on the two-hour trip.

Chapter Four

The driving of small animals from the forest to their slaughter in the clearing was repeated several times over the next few days until the dead and decaying prey covered the entire plot of ground. There were even numerous mounds of carcasses. The animals from the first day's kill had begun to rot. Fur and flesh had fallen away and bones were visible. The wolves had disappeared deep into the woods. Their part in the drama was done. It was now time for the birds of prey to enjoy the carrion feast. The crows arrived first because they were the closest to the killing field. They swooped and fluttered their wings to land. Once on the ground, they strutted from one feeding spot to another choosing the ripest, most delicate morsels of flesh. From the most recent kills, the crows enjoyed the delicacy of plucking out eyes. Their cawing told other birds how happy they were. This called the ravens. These larger scavengers dove from the highest branches. The flapping of their wings upon landing frightened their smaller cousins causing them to hop to other eating stations. Crows and ravens could share food without much squabbling because there was more than enough for all. Then the royalty of scavengers, vultures and buzzards, stopped circling high above the clearing and dove to earth to claim the bounty that was rightfully theirs. The abrupt arrival of the huge birds caused the all the other birds to flutter and hop away to another spot in the landing zone. These latest to arrive ripped at the small carcasses consuming fur and bits of flesh left by others. Their powerful beaks crushed the skeletons which were then partially consumed. Thus, began the last phase of this inexplicable woodland cycle.

The car plied its way through city traffic for fifteen minutes then onto the four-lane state highway heading west. The old man could remember when this was a two-lane road with no state designation. His guess was that it was as recently as ten years ago. As a young man and then as a newlywed, he recalled traveling into the county to buy fresh food and local meats. People took their time on those junkets, because the trip was really a pleasure ride to "the country." Now the posted speed limit was 55, and nearly every driver exceeded that. He feared that most drivers followed much too closely to the car in front. Ever cautious, he kept a distance of three car lengths. This earned him scowls and a few single-digit salutes from passing drivers.

In his rear-view mirror, he tracked the storm. It now seemed to have moved slightly west, still hovering over the city. Joe wanted to put a few more miles between the weather threat and his car. He spied no rain, just roiling clouds and lightning. They were safe from the storm's fury for now. Joe, pondered was heaven trying to tell him something? Were they being followed … or herded by the massive thunder head? Was it a coincidence that he and the storm were headed in the same direction? The old man fretted too much.

Gone were the numerous roadside stands selling seasonal produce and flowers. Gone were the gradual turn-offs into small parking lots. Now, cars sped by entrances to housing developments with alluring names like *Glen Oaks Farms, Millcreek Estates,* and *West Forest.* The original landowners sold their properties to developers who fed a growing appetite to escape urban living. Most of the residents were younger and had small children. So, schools of all levels had been built to accommodate the burgeoning, younger population. It stings the old man's soul that his family contributed to the sprawl that obliterated a natural environment.

Once there was an intersection of a lesser road crossing the two-lane highway every four or five miles. Each intersection was a four-way stop as noted by the stop signs. Now there were intersections with traffic lights every two or three miles. At each new intersection were two gas stations with mini-marts attached. Between the new intersections were strip malls and the occasional large mall with massive anchor tenants. All this "improvement" had created congestion. Ironically, the improvements were made to accommodate the many new residents, who moved into the new developments to escape the congestion of the city. The traffic lights, engineered to safely control the flow of traffic, now slowed it.

"Micah, how did you do in school this year?"

"A's with two B's. I got the B's in Advanced Placement classes – physics and philosophy. They were tough. But I need to take them to get ready for college."

"Any Advanced Placement classes next year?"

"Calculus and 19th Century European Literature."

"Good for you."

"I need the tough classes to get into Brown like you and Dad. The competition for a great school gets tougher each year. How was it for you, Grandpa?"

"Not as competitive as it was for your father and much less competitive than it is for you now. What about sports?"

"I did OK in wrestling. At 133, I placed third in the Tri-County Private School Tournament. I had to cut six pounds to make weight during the last few weeks of the season. It was necessary, but the weight loss weakened me. I know that I will continue to grow and put on weight. I hope to match my growth with more muscle. By next year, I'll be comfortable at 145. That's where the bigger boys compete because they cut from 152. This new competition will be tough, because these guys are older, more experienced, and stronger than the guys at my present weight. Many of them are seniors. So, I'll have to live in the weight room this summer and when school starts. The next wrestling season will be an eight-month event. If I can bulk up, I may even move up to 152. This spring, I went out for the track team to build my stamina. I ran the 400 and the 800. Not fast enough to win, but I was fast enough to get a few thirds."

"It seems you have your academic and sport lives planned. What about girls?"

"No one special."

The old man glanced over at his son, who winked and imperceptibly shook his head counter to the boy's response.

"What's her name, Micah?"

"Who?"

"Your girl."

"Pat. Pat Mossman."

"That's all I'll ask on that subject."

Grandfather's friendly inquisitions were expected, even welcomed but they still made Micah feel uncomfortable just as his father felt when Joe asked the same questions years ago. As the three rode in silence, the old man's right hand slid over to his son's left hand resting on his knee. They squeezed each other's hand – a sign of love tracing back to when the son was a boy younger than the boy on the back seat.

Chapter Five

Mile after mile, the driver noted the absence of family enterprises that were roadside until recent years ... before and after the road expanded from two lanes to four. He wondered how long any small business could hold on in the face of the megastores, car dealerships, and cinema megaplexes. Personal service appeared to have given way to the strident cacophony of discount prices, flapping banners, and the infernal inflatable tube characters beckoning customers. Life had changed, and not necessarily for the better he thought.

"There it is, Grandpa. The sign for Lake Tucquan. The turn is coming up on the right. We're getting closer."

The boy's excitement was manifested in the volume of his declaration.

"Right you are, Micah. One more intersection and we turn."

At the turn the road shrank to two lanes. As he looked in the rear-view mirror, the old man took note that the massive thunderhead appeared to have covered the entire city well behind them. The lightning was visible. The thunder had been muffled by distance. The celestial power was not following or herding them. It's just a big storm that happened to move into the city when Joe was getting ready to leave for the weekend. Coincidence confirmed. He relaxed. Joe began to look for one more roadside enterprise. The intersections on this leg of the trip were farther apart, and there were only a few traffic lights.

Joe recalled how much Mary loved opening the summer cottage on Memorial weekend. She loved the rebirth of family summers. He also recalled how well she planned for it and how hard she worked to make it look easy. To accommodate an easy move-in, Mary would spend the last weekend of the summer cleaning everything. Pots and pans were scrubbed and put away or hung, ready for the next season. The kitchen, main room, bedrooms, and bathrooms were spotless. All items were in their proper places. When the boys were still living at home, they worked especially hard this weekend because they deeply loved their mother. They never complained. Later when it was just Joe and Mary, the cleanup took three days. Completely cleaned, the cottage was a gift ready to be opened in eight months. All this work was necessary so that next year's reopening was seamless ... just move in, put the food away, and enjoy the place and the family. For decades, the goal was obtained.

The old man spied his target, *Stolzfuss Family Farms*. This was the only place where he would buy fresh produce for the cottage opening. He slowed and turned in to the gravel parking lot. There were three cars in front of the store opening. He parked to the left. As he exited, he noticed that the storm appeared to have left its place over the city and was now moving west, just like the three males. The storm seemed to have renewed its following or herding efforts. Very bizarre ... an on-again off-again game of follow the Bickhams. Not a game Joe wanted to play. They entered the open air, multi-stalled market that sold fruits, vegetables, poultry, dairy, pork, cold cuts and freshly baked breads.

"Are we going to buy the usual, Grandpa?"

"Yes, you get the bacon ... four pounds of thick sliced, and twenty-four fresh rolls. Be sure they are the hard kind. Plus, four loaves of rye or pumpernickel bread. Also, please pick up two pounds of sliced ham and two pounds of sweet bologna. Your father and I will select the cheese, fruits, and vegetables."

The three went about their duties and met at the cashier's station with their bounty. Micah held his bags as proudly as a hunter would hold his kill. The elder men have bags containing corn, tomatoes, potatoes, green beans, mushrooms, and three kinds of cheese, sliced swiss for the sandwiches and blocks of gruyere and brie for the adults, as well as bags of apples and grapes.

"Hello, Lester, is your grandfather here."

"No, Mr. Bickham, Grandpa Amos died last December."

Joe's heart sank. Amos Stolzfuss and his market were a fixture in the lives of Bickhams.

"I'm so sorry to hear that. He was a good man."

"My mother is here, I'm sure she would like to say hello."

Lester left his station and walked to the rear. Shortly, the young man and an older woman came to the front.

"Emily, I am very sorry to hear about your father. I truly liked him and greatly enjoyed our conversations. Please accept my condolences."

The plain woman looked deeply into Joe's eyes.

"Thank you. Amos always spoke kindly of you and your family. It grieved him when he learned that your wife died a few years ago. I'm happy to see you looking so well. And your grandson is growing up to look much like you. Now, I must tend to the back room. Have a joyous time this weekend with your family. And be safe."

Her face was nearly blank as she turned on her heel and seemingly drifted away from the counter and back to her work. Joe thought her last comment was odd. He paid, and the boys loaded the food into the car. Joe's heart was heavy, but he kept that to himself. He hoped the excess moisture in his eyes would not give him away. In the short time they were shopping, the storm had not moved but it appeared to have grown and become more ferocious. His interest in the storm had lessen slightly ... from concern to curiosity. But was now back to concern. He asked himself again ... were he and the boys being followed or, in some bizarre way herded. It was all most likely a product of his imagination. Aging increased this aspect of his mind. Regardless, when the car was loaded and the doors closed and locked, he accelerated aggressively out of the parking lot and onto the road. He wanted to put a greater distance between his family and the storm, and he wanted to be in a safe place ... the cottage.

"Dad, will Gabriel be at the cottage tonight?"

"No, he's flying into Harrisburg tomorrow and driving over. He plans to arrive at the cottage mid-morning."

"Will he be taking the company plane?"

"Yes."

"It must be nice."

"Easy, son."

"Just sayin'."

"He has worked hard for his success. And it hasn't been easy. He's had to reinvent himself several times. As jobs disappeared, he reappeared as a different and better applicant. And he kept going. Plus, he's six years your senior. Financially, you'll get to where he is before too long."

"Grandpa, are Lillie and Aggie coming, too?"

"You bet, Micah. You three will have a lot to talk about."

"Grandpa, the storm that we saw when we got in the car looks like it has grown but looks like it is staying in town for a visit. It hasn't moved in our direction. That's a break. I want to get some fishing in before dinner."

Joe drove as fast as he thought reasonable on the final leg of their trip. Micah stared out the window at the passing farm land. Michael's head bobbed in very brief intermittent naps. The verbal silence and a classical music background during the next thirty minutes were interrupted by the old man.

"Michael, how go things with you?"

"My team beat last year's revenue goal by eight percent and was handsomely rewarded. This year's goal is ten percent above last year's final number. I think we can make it. It will be tough, but I have a great team that enjoys the rewards of success. They're motivated. I suspect that at least one, if not two of the other people at my level did not make their revenue goals. If that's accurate, they will most likely be pushed aside or out. If that happens, one or two of my best people will be promoted. It's evilly ironic that the success of my team will mean its break-up. I understand that the company wants to reward the best people with promotions, but I'm selfish and don't relish the

21

break-up of my team leaving me to go through the process of training new members."

"You can do it, and you know you can. If you and your team beat the revenue goal this year, beyond money, what's in it for you?"

"Hopefully, a promotion to VP over another division before the end of the year. We'll see."

"Then you won't have to worry about your present team breaking up and training new people. You'll have the concerns of commanding a new team in a different environment with new goals and different ways of conducting business. You're always moving upward. Always learning more. That's what you're good at doing. Progressing. So, don't worry. You're strong, adaptable, and smart. What about Shelia?"

"She's working fewer nights, and her rotations are more flexible. She's earned all this. She has been with the hospital for eight years, and she is a leader in geriatric oncology. Dealing with that type of patient, she remains positive and never seems to get depressed. I couldn't do that. She's emotionally stronger than me. We are spending more evening time together. Micah sees her more. She'll be up here early in the morning tomorrow, soon after her last rotation."

Questions asked. Answers given. The grandfather was satisfied with the two progress reports. After thirty minutes more of Vivaldi, Albinoni, and Handel's lively Baroque music, the car was deep into the woods. Joe looked to the sky. The churning pitch black in the sky was far behind them. Ahead he saw only the clear blue sky … over the cottage. The game of chase was over.

"Look, Grandpa, buzzards. There must be twenty circling in the sky. It looks like they could be over the cottage. What do you think they are looking for?"

"A meal. They have very sharp eyes and can see dead animals from hundreds of yards away. There must be a large carcass somewhere in the woods that surround the lake. We'll be at the cottage shortly. Then you can check it out."

"They don't seem to flap their wings. How do they stay up there?"

"It's called 'riding the thermals.' They stay aloft by staying in drafts of warm air, or thermals currents, which rise from the ground. The birds float on the warm air until it dissipates, then they gently fly until they find another thermal current. See the length of the wingspans and the breadth of the wings relative to the size of their bodies. Because their wings are so big and wide, their method of transportation is more soaring and floating than flapping and diving. They are not fast or strong fliers, but they can stay aloft for hours and they have a keen sense of vision. Somehow, they can always find a new thermal's updraft and ride it until it dissipates."

The car turned onto a dirt road at the sign that said, *Lake Tucquan*. This dirt road received county road work attention each spring to smooth the ruts created by the heaving of the earth during the fall and winter weather. An accommodation for those who use the public beach and boat ramps, as well as the few home owners on private land. That part of the road had never been paved. Speed was posted at 10 mph. About a mile down the road, there was a fork. Two signs distinguished between private residences to the left and public area to the right. The road to the left was gated.

"Michael, take this key and unlock the gate so we can get to the cottage."

The gate is unlocked, opened, closed after the car passed, and relocked. This leg of the trip was very slow because the way is deeply rutted with frequent dips and bumps. No roadwork was done here because the county considered it a private driveway. Vehicles had to proceed at a snail's pace. SUVs were the vehicles of choice. After this last leg of the trip, they reached the driveway to their destination. A sign was posted on an old oak tree. Micah spoke out…

"There it is, Grandpa – the first letters, *T-u-c-q*."

Chapter Six

They turned at the sign for *Tucquhalla* and came face to face with an explosion of black avian forms that released a thunderous screeching cacophony. A mixed flock of large, black birds bounced and hovered in the back yard, the space between the roadside stand of trees and the cottage. Buzzards, vultures, ravens and crows, frightened by the human intruders, hysterically jumped off the ground in front of the automobile. Seen from the car, the scavengers created an undulating black mass that vaguely resembled windblown waves on the lake. The flock had been feasting on a feral smorgasbord that littered the ground. Some animal corpses appeared to have been recent kills. Blood and pieces of flesh were visible on the ground. Some flesh hung on the bones. Other corpses manifested little or no blood, just dry pelts and cleanly picked carcasses. A few birds lingered over their meals hoping to get the last morsel before the intruders got too close. The beaks and talons of these diners were visibly active, picking and ripping at small varmint flesh. As the buzzards hurried skyward to reinitiate their circling, most of the crows and ravens that left the killing field were perched on the higher limbs of the oak and pine trees near the house. They were poised to return to the carcasses should the intruders leave. Joe pulled the SUV to a halt.

"Micah, stay in the car. Michael, come with me."

Cautiously, the two adults approached the carcasses. Each man had grabbed a stick to shoo away any remaining scavengers, to check the carcasses, and to protect against the return of any birds. Joe felt more than curiosity; he felt confused and concerned.

"I see many rabbits, squirrels, several possums, a skunk, and numerous raccoons."

"Michael, we need to collect and burn the remains, then bury the ashes quickly."

They waved their cudgels and the few smaller birds remaining on the ground squawked and flew away.

"Micah, it's OK. You can get out of the car. Come here."

"Grandpa, what is this?"

"I don't know, but we have to work quickly to clean up the mess. First step. You two go to the shed and retrieve the wheelbarrow, two shovels, and either the post hole digger or the pick. While you're getting the tools, I'll take a few of our bags into the house. We'll meet back here and begin cleanup. Now, let's get to it."

Joe carried two suitcases and his large brown paper bag toward the cottage. He deactivated the alarm, entered the building, and opened all the windows to let fresh air drive away the musty smell of eight months. The stress of the situation, the labor, and the fact that he had been awake since five am began to affect him. His steps were measured as he returned to the Land Rover. By himself, he couldn't lift the cooler and boxes containing food. He had help from his neighbor loading these into the SUV the day before. He needed help getting them into the house. So, he let them stay in the rear of the car.

"OK, here's the plan. Michael and Micah, you guys dig a pit; my guess is that it should be four by four and five feet deep. While you're digging, I'll be collecting the remains of the animals. I'll need one shovel and the wheelbarrow. Michael, you take the pick and Micah the other shovel. By the time the wheelbarrow is full, the hole should be ready. Let's go."

"Where should we dig, Dad?"

"Over there by the trees. But stay about twenty feet away from the stand so that any fire won't hit them. And definitely far away from the house. I don't want the stench of burning animal flesh and hides to get into the cottage. Perhaps dig on the other side of the driveway."

The three generations went about their duties. Joe scooped up the carcasses and any bloody soil near them. A few of the carcasses broke apart during this process. Michael aggressively attacked the chosen plot of land, poking holes in the sod and beneath the topsoil. Micah lifted the loosened dirt and placed it beside the growing hole. An hour of hard work followed, and they were just about ready. Carefully, Joe wheeled his collection of animal parts to the fresh dig. The bending and repetitive lifting, as well as a deep gnawing concern, had taken their toll. He was now fatigued. It had been a few hours since he has had food and he had to work more than he had anticipated. He wouldn't let his son and grandson see his condition.

"Micah, make a small path in the dirt mound for me to push the wheelbarrow to the lip of the hole."

That accomplished, Joe pushed the final four feet. The old man's muscles are trembling, and he was covered with sweat. He lifted the handles of the wheelbarrow and the remains of small animal bodies slid off the front of the it into the pit. Their blood and other bodily fluids lubricated the slide.

"Micah, go back to the shed and get the big can of kerosene."

"OK."

"Dad, what's going on?"

"Michael, we're going to burn the birds' food supply."

"That's not what I mean. How did so many animals die in one place? Why were they here? They didn't just wander into this space, die, and wait to be attacked by the birds. Someone or something had to put them here or drive them to this place. Who? Not our neighbors. The Musselmans and Eshlemans are not here yet. They come down later. If not them, who? What was the driving force? And why?"

"Michael, I don't have any answers. It is, for now, a mystery we can discuss later."

"Don't tell me it has anything to do with the folk tale that the land around Lake Tucquan was once an Indian burial ground?"

"That's just folklore that has little or no basis in fact. The

Susquehannock Indians lived in these parts, but I doubt they would have used this land. I suspect they would have buried their dead on higher ground to be closer to the sky. Besides, dead people don't rise from their graves to collect animals for slaughter and then jump back in their graves. Let's not spend too much time now talking about this subject lest we frighten Micah."

"I found what you asked for, Grandpa."

"Good, pour some of the can's contents over the animals. Pour enough so that it runs down to the bottom of the pit. Pour it all over."

The boy splashed the fluid over the feral mess.

"OK, now splash a little into the wheelbarrow so it can be cleaned of any remaining mess. I'll wipe it down later."

Joe swirled the kerosene around in the wheelbarrow then poured the liquid onto the soon-to-be pyre.

"Stand back. Way back."

Joe reached into his shirt pocket and retrieved matches. He folded back the matchbook cover and struck one. When it was lit, he ignited the remaining matches. As they burst into flame, he tossed the matchbook onto the kerosene-soaked carcasses. When the matches hit their target, there was a *whoosh* as the flames exploded and jumped six feet above the pile of flesh, bones, and hides. The fire's components began to snap, crackle, and pop. The stench of burning flesh was immediate, and it nearly made the boy puke. He gagged and coughed. All three backed far away from the mass grave.

"I'll stay here and make sure nothing goes wrong with our fire. It will need to be turned so that all the carcasses burn thoroughly. You two finish unloading the car, I couldn't carry the big cooler or the boxes. Start to put all the items where they belong in the house. Michael, you take the food and kitchen items. Micah, please prepare three beds for tonight. You'll be in the bunk room. Leave linens for your cousins. Your father and mother will be in the east bedroom. Put linens in the west bedroom for your aunt and uncle. If you would, please make my bed in the master bedroom. When you're done, we can have lunch."

As the son and grandson went about their tasks, Joe leaned heavily on the digging pole and surveyed the killing field. He stared blankly at the large back yard and spied what appeared to be white or light-colored pebbles near each of the carcasses sites. He must have missed these when he was scooping up the animal debris. The pebbles looked to vary in size from a dime to silver dollar. He stoked the fire, turning the carcasses so that all of them could be completely consumed by the fire. The flame was low, but the embers were glowing brightly as they devoured the remains of the small wild bodies. Carrying the pole, he walked to the closest death site and picked up one of two white pebbles. Joe wonders why he did not see the stones when he was cleaning up the carnage.

He had never seen a stone that color and one so perfectly round near the cottage. Or, anywhere near the lake for that matter. It was quite warm … almost hot. Strange for this time of day and time of year. He put both pebbles in his jacket pocket. He moved to another site and picked up a pebble. Also, very warm. Joe was quite intrigued. He visited two more sites and picked up the stones. And so on, until all the pebbles had been removed from the ground and placed in Joe's jacket pockets. The more stones he found, the faster his intrigue became concern. There were thirty.

He walked back to the fire for the kerosene can. With can in hand, the old man walked to each dead animal site and splashed a small amount of kerosene on the area. He then covered the spots with freshly dug dirt. There would be no fires on these small sites. Joe was "killing" the land to ensure that whatever residual fluid or scrap of the animal on or in the land would not be bait for any other scavengers. He looked up at the small murder of crows and ravens in the trees. They were watching his every move. They seemed to be "talking" to one another, or perhaps to the buzzards in the sky. When the last site was splashed and covered, the onlookers screeched and flapped their wings as they retreated to another part of the surrounding woods. They watched, and they learned. This human was wise to them.

He headed back to the pyre pit. It had stopped smoking and smoldering, so he began to shovel the dirt back into the hole. Stench rose with each shovel of dirt that hit the hole. Finally, the entire mess was covered. What remained was a burial mound about six inches above the surrounding earth. It will be watered and tamped flat later.

"OK, the food has been put away, the beds made, and the cottage is ready for occupancy."

"I don't know about you men, but I'm hungry. Clearing the land of the uninvited guests was more than I expected upon our arrival. It's nearly one o'clock and time for lunch. Waddaya say about sandwiches and potato salad?"

"Sounds good to me, Grandpa. After lunch, may Dad and I take the boat out? I'd love to get some fishing in before dinner. Besides, a fresh fish meal tonight would be great."

"If you catch 'em, we'll eat 'em. I have a few more small things to do after lunch ... one of which is take a nap. Like always, the lake was stocked in early April. They put the fish near the mouth of the creek knowing the current would help the fish acclimate to their new home and aid in their dispersion. So, the trout are there, you'll just have to find them. To learn the *where*, will be your first job."

Chapter Seven

Father and son were casually motoring on the lake. The boat slowed, and the engine idled at the halfway point.

"Micah, the water looks still here. This should be a perfect place to start. Dip the oar in the water. We need a depth gauge."

"Dad, looks like the depth is about five feet."

"Perfect. Drop anchor, matey. The water's deep enough for the fish to swim and hide, yet shallow enough that they can rise and attack the small flying insects that come down to the water. See the bugs drifting above the water already? Do you remember how to cast a fly? Be sure the fly will float on top of the water and drag it slowly across the surface."

"How could I dare forget? I am with one of my teachers."

"Cast when you're ready. I'll be right behind you."

"Dad, why are the bugs flying near the surface of the water."

"The afternoon is their time to rest and rejuvenate. The best place to do this is on the surface of the lake. Plus, the water gives them sanctuary from the birds that eat the insects out of the air. The fish know this, so they swim right below the surface then rise up and break the water's surface to claim a meal. The insects drift down to the water to avoid the birds but the fish eat the insects as they land on the water. A life cycle. Hopefully the fish will think our flies with embedded hooks are just dinner morsels. When they bite, we get 'em. Stay alert, we have competition."

"Who?"

"The two red-tailed hawks flying about thirty feet above the water. They don't want the bugs; they want the fish that attack the bugs. They want our catches. When they spy a fish rising out of the water to feed, they swoop down and claim their own meal just as the unsuspecting fish chomps down on an unsuspecting bug. The birds are basically using the bugs as bait, just as we are. Birds, bugs, and fish make up this cycle."

For the next ninety minutes, Micah and his father cast and re-cast into the still water around the boat.

"I got another bite, Dad. And from the tug on the line, he is a big one."

"You know how to sink the hook with a little tug, give him space to run and tire himself out, and then slowly reel him in just like always. Don't let him break the water's surface."

"I know."

Micah knows that his father was only trying to help with some in-boat coaching. Micah had already caught several fish on this lake.

"He's running."

"Let him swim and tire himself out. Whoa, look at that. Your airborne competition is eyeing your catch. The hawk has seen the ripple and splashing in the water. Don't pull the trout out of the water until he is boat side."

The fish was now fighting against the inevitable. He thrashed just beneath the surface, then broke the water's surface. This was what the hawks had hoped for. One hawk dove and sank his talons into the head and neck of the trout. He had claimed his meal and was trying to take the fish back to a perch where it could be devoured.

"Too bad, the hawk just latched on to your fish. You have a tug-of-war over a helpless lake trout."

"What do I do, Dad?"

"There are two battles; the fish that doesn't want to leave the lake and come home with you, and the hawk that wants the fish for his own meal. You have the power to determine which one of you gets the fish. Try to dislodge the bird, by jerking the line. This may also pull the hook from the fish, so be careful."

A single tug caused the bird's wings to flap awkwardly, but he did not let loose his grip. The fish thrashed in the air about two feet above the water. He is trapped between two hunters. He would be the loser whoever won, raptor or fisherman. Another tug by Micah on the line caused the hook to become dislodged from the trout's mouth. The hawk flew away with his trophy, his meal. The fly and line floated gracefully down to the surface. Hawk 1: Micah 0.

"I bet you never had to fight for your dinner before."

"That was exciting. I would have won if the hook had a barb. But Grandpa made it very clear that the barbs had to be removed from all the hooks. He told me years ago, that if the fish can wiggle off a clean hook and get away, he should be able to do so. He calls it fair fishing. I don't think he ever thought a barbless hook would benefit a hawk. I woulda liked to reel in the big one that the hawk got, but I think the three fish we caught already will be enough for dinner tonight. That was exciting. Now, I have a question about the other birds. I mean the birds we saw when we arrived."

"Shoot."

"Do you think it was strange that the birds were feasting on dead animals in our back yard?"

"Very strange."

"How could that happen? I mean, I don't see how all the animals got together and crawled into one area to die. Then, all the birds saw them, flew to the spot, landed, and ate the animals. Were they dead on the ground, or did the birds kill them?"

"I believe something drove the animals on to the back yard to die. I doubt if anyone or anything carried the animals. Crows, ravens, and buzzards didn't kill the animals. Those birds are scavengers. They only eat what is already dead. Road kill, for example. Eagles and your friend, the red-tailed hawk, on the other hand, are raptors. They kill living things, like the fish you lost. We saw no eagles or hawks in the back yard."

"What would drive the animals on to the yard?"

"Perhaps a larger animal."

"But then how did they die? I mean, if a larger animal drove the smaller animals out of the woods, he would have eaten them or killed them and dragged them back to his den. A larger animal would not leave his kill in an open area for another animal to steal it. Some of the animals look like they had been dead for a day or two. They had been picked clean. Some of the critters still had flesh on them as if they had recently been killed. Maybe yesterday or this morning. There's something very weird about the whole situation."

"There are many things in the woods we humans don't understand. This is one of them."

"What did you and Grandpa say when you thought I couldn't hear? I heard a few words, but they made no sense."

"Tell you what … after dinner tonight, why don't you ask your grandpa. In the meantime, we'd better pay attention to the storm that suddenly appeared over there."

The boy turned to the far side of the lake. The waves of rain were a spot-on definition of the expression, "downpour." The rain-filled air was a dark gray and stretched from horizon to mid-sky. It was so dark it hid the land on other side of the lake. The storm seemed to have popped up out of nowhere and was roiling toward the middle of the lake. Lightning flashed from every part of the five-mile-wide thunderhead. The lightning splintered across the sky from left to right and down to earth or the lake. The wind and rain had begun to churn the lake. Waves were actually appearing.

"Dad! Dad! I think I got another one … a big one. At least, he's fighting that way."

"No time, son. Tug the hook out of his mouth and reel in your line. You can get him another day. We have enough for dinner tonight. The storm will be over us in a heartbeat. You best be seated. We have to hurry to stay ahead of the storm."

Micah retrieved his line, as Michael cranked the engine and immediately revved it to full speed. He pointed the boat for home, just as a wave crashed into the side and splashed in. Another. Then a third and larger wave dumped itself into the boat.

"Son, grab the bucket, and start to bail. We don't want to get flooded."

The engine and boy did their best. The strain on the small engine was heard in its high-pitched whine. The rain water pouring into the boat was weighing down the vessel. The water in the bottom of the boat from the waves was augmenting that of the torrential downpour. Both sources had raised the water level inside the boat to six inches. Micah's duties were critical for the return to the Bickham boathouse and dock, now a half-mile away. As they got closer to the boathouse, they seemed to have outrun the storm. It appeared to be holding back from landfall on the cottage side of the lake. The lightning flashes and thunder crashes were over the middle of the lake. It stalled there.

"We made it! Let's show Grandpa our dinner."

Chapter Eight

The young adult man steps through the doorway and looks directly into the kitchen. It is warmly lit by the sun outside. Small plain white curtains rest on the sides of two windows. On the wooden panel between the windows is a small cross. The large oak table and four chairs are ready for diners. The stove is as old as the icebox, not refrigerator. There she is. A comely and plainly dressed woman of average height and build. She has rich dark hair and a trim figure. There are two young boys seated at the table. Neither of them has any facial features. Above the shoulders on each is a head with hair, but no face. The actions of the boys show that they are happy to see the man. They wave. Then, they rise from the kitchen table and embrace him. The woman, standing at the stove, turns away from meal preparation and looks at him. Her eyes express her love for the man. With a small tilt of her head, she beckons him to sit. At the table, the four hold hands and bow their heads. A moment of silence in a silent environment. Hands unclasp. There is no food on the plates. Then it happens. The boys begin to fade from view. First their heads become totally transparent. The transparency continues down from the shoulders to the chest. Finally, they are not there. Then the woman. Her hair disappears. Her head. Her body. The young adult man is alone, seated at the table. He anxiously looks around the room. Where did the woman and boys go? The room is now different. The curtains have changed from white to calico. There is no light streaming from outside. The table seems smaller. The chairs are now ladder-backs. The appliances are clean and modern. The silence that fills the room is shattered by flashing bright lights and thunderous explosions that vibrate through his body.

The old man snapped up from his supine position on the couch. He was groggy. His pulse had quickened. The dream world had been shattered by the noise of the storm. His mind skipped to many things, the dream, the decoration of the room, and the inhabitants. Within a moment, his mind was clear, and he could focus on a chore. Firewood. He must get the logs from the big stack behind the cottage onto the porch before rain soaked them and made them unusable. Although just about June, the evenings and nights were chilly, almost cold, by the lake. He arose, grabbed gloves, and walked quickly to the large stack of logs behind the cottage. His nap had refreshed him, and he had forgotten his dream.

As he reached for the first log, Joe heard rattling and hissing that he recalled from the past. Snakes! He stiffened from the disturbing noise. Beneath and around the first layer of logs, he saw a scaly, writhing mass, a three-foot mass of intertwined rattlers, copperheads, and black snakes. He couldn't determine where one snake ended, and another began. Tiny tipped tails and faces that look like they're smiling appeared on the outer surface of the undulating mass. The reptiles presented a frightening surprise. The man snapped back and slapped his arms to his sides. His heart raced and sweat popped on his upper lip. Joe hated and feared snakes. He believed they were the embodiment of evil. Instantly, he flashed on what to do to get rid of this threat. He walked briskly to the kitchen and opened the small doors beneath the sink. He grabbed two plastic jugs: ammonia and bleach. Perfect. Back to the woodpile. He splashed much of the contents of both bottles onto and beside the top logs, as well as the snakes there. He had to step away from the spot to avoid the toxic fumes of muriatic acid. Standing six feet away, he spotted snakes scurrying to avoid the pain of this poison. Some scurried from the pile into the woods. Some slithered deeper in the pile, down to the holes from whence they came. His heart rate gradually returned to normal.

The wind had picked up and the lightning over the lake was increasing. Flashes of light were followed by moments of gray in the sky. The old man picked through the top logs to find the ones that were not heavily splashed. He carefully looked for snakes before picking up four logs and carrying them onto the front porch. There, he peered through the screen and out on the lake. Searching for the boat holding his son and grandson, he saw nothing but a massive thunderhead, gray sheets of rain, and white cap waves that appeared to be three feet high. The other side of the lake was now engulfed in blackness. He hoped the boys were safe. Michael was adept at boating on the lake, yet the old man was concerned. Another trip to the log pile. Four more logs into the bin. Another round trip. Ten trips and the firewood bin was filled with enough left over for a stack of eight by the fireplace. Half of these would be laid and made ready to remove the chill of the evening air. Then, he heard the voice of his grandson.

"Grandpa, look what we caught."

Joe is relieved. Micah was soaking wet and holding a small string of lake trout, one large and two medium size. More than enough for dinner.

"Glad you guys made it home before the storm hit. I was a little worried. Great catch, Micah. Now, you know the rules … you caught 'em, you clean 'em, but we all eat 'em. You'll have to clean them in the boathouse. After that, both of you must change into dry clothes and take the wet ones to the front porch. We'll finish drying them tonight by the fire."

"OK."

The storm raged. Lightning and rain hovered over the lake. The bright flashing lights revealed the blackness and size of the thunderhead. Huge. But it stopped mid-lake; it did not make landfall on the cottage side of the lake. Outside the cottage, Joe the trees swayed under the wind's pressure. Small limbs snapped and were strewn over the lawn and driveway. Micah turned and headed for the last step in the process of fishing… cleaning.

"Dad, I can't remember seeing larger, blacker clouds swirling with such ferocity. It looked almost primeval. When we first saw the size of the storm, we turned tail and headed for home from near the middle of the lake. We were far from the boathouse, but I knew we could make it. The rain was horrendous. Sheets of it. The lake was churning. Three-to-four-foot waves and white caps everywhere. We were nearly swamped a few times. Micah did a great job bailing. The small motor on the boat wasn't made for racing, but we made it safe at home. It's almost like the storm was driving us."

"I'm glad you made it. I was worried."

"How was your nap?"

"Naps are always good. I had a dream. Strange, but not frightening."

"I mean no disrespect, Dad, but you look overly tired, despite your nap. You're pale and your hands are trembling."

"When I was bringing in the wood for the fireplace, I came upon a nest of vipers in the stack of logs behind the cottage. You know how much I hate snakes. These scared the bejeepers out of me. Lots of them, some of them poisonous. Many of them big. I was able to chase them away, but the scene was frightening. Then, I carried ten loads of wood. That's why I look tired."

"Here they are, Grandpa, fish cleaned and ready for cooking. I put the guts and heads in a garbage bag and put that in the trash barrel."

"Micah, I'll take your wet clothes and mine to the front porch. You'd better wash the fish smell off your hands."

The boy left the living room.

"Dad, taken collectively, the events of today are unnerving. The filthy scavengers and the dead critters on the back-yard lawn. How did they get there? They didn't just walk into the area and lay down to be killed. The snakes in the woodpile. There have never been snakes in the pile. How did they get there? And the huge storm over the lake that appears stationary. Why is the storm not moving to this side of the lake? It's almost as if it were herding us to this shore. But it just stopped. Does it want us to stay here and not on the lake? There's been a lightning flash every thirty seconds for the past hour. Just listen. The thunder doesn't boom, it sounds like the sky is splitting and the wind is screeching like a banshee. If I were superstitious, I'd say something, or someone is out to get us."

Joe looked sternly at Michael as if to say, *let's drop the subject and get dinner ready. We'll discuss this after Micah has gone to bed.*

Dinner prep was interrupted by a knock on the back door.

"Michael, please answer that."

The open door revealed an unshaven man in tattered, ill-fitting, and dirty clothes. He smiled inscrutably as if he knew something others did not. The flashes of lightning behind him emphasized his size and stature. Stooped and less than five and a half feet tall.

"Amon. Is that you? Come in."

"Joe, it's nice to see you. Heh, heh, heh. I'm checking on the houses along the way to make sure everything is safe. I see you're OK. I best be going."

"We're all safe and sound. Boys, this is Amon Kreider. He lives at the end of the road. Amon, this is my son Michael, and my grandson, Micah."

"Hi, boys. I remember Michael when he was a young boy and then a teen. This is the first time I've met Micah. Nice to see you both. Heh, heh, heh."

Handshakes all around.

Michael took note of Amon's dirty fingernails seemingly bitten down to the quick. Beneath the filthy ball cap, Amon's hair was long, greasy, and straggly. The length of facial stubble showed the last time he shaved and perhaps bathed was more than a few days ago … maybe a week.

"Got to get moving before the storm comes ashore and washes out the road. There's already tree limbs and such over it. Glad you're safe. Heh, heh, heh. Have a nice evening."

The stooped man flashed an enigmatic grin, turned, and left the house. Despite Amon's grin, his eyes appeared lifeless.

"That's nice of Amon. To look after the residences like that."

"Dad, what do you mean nice? There are no other people here this weekend. The Eshlemans and the Musselmans aren't here yet. Every year, we are the first to arrive for the summer season. It can't be a coincidence that he suddenly appears at our door. He's not been in this house for years. At least, I've not seen him here. His appearance seems strange to me. He looked dirty and disheveled when I first met him, and that hasn't changed one iota. If I may be bold, he seems like he has an ulterior motive for coming to the cottage … a less than honest motive. Like he was spying on us."

"Michael, be civil. Let the poor man be. If you could see how he lives, you would know that he is a humble man. I know him to be an honest and good man. I seriously doubt that his intensions about visiting us were evil. Now let's get ready to eat."

Chapter Nine

"That was a great meal. Micah, as the youngest, you have earned the right to do the dishes. And because your father and I love you, we will clear and wipe the table and scrape the plates."

The adults completed their respective chores, while the boy washed the dishes and let them air dry in the rack by the sink. Joe did not light the fire. He and Michael sat in comfortably worn chairs near the fireplace. On the mantel was an eighteen-inch high wooden cross. Mary had searched for the perfect pieces of dogwood to make the cross as a spiritual guide and protection for her family.

"Micah, in the time-honored tradition of opening weekend, the youngest male is permitted to light the first fire of the season. How will you do that?"

"First, I will check to be sure the paper, twigs, kindling, and logs are properly positioned. Then, I will open the damper. Next, I will light a few scraps of paper and hold them at the opening of the chimney. This will start the air to draft up the channel and make sure there is nothing blocking the air passage. I will place the burning paper beneath the twigs and wait. A fire can't be rushed. Small scraps of paper, twigs, and kindling will burn in sequence and in their own time. They will heat the air around the logs and then start the logs to burn."

"You have learned well. While you are about that and with your father's permission, I have a special treat for you. Tonight, three generations will sip the nectar of Scotland. The water of life. Is that's acceptable to you, Michael?"

"Yes, Dad. Micah, do NOT to tell your mother. Understand?"

The boy nodded.

The old man grinned and walked to the kitchen. He returned with three small glasses and a bottle of 25-year old single-malt whisky. He poured a dram into one glass and two drams into the others.

"Micah, this is not to be gulped. Good scotch is to be sipped slowly ... almost delicately and in small measures. And you should only drink good scotch. Gently draw the whisky into your mouth and across your tongue. Don't swallow it immediately. Let it mingle with your saliva and caress your taste buds. Only then is it truly enjoyed. Only then can it be swallowed ... also slowly. Remember, when you respect the scotch, you are respecting the skill of the people who distilled it and the years of aging it enjoyed. But most of all, you are respecting the fact that you are putting beautifully flavored alcohol into your body. The liquid is a foreign element, and thus potentially dangerous if ingested in great quantities over time. Always drink in moderation. Drink good scotch ... slowly and in very small amounts."

"Yes, Grandpa."

The boy sipped and immediately winced and stifled a cough. The alcohol flash in his mouth was quite powerful. In struggling to not spit out the whisky, he gulped it down.

"Wow, that's strong. Does it always taste like that, Dad?"

"If enjoyed properly and over time, no. This is your initiation to the fine art of adult drinking. It gets easier. Hopefully, not too easy. And not too soon. Wait a few minutes before you take the second sip. Let the rich smooth flavor caress your mouth and tongue."

During the next hour as the thunder and lightning raged over the lake and the wind whipped the trees around the cottage, the three generations, sitting before a comforting fire, sipped and talked about the upcoming week. Damp clothes were hanging on the screen before the fireplace to dry.

"Dad, I'm going to bed. I'm tired. The scotch has hit me."

Micah walked over to his father and kissed him on the cheek. Then to his grandfather. Another kiss.

"Thanks for the drink, Grandpa. I do hope it gets easier over time."

"You're welcome, Micah. It will. Sleep well."

The two men remained in the big room.

"Well, I think that answered his curiosity. I doubt he'll drink for quite some time."

"I hope you're right, Michael."

"Dad, I want to ask you a delicate question."

"I'm strong. I can handle any question you ask."

"OK. Do you ever feel mom's presence? I mean when you're home, do you ever feel that she is still there?"

"Yes. Occasionally and at odd times, I think of her so profoundly that I sense she is somewhere near me in the house. Late at night, when I awaken and can't get back to sleep, I go to the library and read. Some nights I can feel her in the room with me. As weird as it may sound, I also sense Sarah's presence. I don't see either of them. They make no noise. I just sense them in a pleasant, loving way. Why do you ask?"

"Ever since we arrived here, I have had the feeling that mom was with us. Not like a ghost in a sheet. I just feel her presence and her love. When I was putting away the food and other household items, I felt she was watching me from the living room the way she did when I was a teenager. Lovingly checking on me to make sure I lived up to her household standards. Obviously, she was not here, but the feeling was strong."

"I think we both are recalling her loving spirit and hoping it stays with us. I believe that when we open our hearts and minds to remember her love, the answer comes as the aura of her presence."

"OK, that somewhat religious explanation makes sense. Glad I'm not alone. Now to your pills. I noticed you're taking more pills more often during the day. Why so much medication?"

"My doctor thinks he has found the path to extend my life. I started this regimen at the beginning of the year. It was modified in April after an extensive check-up. My next check-up in July should show improvement. I'll be fine. Maybe I'll live to be a hundred. Let's move on."

"Not so fast, Dad. I also noticed you've lost weight since Christmas. If I had to guess, you've lost ten, maybe fifteen, pounds. It's not as though you were overweight, so that's relatively a big loss. I wonder if the weight loss and the medicine regimen go hand in hand."

"The doctors said there would be some side effects. Weight loss was one of them. Now let's move on."

The impatience in the older man's voice was obvious.

"Another area that needs to be explained. Who is Amon Kreider, except for a dirty little man who lives at the end of the road?"

"Let me pour another drink so I can focus my mind on this delicate subject. You best have another, too."

Joe poured his drink and handed the bottle to his son.

"As you may recall me telling you years ago, your mother's family, the Hess side, owned all the land on this side of the lake; from the end of this road to the far end of what is now the public area. They owned the land, but never built on it. Your Grandparents gave your mother and me this parcel of land as a wedding present. We had this cottage built. After grandfather Hess died, your grandmother sold two parcels of land: one to the Eshlemans and one to the Musselmans. The three families had been friends for years, and we still are. She also donated an expanse of shoreline to the county for use by the public. Now to Amon. Amon Kreider is an older relative of yours. Actually, he's your uncle. He was adopted by Nanna and Neen as a baby. He had been abandoned by his natural parents and turned over to an orphanage. He was a very late child for the couple. Nanna was well past her childbearing age. But she so loved children and was good at raising them. She raised him after her natural children were already grown. He was raised as part of the family … a delayed part. When your grandmother died, she left him the deed to the land where he now lives.

"While Amon was building his house, he fell from a rafter and struck his head on a large rock. He was in a coma for nearly two months and almost died. As he was recovering from the fall and coming out of the coma, the doctors determined he had suffered brain damage. Not enough to incapacitate him, but enough to dim his cognitive powers. It took him nearly two years to recover his basic physical faculties ... walking, talking, and manual dexterity. All the while and afterward, he remained mentally slow. He could not resolve that issue. I doubt he remembers that he is distantly related to us. He probably thinks of you as a much younger pal who lives down the road from him.

"These recent years, he looked after the three cottages during the winter when the owners were at their respective homes. He makes sure there are no break-ins and checks for storm damage. Who do you think cuts the trees and chops the logs that sit behind this building and the cottages of our neighbors? I send him money for his labors and diligence. So do the Eshlemans and the Musselmans. The balance of his money for living expenses comes from a small trust set up by your grandmother. He is decent and law abiding, which is why we trust him. He lives modestly. His purpose in life is that of a caretaker. And, he is good at it. We all need a purpose and hope we can be good at it."

"I never knew any of that. Why was I never told?"

"Your mother and I felt Amon's life story was his alone to tell, so it was not our place to tell you boys. You all were too young to truly understand. Plus, we felt there was no real benefit to you for knowing this story. Then you grew up and moved on with your lives. So, Amon's story just got lost in the family history book."

"I'm glad I know now. I'll look at him differently from now on and treat him with the same respect that you do. I have something else we need to discuss ..."

"Well, that's enough of the third degree. I've been up since the crack of yesterday, and the scotch has worked its night-time magic. I'm going to go to bed. I leave it up to you to scatter the embers in the hearth and make sure the screen in front of it is secure and free of your clothes. They can be draped over the chairs in the kitchen to finish drying. Unless you have a strong desire to watch the lightning flashes any longer, I suggest you turn in, too."

"I'm right behind you. Thanks for the talk. Love ya."

"Love you too, son."

Joe sat on the edge of his bed and pondered today. His hands were trembling as Michael noted. His heart was beating more rapidly, and he was sweating. The scotch or the events of the day? The move-in events he had seen before in one form or another, most of them when he and Mary had two very young sons. But he had never seen the dead animals, the scavengers, the pebbles, and the spots on the lawn all on the same day or in such volume. There were a few dead animals forty-five years ago, and they were found on warm ground. Scavengers were always flying around looking for a meal. Once he found three small, white stones that were warm. But, today. Are these new omens or just repeated coincidences? If something repeated, it was not a coincidence. Was something happening or about to happen at the Bickham's retreat. Something substantial? Something evil? What was wrong? With him? With this week end?

Chapter Ten

Joe was up before the sun. He used to joke that it was his job to ensure the sun rose every morning, so he had to go outside and pull it from its resting place in the east. When his boys were toddlers, they loved to watch him "bring in the day." Once, Michael asked his father to "do it again" and was told "tomorrow." This morning, dressed in comfortable work clothes, Joe was staring at the coffee pot hoping to speed its brewing process. It never worked. Finally, coffee. A touch of sugar and some milk in his big mug that Micah gave him. "World's Greatest Grandpa" was written in bold red letters on the off-white surface. Mug warming his hand, Joe stepped through the back door. The morning was chilly and damp. Summer mornings were not yet here.

He surveyed the killing field and focused on the overturned earth mound, the burial pit, and numerous vague outlines of freshly turned dirt, each the size of a serving plate. Spots where the dead rodents lay, and where he doused the kerosene. The dimness of night hid the details of the landscape, but not the shadows. The turned earth was visible because it was different. He sat on the back steps and stared at the strange checkerboard in his back yard. While he inhaled deeply the fresh air of the new day, he sensed other aromas mixed with the traditional smell of damp woods. Kerosene he recognized, but there was something else.

Joe also sensed he was not alone. He surveyed beyond the mottled ground into the woods trying to discern the presence of any other being. He remained stock-still and took shallow breaths to minimize any noise. Staring to his right, he spied motion. An animal was gracefully walking among the trees about forty yards away. Joe watched as the shape traveled cautiously around the perimeter of the yard. Was the shape stalking, reconnoitering, or just going somewhere? In the shadows, the shape looked to be a canine of substantial in size. Joe guessed over two and a half feet high and four feet long and solidly built. In the first hint of the morning light, the shape was darker than its surrounding environment. Was it a wolf? Wolves hadn't been seen in this area for decades. Whatever its purpose, the beast did not seem to be in a hurry or in an attack mode. Joe felt the canine was scouting the cabin and those who were there.

More shapes and more motion. The large animal was followed by four similar nut smaller shapes; Joe thinks he sees four. A pack of wolves? A scouting party? A raiding party? The followers were not petite or stunted, just smaller than the leader. The leader was large. Each follower was in lockstep with the alpha wolf. The overall pace was deliberate as if they knew where they were going. Occasionally, one of the four followers turned his head and sniffed in Joe's direction. There was no growling or howling from the five. The subtle beginnings of daylight clarified the outlines of the moving shapes. He stared at the leader.

The burly all-black beast turned toward Joe and stared. Joe was sure he saw the animal's eyes … probing eyes that did not glare. The beast's eyes were not yellow or golden; they appeared to be blue-gray. The eyes of beast and man meet and locked on. There was no anger in the animal. Joe felt no threat. He felt he was being examined; scanned for something. A feral MRI. In a strange way, he felt the pack leader was trying to communicate. Joe yawned. As with any deep multi-breath yawn, his eyes closed briefly.

As his eyes automatically opened, he noted the five have vanished. Just as suddenly as he saw them, the five shapes had disappeared. Did they run away? There was no noise or flurry of motion. Were they really there or was Joe seeing something in the dim early morning haze? Was it something he wanted to see? Something his mind told him to see. He continued to stare and scan the woods but saw nothing. His trance-like state was interrupted by noise in the kitchen.

"Dad, good morning. Thanks for starting the coffee."

"You're welcome, sleepy head."

"You're all dressed for a work day. Are you helping the sun rise? Did you pull it up from the east? Or are you sittin' on the back stoop just staring into the woods looking for answers to the mess we found? Waddaya see?"

"Nothin' except the trees. Thinkin' about all we have to do today, and it's a lot. You'd better get dressed. And while you're at it, wake up Micah. I'll start breakfast. Bacon and eggs."

"That'll be great. Be back in a few minutes to help."

Joe stood and walked into the yard to the closest spot where a critter had died. The smell of kerosene floated above the spot. But there was another odor mixed with that of kerosene. The heavy petroleum odor only partially masked the second scent. Upon inspection, he saw animal tracks in the grass around the dirt-covered spot. Canine prints. A few of the prints were massive – about the length and breadth of the back of his hand from his wrist to the major knuckle on his fingers. The grass had been matted down by the weight of the leader beast. He also discerned slightly smaller prints of the alpha's followers. Were they sniffing around looking for scraps or just investigating the area? Joe noticed the larger prints seemed to circle the first area, then the second, and the third. The big wolf walked around each spot. The other tracks indicating the followers, did not. It seemed the followers simply came to the spot, stopped, and moved to the next one, following the alpha.

Joe leaned closer to one of the spots and inhaled. Now he knew the second odor … urine. The wolves were marking this territory: one dead-critter spot at a time. Joe was puzzled. Why mark around the places where the critters died? Was the entire back yard marked? What was so special about the spots? He reached down to one dirt-covered spot. About a foot from the ground, he felt a subtle warmth rising to meet his hand. The same heat he noted on the round white pebbles. There was no heat from the area a foot to the right and a foot to the left of the spot. Heat was only found at the spot that had held a dead animal and had been covered by dirt. Very strange. At three inches above that

49

spot, the temperature became almost hot. A hot smelly spot. What the hell was all this about?

Joe walked to the back stoop. The smell of wolf urine was now recognizable here. Bent over, the old man walked around the cottage sniffing and deeply inhaling every six feet or so. In total, he smelled six places where a wolf squirted territory markers. Then he went to the edge of the woods where he had seen the wolves. Trudging amidst the undergrowth, he leaned over to inhale any odor of territory marking … nothing but the smell of decaying leaves and branches. No urine. The spots and the cottage were marked, but not the land that surrounds them. Puzzled, Joe returned to the back door and stepped into the kitchen for his breakfast chore.

Chapter Eleven

The three generations set about their morning tasks; Micah was in the boathouse making sure the boat was ready for an afternoon on the lake with his cousins. He had to complete the water bailing, dry the vessel, and check the vests. Then he had to be sure the engine was dry to start and there was enough fuel for the day. Michael was clearing and cleaning the flagstone patio in the front of the cottage facing to the lake where the family would enjoy outdoor meals. Joe put a second layer of dirt on each spot in the back yard in an effort to completely mask what was beneath. After wetting each mound stomped the second layer into the earth. Then he re-tamped the pyre pit. Some things were better securely covered. The threesome's tasks were interrupted by Shelia's car horn announcing her arrival at the gate. Micah, running from the boathouse, grabbed the key from his grandfather and sprinted to unlock the gate. Mother and son arrive in a few minutes.

"Good morning, Shelia. You worked all night then drove nearly four hours. Wow! You must be tired."

"Good morning, Joe. I'm a little tired. Where is my big boy? I need a manly hug."

"Hey there, lady. Happy you're here."

A big hug from her husband. Michael returned to his chores. Micah stood ready to help unload the car. Joe sensed something. He stood back and stared at his daughter-in-law from the rear but saw nothing unusual.

"Micah, grab the bags from the car, please. Joe, I brought some food and my homemade sauce for the bar-b-que. No offense, but the bottled sauce you buy is mostly vinegar. Mine is mostly molasses with a touch of vinegar and lemon, and my secret spices."

"No offense taken. I was hoping you'd bring your sauce."

There was something about her that was different, but Joe couldn't determine what it was.

"I don't want you to interrupt your work, but I'm famished. I need to eat."

At that moment, Shelia turned sideways, and Joe spied the difference. His daughter-in-law was pregnant.

"When's the baby due?"

"You noticed. Late October."

"Hard to miss the bump from this angle. Congratulations to both of you. Do you know if the child is boy or girl?"

"We don't know. We wanted the joy of surprise. But with all the fussing going on inside me, my guess is we will have a second son. Regardless, we have a flexible name; Christian for a boy and Christina for a girl."

"Now, I'll take a hug."

The embrace was deep but brief.

"I really have to eat something. I am being ordered to eat by the life force within me. It's becoming cranky. Then I want to take a quick nap before Gabriel and Martha arrive."

"Scoot. There's plenty of food in the kitchen. I want to talk to Michael. We'll wake you when the Illinois tribe arrives."

Joe left the back yard and walked to the front of the cottage. Michael had policed the area of small branches, large twigs, and trash blown by the storm. He was now raking what remains from the area.

"When were you going to tell me?"

The son lowered his head in reaction to the father's inquiry.

"It seems you already know. We have been trying to have a second child for the past few years. We'd almost given up hope. Then it happened. We lived through the first-three-months' thing of telling no one. Finally, we told Micah and swore him to secrecy. We decided to wait for this weekend, so we could make a big family announcement.

We didn't mean to exclude you. Sorry, if we hurt your feelings. I thought you'd understand."

"I'm not hurt, and I understand. But I just wanted to make you feel guilty and uneasy."

"You succeeded."

The two men smiled and hugged.

About two hours later, the quiet of the woods was shattered by a blaring claxon and the revving of a big engine. The rest of Joe's family, the bombastic side, had arrived, but they couldn't get through the locked gate at the road's mouth.

"I'll go down the road and admit the crown prince and his three angels."

Michael walked very slowly toward the locked gate to piss off his older and demandingly impatient brother. Michael was in control. The flashing lights and honking horn of the SUV confirmed that Gabriel was aware he was not in control. He was at the mercy of his younger brother, dangling the gate key in front of his face for everyone in the car to see. Michael could easily walk the quarter of a mile in a few minutes, but his pace was so deliberate that it would take ten minutes or more. Grinding his brother's nose in it was the fun part of control.

"Hurry up, slow poke! What's taking you so long?"

"Always the charmer. Are you practicing to be a diplomat? What's your hurry? The cottage will be there when you get there. It's not going away. And we saved you lots of chores. By the way, I can't help but notice the huge size of your rental. Are you compensating for some deficiency?"

"Screw you, Mikey!"

"Easy, Gabby. Stop the commotion. You're scaring the neighbors."

"Who are the neighbors except for that creep at the end of the road. What's his name?"

"Amon Kreider."

"I'll bet the dirty little man is peering from one of his windows at me and my car.

With that, Gabriel raised both hands with each middle finger extended in the direction of Amon's house.

"Take it easy, Gabe, until you know the whole story about Amon."

"What whole story?"

"Well, for one thing, he's your uncle."

"No way! That bum can't be my uncle."

"You can ask Dad, but only if I let you through the gate."

"I gotta hear this. Hurry up."

"What's the magic word?"

"Please."

"Thank you."

When Michael unlocked and opened the gate, Gabriel accelerated aggressively. The big SUV bounced rudely on the rutted lane. The three female passengers bounced off their seats like rag dolls. Michael could hear their complaints. He closed the gate, locked it, and began to jog alongside the automobile. The car had slowed to a snail's pace. The ladies insisted upon slow travel. Michael passed the car before it reached the *Tucquhalla* driveway.

"Dad, I give you the boy prince."

"Hey, pops, howyadoin'?"

"I'm fine Gabriel. How was your trip?"

"Easy peasy. I do love flying first class without the riffraff around me."

"Pomposity, thy name is Gabriel."

"Do I detect jealousy, little brother?"

"Jealous of you. Not likely. By the by, how long did you have to grovel before the HR manager to gain access to the plane?"

"After I scheduled an appointment with an important client, I put my name on the list, detailed the reason and time I needed the plane, and I'm in like Flynn … in the comfort of a private jet. Which, by the way, allowed me to bring a case of very expensive wine for late afternoons and dinners. Girls, help your mother unload the car. Make your beds. You're sleeping in the bunkroom with Micah. And, Micah, be careful with the case of wine. We don't want it to be bruised or a bottle broken. If the wine is bruised, all the money I spent on the rare vintage would be wasted. We don't want to waste that much money, now do we?"

Michael and Joe winced at the arrogance. It had always been Gabriel's way. He approached his father and extended his hands and arms to initiate a hug. The old man looked onto Gabriel's sallow skin and puffy face and was taken back by the signs of overindulgence. Too much alcohol and rich food, most likely well after nine in the evening. As he gripped his son, Joe felt a soft and bloated midsection. The sickeningly sweet odor of juniper seemed to ooze from Gabriel's pores. Gin. All the signs confirmed that there was something awry with his son's physical well-being. Most likely driven by an issue with his emotional well-being. Are these the manifestations of work stress, or are they the self-indulgent rewards of ego-enhanced success?

"Gabriel, get changed into work clothes. You have a lot to do before dinner. Martha, Shelia is resting, but she wanted me to ask you to wake her when you arrive."

Chapter Twelve

"OK, Dad, the beds are made, and our clothes put away. We're ready for our chauffeured lake excursion. Where's Micah?"

"Girls, he's down at the boathouse making sure the boat is ready."

"Thanks, Grandpa. See you guys later."

Lilith and Agnes, or Lillie and Aggie as they want to be called, were Gabriel's daughters. Lillie would be a high school senior this year, while Aggie was two years behind Micah. They got their good looks from their mother, Martha, a beauty, who had won several pageants in her youth. It was their attitude that bothered Joe. He thought their attitude was a mixture of aggressiveness and arrogance. Lillie's aggressive and arrogant attitude was far more pronounced than Aggie's. But the old man feared that Aggie would get to that point soon. Maybe the girls acted as they did because they've been spoiled since birth and felt entitled to have whatever they wanted. Or maybe they're just teen girls acting like they're hormonally programmed to act. Given their good looks, Joe sees how they could get almost whatever they wanted, particularly from the male of the species. If that's the case, the old man should have felt sorry for Gabe, but he did not. Maybe the girls' behavior contributed to his drinking. Or was a reaction to it.

The 17- and 12-year-old girls charged through the front porch, the screen door slammed, and they ran giggling to Micah. Joe was happy he and Mary had boys. He could deal with boys as an older peer, and because the boys adored their mother, they obeyed her every wish.

"Gabe, please help Michael make sue the outdoor eating area will be ready for dinner tonight. You'll need a bucket, some spray cleaner, and several rags to wash and wipe the chairs and table. Also, please scrub down the flagstones. They're covered with algae. I don't want anyone to slip and fall."

"Aye aye, Captain."

"That's wonderful, Shelia. When's the baby due? Is it a boy or girl? How do you feel?"

"Slow down, Martha."

"I can't. I'm so excited for you. A baby. There's a large part of me that wishes I could have another. But Gabriel made sure that could never happen. And, he never consulted me when he made that decision. In fact, he rarely consults me on any big issue."

"Well, since you asked … late October, we're not sure of the sex because we wanted to be surprised, and I feel healthy and truly alive. The only issues are fatigue and food. I get tired quite quickly during my rotations. I sit as often as I can. Can't have coffee or tea to boost me, because the caffeine is not good for the life force. I work slowly. I'm lucky because with my patients, speed is not normally critical. But food is a big issue for me. I seem to eat everything in sight that isn't nailed down. If I don't eat something every two hours, the baby becomes agitated. It almost seems like he wants to kick through my stomach and grab food for himself. Based on this level of frenetic activity and constant clamoring for food, I believe the child is male. No dainty little girl would be so rude."

"Yeah, sure. Both my girls moved around so much that I feared they were going to punch a hole in my stomach. I think the level of their kicking and fussing can be traced directly to Gabe's bombastic approach to life. Can't say the same about Michael. He always seems so calm and in control. The opposite of the bull I married."

"Micah, take us around the lake, and make it snappy. We want to see everything."

Thus, began the excursion. Two teenage girls relaxed ... leaned back to soak up the sun. He thought of two Cleopatra wannabes on their own version of the barge floating on the Nile. He saw that painting at the Philadelphia Museum of Art. But there was no sail and Micah was not a Nubian.

"Micah, do you think anyone on shore can see us?"

"Not sure, Aggie. If we go nearer the middle of the lake, for sure no one can see us then. They'll see just a small boat. Why do you ask?"

"Take us to the middle, now, knave."

"Aye aye, milady."

The boat moved to the midpoint then slowed to a stop.

"Here we are. Now what?"

"Now we're going swimming. But, since we have no suits, you'll have to look away as we get out of our clothes."

Micah turned away and stared back at the cottage. He wished he were there. This was embarrassing.

"I don't think swimming is a good idea."

"Why? Will some horrible, giant fish attack us?"

"No, it's not dangerous, it's..."

Two splashes interrupted his response.

"...very cold."

The screams and thrashing confirmed the girls' surprise at the water temperature.

"Get us out of here. Hurry! It's too damned cold! Why didn't you warn us?"

He heard Lillie, but Micah did not move from his position aft. He couldn't extricate his cousins from their predicament without gazing upon them. He tried to warn them. They chose not to listen. Let them live and learn.

"Help us out of the water. Now!"

"I'll move to the starboard side of the boat, so you ladies can climb aboard on the port side. One at a time or the boat will tip and take on water."

He returned his glance to the cottage but had a difficult time not laughing at the girls. He coughed to relive this emotional pressure. First Lillie, then Aggie struggled to hoist herself aboard. Despite the warm sun, they were trembling. Shaking like frightened puppies.

"Where are the towels?"

"Back at the boathouse."

"You mean, you didn't bring towels for us. We have nothing to dry ourselves?"

"I didn't realize you were going to take a plunge. In less than thirty minutes, the sun will warm you. Your clothes will absorb much of the water from your bodies. But they will take about an hour or so to dry."

"Thanks for the big nothing."

He turned to confront this accuser, Aggie, and only glanced at her small, yet-to-be-fully developed teenage body. He shifted his gaze to Lillie. He was intrigued by the sight of this nude older teenage girl. He tried to avert his eyes, but he stared uncontrollably. Micah wondered if this is what Pat's body looked like after a shower. Or was she more like Aggie. Lillie had small, but apparently firm breasts, a slim waist, and a tuft of hair below the belly button. Her hands were on her hips, as she stood defiantly, almost daring him to look at her or say something. Her gaze was fixed on Micah's crotch. Aggie had strategically placed her right hand on her lady parts and her left arm over her emerging breasts. She was embarrassed. He was also embarrassed at staring. Lillie was not embarrassed. She was defiant in her nakedness.

"What are you gawking at, Micah? Haven't you seen a real girl in the flesh before? Do you like what you see?"

He was blushing, and she saw it. A weakness on which Lillie pounced.

"So, we went skinny-dipping. And now we are naked standing before you. It's no big deal to us. But it appears to be a big deal to you. Are you getting excited? I think I see your excitement rising."

"Not a big deal for me either, just unexpected. I can't wait until your parents see you both in wet clothes, and with hair all matted like a rat. You guys'll catch hell."

"Give me your T-shirt to dry off."

"No, Aggie. You're on your own. Perhaps if we go around the lake a few times, your dilemma will be less obvious."

"OK. Let's do that."

The moving boat caused the two girls to struggled to put their dry clothes on their damp bodies. With the clothes clinging to every curve of their bodies, the girls sat on the boat's front bench to take maximum advantage of the air and sun. Micah headed for a trip around the lake. A large Cheshire-cat grin crept over his face.

"Mikey, all this work has made me thirsty. Gonna get a beer. Want one?"

"No thanks, Gabby."

Gabe had been working less than thirty minutes and he had already sweated up a storm. Not just his underarms, but the back and chest of his T-shirt was soaked through. This was strange. According to the large round thermometer on the side of the house next to the patio, the temperature was 68. The breeze off the lake would keep the temperature at that comfortable level or lower all day. In addition to seeing Gabe's sweat, Michael smelled the ambergris-like sweetness of alcohol oozing from his brother's pores. Gabe returned with two beers.

"I said I didn't want a beer."

"These are both for me. I'm really thirsty. Although I don't know why. I had a lot to drink last night. Ha, ha."

"Very funny, Gabe. Let me ask you something personal."

"Fire away."

"Do you ever think you drink too much?"

"No. But often I think I haven't had enough to drink."

"I'm serious. Does your drinking ever interfere with your work? Or your family life?"

"No! And that's enough on the subject of my lifestyle."

"OK. Sorry for scratching at a sore spot."

"It's not a sore spot. It's just none of your damned business!"

Joe was sitting on the back stoop holding a paper bag that held the eighteen white stones he collected yesterday. He reached into the bag and was startled by the heat. He thought the stones were as hot or hotter than they were when he found them. He gingerly retrieved two and placed them on the wooden step beside him. He stared at them trying to discern something that may or may not be there; some telltale mark or clue to the stones' origin or meaning. He saw nothing.

"Joe, it's almost time for lunch. I know the day laborers on the patio will want something. How about you?"

"A sandwich will be great, Martha."

"I know you and your sandwiches. So, I'll leave the construction up to you. Shelia and I will leave the fixin's on the kitchen table. Bread, meat, cheese, lettuce, tomato, mayo, and mustard will be there when you're ready to build. What do you have there? Oh, white stones. I never saw anything like them around the cottage before. Where did you find them?"

"They were scattered over the back yard. I agree. I've never seen anything like these in the many years of coming to the cottage. Very interesting."

"Let's take a closer look at them. Shelia, come out here. Joe has found something very interesting."

Joe emptied the contents of the bag. The three adults scanned the pile of stones.

"I see fifteen or so light-colored or white pebbles. Nothing unusual there."

"Feel them, Martha."

"Whoa, they're hot, Joe. I guess the sun worked its magic on them."

"They have been in this bag, which has been inside the cottage since I found them yesterday. The sun has had little or no effect on them. Shelia, what do you see?"

"I see eighteen stones and I can feel the heat. Based on a cursory view of the stones, I see two possibilities for the heat. Some type of chemical reaction is occurring within the stones or are they transmitting heat from another source. If the first is accurate, we're looking at living organisms. Now that's more than strange. Stones as living beings is impossible. And it's unlikely that a chemical reaction would be occurring within the stones. If there were a chemical reaction, it would most likely come to the surface or crack the stone due to pressure from within. I would rule out internal reaction as a viable possibility."

"What about the second possibility?"

"The second possibility is based on the theory that the stones are somehow connected to a force beyond their location. It would be like the electrical sockets in a house. The only power they have they receive from the utility company. The heat of the stones would thus be generated from somewhere outside the stones themselves. In the earth or outside the property. But that is such a bizarre hypothesis that it's simply not reliable. Where exactly did you find them, Joe?"

"Scattered in the back yard."

"Does Michael know of these warm stones?"

"No, you two are the first to see them."

"I can't deal with this now. It's too strange. I've got to make sure everyone is fed. Shelia, are you coming?"

Martha rose abruptly and quickly went to the kitchen. Shelia followed.

After his daughters-in-law left, Joe saw something interesting. The eighteen stones could be grouped by size. From smallest to largest, there were three groups of six each: a group of small stones, each about the size of a dime: a group of medium size stones, about the size of a quarter;

and a group of larger stones, about silver-dollar size. Three groups of six each; six, six, six.

If Joe believed in the biblical prophecy, that 666 is the sign of the devil or the great evil the stones could mean that an evil force was here. Most likely, the stones were another example of the folklore that was centered on this property. If he believed the lore, the stones could help explain why the vermin were found dead in the back yard. It could help explain why the birds came to find the vermin. Balderdash! Folklore was a distorted conspiracy theory; each part of an expansive and overriding theory confirmed the other parts when examined on an *ex post facto* basis. Everything fit into a neat and believable construct. Circular logic confirming the illogical.

Folklore was crazy. In fact, it was unbelievable. And definitely not repeatable by rational men. While it could make for an interesting campfire story, the concept of a great evil revealing itself through dead vermin, scavengers, scorched earth, and hot white stones was simply beyond man's ken. What Joe had here were eighteen white stones that were hot. That in and of itself was strange enough without introducing a supernatural force from folklore. Joe was hungry.

Chapter Thirteen

The screaming and crying that emanated from the boathouse could be heard inside the cottage, and probably down at the entrance gate.

"Mom! Dad! Come here quick!"

Micah's cry for help was met with an immediate response – five adults stopped washing-up and getting lunch ready and ran to the boathouse. Michael was the first to arrive. He threw open the door and was immediately attacked by three yellow jackets. They bit his arms and hands as he tried to fend them off. The searing hot stings were minor distractions as he rushed to protect his son.

"Micah, are you OK?"

"I think so. But those damned things hurt a lot."

"Get out of here and run back to the cottage. What about the girls?"

"They're lying on the bottom of the boat. I tried to cover them with beach towels."

The swarm was hovering over the bodies beneath towels. It seemed to be poised to launch a well-coordinated and massive strike against the two girls. They were wailing hysterically and thrashing their arms and feet in an effort to ward off the few yellow jackets that found their way beneath the towels.

Their father arrived.

"Gabe, give me a hand. Grab two towels. Cover your head and shoulders with one. Roll down your sleeves to protect your arms. That should be enough to keep us safe while we get the girls. Use the second towel to shoo away the jackets. We need to get the girls out of here at once."

"Right with you."

Michael took the lead, flapping a towel as he moved forward. The air currents created by the activity were enough to disperse many of the winged attackers. Leaning into the boat, he lifted hysterically screaming Lillie. Gabe grabbed Aggie. The men stood the girls upright and wrapped towels around them. This did not provide complete coverage. The yellow jackets spotted vulnerability and dove at the exposed legs. Michael took the towel from his head and swatted the attackers. Gabe did the same. None killed. Many dispersed. The men hoisted the girls, rushed to the door, slammed it closed, and headed for the cottage. Joe, Martha, and Shelia, waiting outside, followed. The entire family was in the main room. The girls were on couches. They were in intense pain, screaming, crying, and scratching.

"Shelia, what should we do?"

"First, Michael, would you go to my car and retrieve my bag. I need some things to help me with the girls."

"Mommy! Daddy! Help me! It hurts so much."

"Aunt Shelia will take care of you, Lillie."

"Mommy. What about me?"

"You, too, Aggie. Aunt Shelia is a doctor."

Amid near panic manifested by tears and loud adult voices, Shelia calmly assumed the mantles of leadership and control … her style at the hospital.

"My area of expertise is geriatric oncology not yellow jacket stings. My immediate concern is that the girls may go into anaphylactic shock. To avoid this, we should seek emergency medical attention at once."

"Why immediate medical attention? Wouldn't rest be the best medicine?"

"Gabe, anaphylaxis can quickly result in an increased heart rate, sudden weakness, a drop in blood pressure, shock, and ultimately unconsciousness. There is only one rapidly effective treatment for anaphylaxis – epinephrine by injection. Epinephrine is adrenaline and it rapidly reverses anaphylactic symptoms. It is typically given through an automatic injection device called an EpiPen. In the absence of straight epinephrine, antihistamines may be taken orally to mitigate the symptoms. Does anyone have any antihistamines?"

No offers.

"Thanks for the bag, Michael. I need to monitor the girls' temperature and blood pressure."

"We need to do something. The girls are in agony."

"I know, Martha."

"Mommy, help me! Please!"

"We need to do something to retard the spread of the toxin injected by the yellow jackets. We need a stop-gap measure before we can get help from a local ER. The closest town is about eighteen miles away. My guess is that they have a small hospital or clinic and EMS. Given the condition of the rural roads, it will take the EMTs at least thirty minutes to get here. So, Gabe, please call them now! There is no time to waste."

"We have no epinephrine and no antihistamines. What else is there that will help my daughters while we wait?"

"I know an old-fashioned remedy that will partially relieve the pain. Salt will draw the poison from the sting site. We need to make a salt paste and slather the paste on the sting sites. Joe, can you gather all the salt in the house and pour it into a mixing bowl?"

"Will do."

"Shelia, I have no service on my phone. Can anyone get a signal in this god-forsaken place?"

Three more phones checked, and three similar negative responses.

"Joe, do you know of a landline we can use?"

"No, but Amon probably has one. I'll go to his house and ask."

"Somebody, go now! Martha, take over Joe's salt duties, we really need the mixture, immediately. Time is critical. The sooner it is applied, the sooner the toxin will begin to be drawn from the girls' bodies. Mix the salt with a few drops of water to make the paste. Be careful not to add too much water or the result won't be the right consistency. It will be too runny. I need a thick paste, like plaster."

"I need to remove the girls' clothes, so I can find all the bite marks. Gabe, while Martha is mixing, go into the bunkroom and get me three sheets. For propriety's sake, the girls need to be covered while I examine them. Micah, you had better stand in the kitchen away from the girls. While your back is turned, remove your shirt. Leave your underpants on and wrap a sheet around yourself. I'll examine you after the girls."

Joe turned to leave for Amon's house when the flurry of activity was interrupted by a knocking on the back door.

"I got it."

Standing on the back stoop is Amon Kreider. He was holding a small bottle and a medium-size bowl.

"Amon, thank gawd you're here. I need to know if you have a landline telephone. We need to call for emergency medical help."

"I know. I came to help."

"Help? How did you know we needed help?"

"I have this tea that will help calm the girls' fever. And a mixture of herbs, wild plants, and flowers that will fight the poison of the yellow jacket stings."

"Before we apply any backwoods remedies, I need to know how the hell do you knew about the girls' condition."

"I had seen the three children on the lake as they headed back to the boathouse. Late spring is the time of year when the yellow jacket queens begin the reproduction cycle. They build their nests in protected places like the boathouse, which is damp and dark. The males like to swarm around their queen. Then I heard the girls crying out for help. I knew they had been attacked by the yellow jackets. I just put two and two together. I'm only trying to help."

"Amon, please come in. The girls can use all the help we can give them. We may be able to use your remedies before the EMTs arrive."

"Joe, my door is unlocked. You can go to the house and call for help."

Joe exited and walked as fast as he could to Amon's house.

"Ma'am. You must be the doctor who's married to Michael."

"Yes, my name is Shelia. Now what have you brought?"

"The tea is brewed from flowers and tree bark found around these parts. It calms fevers and it strengthens the body to fight illness and poisons. I use it whenever I have a bad cold. It's safe to drink, but it should be warm to the touch. Not hot. Just warm. I must warn you that it does not taste good. It is bitter, and the smell is unpleasant. The children will not like the taste, but it will help them. The mixture in the bowl should be applied directly to the bite sites. It is made from herbs, wild plants, and roots. It looks like mud and smells like the earth, but it relieves the pain of the bites and fights the venom of the sting."

"Easy there, Amon. How do we know these rural remedies are safe, or that they will actually help the girls? How do we know this isn't just some backwoods hokum? Where did you learn to make the tea and the goop in the bowl?"

"My mother taught me which natural plants to use and how to mix them the right way. She gave me the tea when I was young and used the mixture on me a few times. They're both safe and they work."

"Shelia, I don't feel comfortable using these untested natural remedies on my girls."

"Gabe, if Grandmother Hess showed Amon these remedies, I have faith they're safe and will work on the girls just as he says. We must do something before the EMS truck arrives. It could be a while."

"I dunno. Martha, what do you think?"

"If your grandmother taught Amon, we should trust him."

"OK. You're the boss."

"Michael, please warm the tea."

"Michael, be careful not to boil it. If boiled, it will stink up the whole house. And, it will lose its healing power."

"Thanks for the warning, Amon."

"Amon, please bring me the bowl and show me how the mixture should be applied."

"I don't want to come too close to the little girls. They're naked, and they would be embarrassed if a stranger gazed upon them. So, while you are treating the girls, I'll stand back here and answer any questions you might have. Heh, heh, heh."

"Thank you for your consideration. Gabe, take the bowl that Amon brought and hand it to me."

"Just put the smallest amount on each site. A small dab directly on the site where the stinger entered the skin. Then rub it into the site until it begins to dry. It dries quickly. Then leave it alone for about an hour. It can be washed off after that. A second dose can be applied to certain spots if necessary."

"Gabe, will you get a pen and piece of paper to write down what I tell you? I'll need the information for a baseline."

"Gottit."

"Lillie: Temp 102.1, Pulse 84, and BP 125 over 73."

"Aggie: Temp 101.9, Pulse 88, and BP 130 over 81."

"I need to hurry. Martha, I'll apply the mixture first to Lillie. Please pay close attention. For the sake of prompt treatment, I will need you to do the same applications to Aggie. Micah, can you hold on a little while longer while I treat the girls?"

"Sure, Mom, but hurry."

"Good soldier. I'll be with you very soon."

"Amon, I'm going to apply the mixture to a site on Lillie's arm. I want to be sure that I'm doing it correctly. Can you see from the kitchen?"

"Yes, doctor … er Shelia. Just use a little bit. The rubbing is important to make sure the medicine gets into the sting spot and the skin around it. Yellow jackets don't leave stingers. They bite."

"Martha, after watching me take care of the first two sites, you can begin to apply the mixture and rub it on the Aggie's."

"Good gawd, I've never seen so many welts on my poor babies."

"Michael, someone better unlock the gate at the end of the road for the ambulance. Martha and I will start the application with the arms and shoulders, then the legs, and finally the back and stomach. Hang tough, Micah, you're next. OK, here we go."

As the parents assumed their appointed duties, they realized that the girls' screaming and crying had morphed into moans of extreme discomfort. Michael found the key to the gate lock and headed down the road.

Chapter Fourteen

The *worp-worp-worp* of the EMS truck was heard getting closer and closer. Its arrival at the cottage was slowed by the road from the gate. Then two technicians, one male and one female, were at the back door.

"Come inside."

"Can anyone tell us what happened?"

Shelia asked everyone to be quiet while related the events from the boathouse to the cottage. She was speaking in terms the technicians understand and follow.

"Who are you, ma'am?"

"Doctor Shelia Bickham. I'm an attending physician at University Hospital in Philadelphia. These girls are my nieces and the boy is my son. Here is my ID."

"Well, Doctor Bickham, we'll take over now. Thanks for your help."

"The three children are all yours. When you take the girls' vitals, would you mind reading them to me.? I have a baseline."

The female technician took over.

"Sure thing. Now let's take a look at you, young lady. What's your name?"

"Lillie."

"Well, Lillie, as a first step to helping you, I need to read your temperature, heart rate, and blood pressure. OK?"

"Yes."

"Your temperature is 100.1. Pulse is 70. And your blood pressure is 105 over 70. It seems that given what you went through you're in pretty good condition."

"What's all this gunk on your body?"

"Excuse me. The gunk, as you call it, is a homeopathic remedy which will reduce the bite site swelling and minimize any infection caused by the venom of the yellow jacket stings."

"Doctor, is it on both girls?"

"I applied it to all three children."

"We need to wash it off until we can determine if it is safe."

"No! It must stay on the sting sites for at least an hour."

"And who are you?"

"I am the children's granduncle. I've lived in this part of the country since my childhood. My mother used the mixture on me after I got stung. It is safe and it works. The important first hour will be up in a few minutes. You must let the gunk, as you call it, alone. Heh, heh, heh."

"I'm not sure it's safe. And I'm very sure it does not meet any accepted medical protocol. Home remedies are just that – remedies. They are not medicines approved by the FDA or the medical profession. The gunk must be washed off so we can examine the stings."

"As a licensed physician and the girls' aunt and boy's mother, I take full responsibility for the remedy. Therefore, I insist that it remain on their bodies for another fifteen minutes. Then you can remove it to examine their skin. In the meantime, would you please go to your truck and get three vials of injectable epinephrine just in case the mixture is only temporarily effective and anaphylaxis occurs. I'll write scripts for them. Now, what are Aggie's vitals?"

The male technician leaves for the truck.

"The readings are Temp 99.5, Pulse 70, and BP 110 over 68."

"Please look at the readings I took as baselines for both of them about an hour ago. See the incredible improvement in such a short time. The gunk is working to relieve the sting reactions and it's working fast."

The EMT was silent ... stunned.

"Well, I guess we can leave it on the skin for a few more minutes. After that, I will need to wash it off and examine the sting sites."

"That'll be fine. Thank you for indulging us."

"How about your son? Is he as covered by the stings as the girls are?"

"No. He received only five stings, while the girls each received between twenty and thirty."

"I still need to read his vitals. Do you have a baseline on him?"

"Yes. I noted it on a separate piece of paper. Go."

"Temp is 98.8, his pulse is 66, and BP is 100 over 60."

The technician looked at the baseline readings.

"While your baseline readings were not as high as those of your cousins, young man, your present readings are excellent. You must be an athlete."

"I wrestle and run track."

"Fewer stings and solid athletic conditioning are the root causes of your near-robust readings."

"Love ya, Micah."

"Love ya, Mom."

The faces of the family seemed to relax and small smiles of relief appeared.

"While we are waiting the prescribed hour, I need to take down some information from you."

With the completion of the three forms, all reticence and potential animosity had disappeared. The family had stared down a crisis, and the two EMTs had been cordial and understanding of the family's wishes. There was no reason to tell the technicians about the tea. The female technician washed the dried mixture from the sting sites. There were bite spots with redness, but very little swelling. The children admitted the pain was gone.

"It seems that your home remedy has worked to mitigate the issue. I suggest bedrest for the children to allow their bodies to regain strength lost in fighting the venom. Doctor, if you will, please take another round of readings in an hour just to be sure the children are on the right path."

"Yes."

"Now a final housecleaning item. I will need you to sign this release form and enter your medical license number. The form states that we have been here, found no reason to take the children to the hospital, and have left them in your care."

"Not a problem. Again, thank you for being there when we needed you … and for understanding our position."

The male technician handed Shelia the vials in exchange for the prescriptions. Joe stepped forward.

"I'll walk you back to your truck."

"No need."

"I insist."

Upon arriving at the EMS truck, Joe reached into a large brown bag and withdrew two bottles of his favorite Scottish nectar.

"I want you each to have one of these."

"We really can't accept gifts."

"They are not gifts. They are payments in lieu of cash. People in these parts have been working this way for years. They call it barter. You don't have to tell anyone or report them on your taxes. Just promise me you won't drink the contents before your shift is over."

"Thank you, Mr. Bickham. And we promise. Now we must leave."

The truck cautiously lumbered down the road. Joe followed it to lock the gate. His pace was measured. He avoided the pitfalls of the uneven earth. The return to the cottage took longer than the trip to the gate. At this time of day and after all the commotion, Joe was beginning to feel tired. The frenetic crisis of the past hour had energized him, but now it enervated his old body. The children have had a drink of Amon's tea and were resting in the bunkroom.

Chapter Fifteen

"Shelia, it's been quite a while since the children had their first drink of the tea. Before they lie down to sleep, we should be sure to give them another small cup. It will help them sleep. And sleep is what they need now. Let their young bodies regain the strength lost fighting the stings."

"Amon, you are a godsend. How can we ever repay you?"

"You're family. I only did what any family member would do. Now I must get going. Heh, heh, heh."

"Not so fast, Amon. You're staying for dinner. We insist. Getting to know you as family is long overdue."

"I don't want to be a bother."

"As family and a good neighbor, you're not a bother."

"Thanks, Joe."

"Joe, you and Amon, get out of here and sit on the patio while the four of us prep dinner."

"Shelia, I normally don't like taking orders in my own house, but this is a special occasion. Your mastery of the crisis was impressive. You marshaled the confused army to deal with a family problem. You must be terrific at the hospital. With that talent, I place you in charge of the dinner preparation. You have the authority over the other adults. Amon and I will repair to the patio. Amon, do you drink scotch?"

"I rarely drink alcohol. When I do, I have a beer."

"Tonight is special. You have saved my grandchildren. Tonight, you and I will celebrate family: past, present, and future. I have two glasses and the bottle. I will teach you the time-honored method of enjoying very good scotch. Now we must make space for the kitchen commandant and her help. We are not needed here."

"Shelia, how can we really trust what Amon said about the tea and his herbal stuff you applied to the bite sites?"

"Gabe, your skepticism is natural, but unwarranted based on my readings of the children's vitals. Besides, since he learned the remedy from our grandmother, I feel all of us can trust him and it."

"I am just not sure. What happens if the remedy is only temporary or makes matters worse and anaphylaxis occurs? What then, Doctor?"

His tone was demeaning.

"I have three vials of epinephrine, and we can recall the EMTs."

"Gabe, shut the hell up. I trust Shelia even if you don't. Our girls have already begun to slowly get out of the woods. So, drop the subject. Damn it! Now!"

Martha, perceived to be normally a passive-aggressive, was following her motherly instincts. The girls were out of danger, and that's all she cared about.

"But I am only saying …"

"Enough, Gabe! Enough! Damn it, Gabe, drop it!"

Michael grins. Big brother has just been verbally bitch-slapped by his own wife.

The four got busy getting dinner ready. While Michael, Gabriel, and Martha found and wiped clean the flatware, plates, glasses, and serving utensils, Shelia was working on the side items: tomatoes have been halved and sprinkled with breadcrumbs and parmesan cheese for grilling; potato salad and cole slaw have been spooned into serving bowls; carrot sticks and celery stalks stand in ice water; and fresh green salad, rolls, condiments, as well as chips were placed on a three-foot-wide serving tray. Then she dumped four pounds of 80/20 ground sirloin into a massive mixing bowl. Beside this bowl were items from her "Culinary Crash Cart:" salt, pepper, a finely diced onion, garlic powder, Worcestershire Sauce, and seasoned breadcrumbs. Small amounts of these ingredients would be mixed with the ground sirloin to produce her special burgers, fit for every king and queen of the family.

"What should we do about the kids? They're asleep now, but they'll wake up soon and be hungry. I know Micah will be famished, that's for sure."

"The girls, too. We'll let them sleep for now. I'll wrap three burgers and put them in the fridge for when the kids are out of bed. If they don't wake before we go to bed, I'll put their burgers in the freezer. Joe can have them next week."

"Good idea, Martha."

"Thanks, Michael."

"If that's what you want to do, Martha, it's OK with me."

"Thanks for your approval, Gabriel."

The snap of sarcasm in Martha's response was not missed by Shelia or Michael. The tension of the last hour had raised her hackles.

"Gabe, would you put the plates, serving spoons, and cooking utensils on one of the big trays so they can be carried to and from the patio? Michael, you'd better start the fire. It takes about fifteen minutes before the flames have died out and the coals are the right temperature for proper grilling. This year go easy on the starter fluid. You have a history of fire-starter abuse, thus making the burgers smell and taste like a gas station."

Shelia was orchestrating the goings-on in the kitchen. She was in control as Mary was for many years. As Gabe exited the cottage with his big tray and headed to the patio, he noticed his father and uncle sitting side-by-side talking in soft, nearly intimate voices. Each was holding a glass of whisky. They take a sipped at the same time. Joe smiled beatifically, while Amon winced at the alcohol flash.

"Just to let you gentlemen know … dinner will be served in about thirty minutes."

"Thanks for the heads up. Amon, we'd better wash up."

"Right, Joe."

The two older men slowly shuffled back into the cottage.

"We're ready to grill. Thanks for your patience, I realize prep time may have seemed to take forever. Gabe, will you do the honors?"

"Glad to. Who wants rare? Who wants medium? Who wants well done?"

Gabriel seemed to slur his words a little bit and his actions were measured and unsteady. He had placed an empty bottle of wine in the recycle bin before he walked outside. His condition could make for interesting mealtime conversation.

"Hey, Mikey, fetch me a brew. I need to quench my thirst while I sweat over this hot grill."

"Before we eat, let's say Mary's grace. Everybody hold hands and pray together. *Heavenly Father, grant us the grace to accept your teachings and to be faithful stewards of thy bounty. Bless this family, both present and in our thoughts.*"

"Amon, I can't properly express my deepest appreciation for your remedies and the fact that you brought them when they were dearly needed."

"Shelia, I am only too glad to help. One thing I forgot to mention is that the tea will help the three teens sleep. It's not a narcotic … at least I don't think it is, but it relaxes anyone who drinks it. After the tea and the mud mixture, rest is what their bodies need. When they wake up, they will be thirsty. They will feel dehydrated and, I'm sure, they'll be very hungry. Heh, heh, heh."

"We're prepared for that. Again, thank you so very much."

"Amon, if you're so smart in the ways of the woods, how do we rid the boathouse of yellow jackets. Some of us would like to go fishing tomorrow."

Martha scowled at Gabriel. Alcohol and arrogance were not a good combination. Shelia shifted uneasily in her chair. Joe simply stared in disbelief.

"Smoke pots."

"What the hell are smoke pots?"

"Any metal container that can hold oil-soaked rags to be lit and give off lots of smoke. Yellow jackets hate oil-based smoke, just like hornets, other wasps, and honey bees. The thick smoke gets on their delicate wings, and they can't fly properly. They can get airborne, but the weight of the smoke on their wings will cause them to fly very slowly and inaccurately. They will wind up flying into walls and other objects before they figure out that the best course of action is to flee the smoke-filled space. They will leave the boathouse."

"OK. But what about the queen or queens and any nests?"

"You'll have to find the opening to a nest and place a smoke pot in front of it. Make sure the pot is against the nest opening. The smoke will drift through the opening into the nest and block any exit for a while. Finally, the queen's wings will be coated, she will lose mobility, and die of dehydration in a day while remaining in the nest. The nest opening will probably be near the floor or under a tarp or something big and heavy."

"OK. Tomorrow mid-morning, Mikey and I will attack the yellow jackets' fort."

"Gabriel, the smoke pots must be placed and ignited before sunrise, while a few yellow jackets are drifting near the opening. They are the guards. The remainder of the swarm is asleep in the nest. The pots must be put down before any of them leave the nest to hunt for food for the queen and her brood."

"What? Before sunrise? I'm on vacation."

"That's up to you, big brother. I'm sure I can handle the job without you. I know you need your beauty sleep. It is obvious from looking at you, you have missed it for some time."

"Screw you, Mikey."

"Easy, you two."

"Any time you can get up, I can get up earlier. We'll both attack their fort. Waddaya say we meet at five thirty on the back porch. That will give us time to get all the materials ready for our invasion."

"Great. Five thirty, it is then."

"The burgers are ready."

Michael felt smug. He has just goaded his older brother into something that Gabe didn't want to do. Perhaps couldn't do. Michael 1: Gabriel 0.

Alcohol, hunger, and scrumptious tasting picnic food cause the six adults to be nearly silent ... except for the smacking of lips, the subtle moaning of pleasure and praise for the food for the next twenty minutes. Shelia - prepared juicy and delicious half-pound burgers which, were grilled to perfection.

"Super burgers, Shelia."

"Thanks, Joe."

"Hey, don't I get some credit for grilling them perfectly."

"Hooray for grill master, Gabby."

"Thanks, Mikey."

Dinner wound down. Gabriel consumed his fourth beer. Joe's and Amon's stomachs were full and they look exhausted. Ready for sleep.

"Well, ladies and gentlemen, the sun has disappeared and the embers are burning themselves out, so I officially call dinner over."

"Is there anything I can do to help with cleanup?"

"Amon, you have already done more than enough. You saved our babies. Something we'll never forget."

"At least let me take the trash out to the large garbage can at the road on my way home."

"That's a deal. Michael ... Gabriel, please clear the table and scrape the dishes into a large trash bag. Also, take the untouched food back into the kitchen so Martha and I can put away the leftovers. Joe, I don't mean to be presumptuous, but you look ready for bed."

The old man abruptly sat up straight, smiled faintly, and nodded.

"To my sons, their wives, and all of my family, I bid you all a fond adieu. I am retiring to my room to be wrapped in the arms of Morpheus."

Amon helped Joe haltingly rise for the short walk to the inside of the cottage. Joe's pace was unsteady, but he had Amon to hold on to along the way. His sons wanted to help, but Joe was in good hands.

"After I walk Joe to his room, I'll be ready to take out the trash. Heh, heh, heh."

"Mikey, hand me another beer."

"OK, Gabby."

Chapter Sixteen

The screeching was horrible. The sound was vaguely like that of adult human wailing: stronger and deeper than that of a teen. Was the noise coming from a woman or a man? From inside or outside the cottage? The sound pulses were very violent: long screams offset by short periods of low moaning. Almost as if the source paused to take breaths. Joe heard no words, just frightening screams. Extreme pain mixed with rage. He hesitated to get out of bed to determine and to quiet the source of the noise. If it woke him, it must have awakened his family. The small bedside table held a flashlight he needed to negotiate the black space. Click! A small LED field of light hit the floor where he placed his feet. The floor was chilly. He put on his shirt and pants and walked barefoot from his room.

Nothing and no one were in the main room or kitchen. But the violent screaming continued. He thought this was the spot-on definition of the phrase, "Scream like a banshee." Joe opened the back door and stepped onto the small stoop. His feet hit the damp cold wood. The noise became louder. It came from somewhere out here. The crescent moon cast delicate shadows on the lawn and in the woods nearby. There was a form on the lawn that appeared to be female with long hair. Gracefully twirling, dancing. She waved her hand, as if she were inviting Joe to join her. No face, just a thin body wrapped in gossamer. The form floated above the ground. She did not seem to have feet. A second form approached the dancer. She was joined by what appeared to be a male figure, taller and visibly more muscular. No face or feet, just a bodily form. The male figure took the hand of the female figure and pulled her close. They stared at each other. The horrific screeching continued. Now the two forms were moving as one: dancing. Their embrace was tight. The movement suggestive. The male form grabbed the buttocks of the female form and pulled her loins to him. She reciprocated. They began to grind pelvises.

Out of the corner of his eye to the right, Joe spied a four-legged shape on the border of the back yard. It did not look like a shadow. It had form and substance. A massive wolf. The big black wolf was back. This time the alpha wolf was flanked by ten, no twelve, other wolves. More than Joe had seen before. They were silent. No growling, only staring. Joe tried to cast the light on the pack, but the beam was not bright enough to illuminate the animals. They were too far from the flashlight. He saw only their shapes in the limited blue-gray of the moonlight.

The gyrating couple took notice of the wolves and stops dancing. The pair moved away from the alpha's pack, very slowly. Their actions showed deference. They slowly moved away so as not to show weakness and invite an attack. Then Joe heard a deep guttural growl. So deep it sounded as if it were not of this earth. Not unlike the rumbling of a volcano, the distant roar of a large storm, or an artillery barrage. The alpha wolf raised his hackles and his shadow grew to the size of a bear. His growl became louder. No pulsing. No stopping for inhalation. The couple moved to the other side of the back yard where they were greeted by six wolves from the pack. The dancers seemed to be trying to escape. The pack members, expressing low warning growls, blocked any escape. The couple stopped. They looked at the small pack, then back at the alpha. Joe focused on the suggestive dancers as they separated and stood side-by-side. The male figure bowed his head in supplication. The female followed. A bolt of lightning hit the ground near the couple. They dropped to their knees. A second bolt struck the female and she disappeared. A third bolt caused the male figure to vanish. No smoke from the strikes. In less than five seconds, the dancers were gone and the back yard was still. No motion. No growling. No screeching.

Joe could not find the six wolves that had confronted the couple, so he turned to see the alpha wolf. Gone. Just as quickly as all appeared, all have disappeared. The screeching was replaced by nature's woodland silence. The old man was dumbfounded. Who? What? How? Why? These questions will have to be contemplated in daylight.

Joe sat up in bed. He was not sweating, but his heart was racing. He guessed his pulse rate was well into the eighties. His bizarre dream had spurred him to awaken. The digital clock told him it is 3:35. He remained on his back and stared at the ceiling trying to recount the details of the dream. He hoped to fall asleep again. After thirty minutes, no such luck. He might as well get out of bed and be productive. He reached for his small, "bathroom" flashlight. Groping the bedside table, his hand came up empty. Strange. He dressed, put on shoes, and cautiously walked in the dark through the cottage to his destination, the shed outside. There he would find three coffee cans holding various nuts, bolts, screws, and nails necessary for repair of minor cottage issues. They would serve different and immediate needs.

As he placed his hand on the kitchen table to steady himself in the dark, he felt the small flashlight that had been in his bedroom. How did it get there? Now he could walk outside without fear of stumbling. He had light to find what he wanted in the shed. Inside the outbuilding were three cans, several old and dirty rags, and an unopened can of motor oil. It's years old. It was needed the last time one of the boys mowed the back and front yards. Now Amon did this work with his own mower. After emptying the cans of the metal items and ripping the rags into strips, he carefully poured a bit of the motor oil in the cans until they were one-quarter full. Finally, he dumped the remainder of the oil over each small pile of rags.

Cans in hand, he headed back to the back porch. There he placed the soon-to-be smoke pots and a big box of matches for Gabriel and Michael to take to the boathouse. He sat on the top step and rested. He was tired. Although it was early in the day after a long sleep, the disturbing dream sapped him of emotional energy. As he caught his breath, he took in two distinct odors. One he recognized but can't place. The other was foreign. He shone his light onto the yard. Unfortunately, the light throw was neither far nor wide. Ideal for in the house and shed. Not good for outdoors, particularly in pale moonlight. He arose and walked into the yard. He must find the source of the odors. Walking through the yard, he became enmeshed in spider webs. There were many of them ... long and clingy. Joe hoped he did not meet the spiders.

Snakes and spiders head Joe's list of things he feared and loathed. At his feet, he spied volleyball-size clumps of the gossamer. The creepy crawlers had been very, very busy.

He thought he knew the first odor. Feral urine. Again! It was all over the place! As he walked toward the front of the house, the smell became stronger. The damned wolf had come back to re-mark his territory. Why the house? Why now? The markings were at every corner and by both the front and rear doors. The cottage was in the wolf's territory. Was it a protectorate?

As he returned to the back of the cottage, his flashlight came across three burn marks on the lawn. Each was about two feet in diameter. He now recognized the second odor, sulfur. Once called brimstone. It stank like human waste. Were the three lightning strikes in his dream real? Joe couldn't recall hearing thunder. So, the lightning must not have been part of a storm. Who were the dancing forms? Why were wolves there? This was too much for Joe this early in the day. He could not address these issues now. Maybe later. Maybe never. He walked with purpose back to the house to make coffee for his sons. All the while, the events occurring on the land were churning in his psyche.

"Thanks for the coffee, Dad."

"You're welcome. Thought you would need it this early in the morning."

"Have you seen Gabriel?"

"No, and I doubt he will be up and about very soon. I think he had a lot to drink last night. A bottle of wine and a six-pack, but who's counting?"

"Keeping tabs on your big brother, are you?"

"Not really. It's just that he seems to drink a lot. At least a lot more than I remember and he's my brother, so it concerns me."

"I'll give you a hand with the smoke pots after you've had your coffee."

"I see they're all loaded. And big wooden matches to boot. You prepare for everything. Like always … since as far back as I can remember."

"I had time. Couldn't sleep so I decided to get out of bed and help."

After a few gulps of coffee, the two men slowly walked to the boathouse. Opening the door, Michael stared into darkness. Joe shone the light toward the corners. At one, he spotted three yellow jackets lazily hovering near a small hole about two feet off the floor.

"Look over there, just above the corner. I see at least one nest opening. Before we set the pots, let's make sure we have found all openings."

"Dad, I can make out two jackets slowly flying near the tarp in that corner."

Joe, swept the light across the space several times. Stopping whenever he thought he saw a yellow jacket. The thorough search took about ten minutes.

"Good. Those two places seem to be the only nests. We need to place one can near each and the third can in the middle of the room. Take this can opener and punch two holes on the side near the bottom of each can to ensure an updraft. Place the pots, then light the rags."

Three minutes later, the cans had been strategically placed and contents ignited. The boathouse door was pulled down to prevent escape of the yellow jackets. The two men exited, making sure the entry door was closed tight. They walked back to the cottage. Dawn was slowly breaking.

"How long should we wait before we re-enter the boathouse?"

"Let's wait until the afternoon."

"What the hell are those, Dad?"

"What?"

"The three circular marks on the lawn. What are they? How did they get there? Who did it? Is this something else that you don't want to talk about?"

"Easy, Michael. They look like burns. Don't know how they got there. Don't know who burned the lawn."

"Dad, something very strange is going on here this weekend. First the dead animals and the scavengers. Shelia told me about the warm white pebbles you found. The storm that chased Micah and I off the lake but did not come onto our shore. Yesterday, the yellow jackets, and now the burn marks on the lawn. I don't believe in coincidences. Something or someone seems to be trying to communicate with us and tell us to beware of something … or does this something want us to leave."

"I'm not sure what is happening, and I don't know what we should do. Let's talk about it … I mean, let all the adults talk about it at dinner."

"I agree. Everyone must be of one mind about the events and their meaning."

Michael left the stoop, walked to the three burn marks, and sniffed the air above them.

"I smell sulfur. That is confounding. Who would burn sulfur near the house? Something else to put into the discussion tonight. Enough of the mysteries for now. Dad, let's start breakfast."

"First, let's sit on the back porch and enjoy the glorious awakening of nature."

"Are you going to raise the sun?"

"Not today."

As the sun rose, the two men silently communed with nature. Birds and small creatures of the woods were doing all the talking as they greeted the day. The back door was opened.

"Hey, Mikey, let's get a move on and attack those yellow jackets."

"You're a day late and a dollar short, Gabby."

"Dad and I set the smoke pots about an hour ago. By the way, where the hell were you?"

"My alarm didn't go off."

"You mean, you slept so deeply that the alarm didn't wake you. That's what a bottle of wine and a six-pack will do to anyone."

"Easy, baby brother. Alcohol had no influence on my arising late. It was the alarm's fault."

"If you say so, Gabby. In a few hours, you can go to the boathouse and check on the effectiveness of our efforts. Dad and I killed 'em, you can sweep 'em."

"Are you assigning chores for the day, little boss?"

"No, I'm asking you to do your fair share. If you're up to it."

There was deep-seated anger in both their voices.

"Boys, let's be civil. We better start thinking about your families. I think I hear them stirring. The kids missed dinner so they'll be hungry. Let's get a move on."

Gabriel and Michael left the back porch. Joe sat and stared. His energy seemed to fade faster after each dream during a night's sleep or daytime nap, as well as with each passing day.

"That was a great breakfast, Mom."

"Yes, it was, Aunt Shelia."

"Two questions, Lillie: How do you feel? And, what are your plans for today?"

"I feel fine except for a little itchiness on my arms and legs. No soreness. No swelling. I'm rarin' to go."

"How about you, Aggie?"

"I feel punky. My skin itches all over. My stomach is upset. I have a headache. I want to go back to bed."

Her tone of voice caused Martha to lean into Shelia's ear and whisper. Shelia acknowledged the message: Aggie's "friend" was visiting for few days.

"Aggie, if you want to lie down until you feel better, you can. The events of yesterday would certainly be exhausting for anyone."

"Thanks, Momma."

"How about you, Lillie?"

"I know one thing I don't want to do; I don't want to go near the boathouse. I'm staying as far away from the yellow jackets as possible."

"That's a good idea."

"How about you, Micah?"

"I was thinking about exploring the other side of the road. There's the big meadow, with the woods on the hill behind it. I want to see if there's anything there worth looking at. I think I remember seeing a farmhouse up on the hill. Besides that's about as far away from the yellow jackets as I can get without going home."

"I'll go exploring with you."

"OK, Lillie. Let's leave in thirty minutes."

"Hey, you two, wear long pants and long-sleeved shirts. In the woods, thorns can scratch you and the poison ivy can be a problem for the skin on your arms and legs. I think you guys have had enough skin irritation for one weekend. Micah, you should wash off the rest of Amon's mixture before you go. Then rub some bug repellant on your exposed body."

"You too, Lillie."

"Lillie, you can have the indoor shower. I'll use the one outside."

"Well, aren't you the perfect gentleman."

"Lillie, be civil. Micah is being polite. No need to get snotty."

"Sorry, Mom."

The two teens headed to their respective showers, while Aggie went back to her bed. Before Shelia and Martha could finish a second cup of coffee and kitchen cleanup, Lillie and Micah were standing at the back door. Obviously, they used no towels. Their plan was to air dry.

Chapter Seventeen

"See you guys later. We'll be back well before dinner."

Off the teens ran to the driveway and over the road. The mothers sipped coffee in the kitchen.

"Sometimes I wish I had the vitality of my younger years."

"Martha, that sounds like the complaints of a very old woman. You are too young to feel that way, and besides, you have many, many active years ahead of you."

"Shelia, that sounds like it came from a TV commercial."

"I guess it did sound that way. I didn't mean it to."

"That's OK. I'm feeling a little sorry for myself. I'm having a little pity party in my head. The girls are fast becoming young women. Before I know it, they'll be off at college, then married. All the while, I stand on the sideline and simply get older. I'm spinning in place, while they move forward."

"I don't mean to pry, but from a professional standpoint, are you and Gabriel OK as a couple?"

"No."

"If this is too delicate of a subject, we don't have to go further."

"Look Shelia, we are both over thirty and have had children. So, nothing is too delicate. The truth is, my husband is rapidly becoming a drunk, we are dangerously deep in debt, my body that once was shapely now has the shape of a potato, my sex life is almost non-existent, and my babies are becoming adults, who will soon have no need for me. Other than all that, my life is just peachy."

"If you would feel more comfortable talking about this away from the house, we can go for a walk."

"Good idea. Gabe, I'm going for a walk with Shelia. Be back in a bit."

No response.

"Micah, what do you think we'll see in the field?"

"I have no idea, but that's the thrill of looking; if you find anything that is new to you, you've been successful."

"Whatever."

"Be careful where you walk. You don't want to step into the mouth of an animal's den. You could twist an ankle."

"But if I'm always looking down, how will I see what's in front of me?"

"Just don't look at the horizon. Focus your gaze about fifteen feet in front of you. Occasionally, you can look up to the horizon or the hill straight ahead."

"There's nothing in this field but tall grass, dirt and rocks."

"It seems nothing has been planted here for a long time. Perhaps this was a pasture for sheep or cows."

"Great, now I have to watch out for animal crap."

"Given the height of the grass, I doubt any animal has been in the field for years. So, you and your shoes are safe."

"Up on the hill, I can see a building set back in the woods. Is that the house? How far do you think it is from here?"

"About a half a mile."

"Half a mile up hill. That's comforting."

The pair walked side-by-side across the meadow to the ascent. The climb started.

"There's the building. Doesn't look like anyone lives there. I see broken windows, and the front door is wide open. I'll race ya to the house."

With the challenge to Micah, Lillie started her sprint. Taken by surprise, the boy picked up the challenge. In less than fifty yards, he was beside her. He slowed down so as not to pass but ran just fast enough to push her. In a few minutes, they were standing at the steps to the front porch gasping for breath.

"Now what, Micah?"

"Now we enter and explore."

She bounded up the steps and stood before the open door.

"Be careful. I wouldn't trust the wooden floor. The boards are probably weakened by time and weather."

"Are you coming or are you planning to stand back and give me advice?"

Micah couldn't resist the challenge. He ran up the nine steps and stood beside his cousin. They entered.

"This must have been the living room. There's the entry to the dining area, and beyond that the kitchen."

They walked cautiously through the first floor.

"The room over there may have been a den or something. Right, Micah?"

"I'll bet it was a bedroom. The people who lived here worked the land. They had no need for a den. But, with several children, they had a real need for sleeping space. Come here and look toward the back of the house. There are big windows in the front of the building and two regular size windows in the kitchen. There's also a window in the small room off the dining room. The people most likely opened the windows in the summer to get a breeze going through the first floor. In the winter, they tried to keep warm with a Franklin Stove that sat over there on the iron plate. The large exhaust pipe went upstairs to warm that space, too. See the hole in the ceiling?"

"Well, aren't you the architect?"

"Why are you such a snot? I was just trying to understand how the people lived."

"Whatever. Let's check out the upstairs."

They climbed the rickety stairs. At the top, they saw a single large room. Again, windows in the front and back. There were several large dark areas on the floor as if something had been spilled and soaked into the wood.

"I'll bet this is where the children slept. The pipe from the Franklin Stove came into this room over there and went up to the roof. See the metal plates on the floor and wall?"

Micah felt Lillie's hand. He turned and looked. She was staring at him in a strange way.

"Do you have a girlfriend?"

"No. Not really. Why?" He stammered.

"Which is it? No or not really?"

Her countenance was as stern and her eyes as piercing as a modern-day Torquemada.

"I don't think that's any of your business."

"So, I can safely guess, you've never done it with your maybe or maybe not girlfriend."

"That's not appropriate, and it's none of your business."

"Would you like to do it with me?"

"I'm not going to answer that."

"Then your answer is yes. When you looked at Aggie and me yesterday after our swim, did you like what you saw?"

"I'm not going to answer that either."

"Another yes. Now we're getting somewhere."

"Would you like to see me naked again?"

"You are making me uncomfortable. Please stop."

"My gawd, my first virgin. Soooo shy and soooo cute."

Lillie was standing about four inches from him. He felt her hot breath. Her hands were now holding his upper arms. He did not look into her eyes but stared to the left like a deer in the headlights of an oncoming vehicle and certain death. She moved her face to his and kissed him softly on the lips. Her mouth was open slightly.

"Wait. Stop. This isn't right. You're my cousin, and you're trying to seduce me? That's wrong."

"Right or wrong does not matter. The only thing that matters is how good we are together. That will be between us. Whether we are good or not, I won't tell anyone, and it's a safe bet you won't either."

She kissed him again. This time longer. He did not pull away. His heart was racing, and his breathing was shallow and rapid. He was panting almost like a dog. Her hand left his arm and slid to his crotch. She gently massaged him. He was almost ready. Suddenly, she stopped and stepped away. Micah was simultaneously excited, anxious, and very confused. He remained still like a small animal in a trap. Not sure what's next. She rapidly removed her top shirt and the T-shirt beneath it to expose her soft skin and small firm breasts.

"Touch them. Rub them. Better yet, kiss them."

Like a robot, he obeyed her instructions. Micah had become fully aroused. He began to throb.

"You look soooo scared. Don't be. I won't hurt you. In fact, you're going to enjoy it. I know I will. Just relax and let me lead the way. Since you have no idea what to do, I will be the leader. So just follow the leader. Take off your pants and lie on the floor."

Micah was torn between obeying her command and stopping this awkward event before it goes further. He yielded to his primal urge and remained silent. They each removed their pants. Micah placed his atop one of the dark irregular areas on the dirty floor. He lay down on his pants. Lillie stepped over him and stood there completely naked. He looked up at her. Knees, thighs, the tuft of dark hair, ribs, breasts, and her face. Around the tuft, he noticed hair stubble like his dad's beard on weekends. Did she shave down there? Why? Her eyes appeared glazed. Her breathing was deep and she grinned … a sardonic smile as she stared down at him the way the hawk must have looked at the fish. He was her prize. Gently, Lillie lowered herself, straddling him and rubbed herself on him from his naval down one thigh and back again. Then to the other thigh. All the while she kissed him, driving her tongue deeper with each kiss. Slowly, she lifted her chest. Her breathing had become rapid.

"Grab my tits and squeeze them real hard. Pinch my nipples. I like that. Close your eyes and relax, newbie. I'll do all the work."

The boy didn't know what to do or what was next, so he willingly obeyed the directions of the leader. He raised his hands and cupped her breasts. As he massaged them, he felt the nipples between his thumbs and index fingers harden. He gripped the protrusions, and pinched them, at first delicately, then harder. With each pinch, Lillie emitted a whimper of pleasant pain and showed a wider grin. She took his staff in her hand and placed the head in the mouth of her chamber. After four phases of partial insertion and withdrawal, each time going a little deeper, he was completely inside her.

"When I slide down, raise your hips to go deeper inside me. Deeper is how I like it."

From within her moist body cavity, her warmth was transferred to him. A very pleasant sensation spread to his stomach and over his entire body as she aggressively rose and fell. Her eyes were now tightly closed. Her grin had been replaced by a grimace, but not of pain. Her lips were partially closed so the air intake and exhalation make a hissing noise. Her head was swaying. His pleasure was increasing as fear and confusion dissipate. A powerfully visceral instinct had taken control of both teens.

She balanced herself with her left hand on his shoulder and lowered her right hand to the tuft of hair, rubbing up and down, right and left. Suddenly, her eyes and mouth popped open in an expression of amazement. Her face was contorted. Her eyes rolled back so that only the whites were visible. Her body suddenly snapped to attention and became rigid. Then it began violently jerking and bouncing. Micah had never seen the violent throes of female pleasure. Her spasms lasted about ten seconds. She let out a loud squeal, then a whimper and collapsed onto her stupefied partner. Her lips locked on to his. Then she kissed him tenderly on his cheeks and forehead. Lillie slid her head onto his shoulder. Gradually, normal breathing return. She rose and extracted him. After she lifted her body off him, she curled up at his side. His penis stood for a few seconds, leaned to one side, then flopped to his thigh.

"Whew, I needed that. It's been six weeks. It was good for me. For you … not so much, I think. Poor bunny. Not bad for a first timer, but you'd better improve before you try your moves on your girlfriend. Look, you're still hard. Well, almost. Let Lillie take care of that."

Lillie reached over and delicately wrapped her fingers around Micah's moist staff. Slowly, she massaged and stroke it until his powerful basic urge returned. Pleasure rose within him. It encompassed his entire being. He closed his eyes as rapture was reached. The throbbing he feels in his loins peaked as bodily fluid pulsed over Lillie's hand and onto his stomach. He's embarrassed.

"The little bunny made a mess. You'll have to clean yourself. I don't clean boys who make messes. I'll wipe my hand on your underpants. I wish I had that inside of me. Maybe next time you'll do that inside so I can enjoy you even more. Now let's get out of this place; it's beginning to scare me."

Almost as quickly as his first sexual encounter began, it ended. It was pleasant, troubling, incomplete, and embarrassing. He felt anxious, mystified, and empty. Was this the way sex was supposed to feel?

Chapter Eighteen

"Shelia, I don't know what to do … I need you to help me get my life back … my life is a train wreck that happens every day over and over again like a bad movie … I've started to have more than one cocktail before dinner … but when Gabriel is home for family dinner which is becoming less and less often, we drink ourselves silly then flop into bed … he hasn't touched me in three months I am sagging in areas of my body I thought wouldn't sag for years … I'm gaining weight that I can't seem to lose even going to the gym four times a week … my clothes make me look dowdy … the girls get new clothes for each season and they are growing up too fast … Lillie has become sexually active and I suspect *really* active … certainly more active than me … Aggie has yet to learn what boys are good for … she's a late bloomer like I was … Aggie has just entered the first stage of being a woman so she leans on me for advice … I try to guide her but I'm distracted by my feelings of failure … Lillie and I don't talk … her grades are slipping … I'm not sure she'll be able to get into a good school … hopefully she'll qualify for the University of Illinois or a community college …

Gabe seems to view our home and me as accoutrements to his climb up the corporate ladder … he was promoted four years ago but passed over last year … he's bitter about that … he stays out too late almost every evening claiming he has to work but I suspect he is having an affair … maybe with his admin or maybe the new woman the company hired to run another division … he is getting fat and soft … Gabe is no longer the good physical specimen he was five years ago … we can pay most of our bills mostly on time but the situation is becoming worse and leads to arguments … he hasn't gotten a raise in two years and no bonus last December … we use credit cards to pay for our day-to-day living and the expensive toys he and the girls simply must have … recently we've had to take money from the girls' college funds and sell a few investments to pay off all our credit cards … I don't understand why we need two very expensive cars but Gabe craves the status of new cars every two years … he has all the electronic devices known to mankind … I am losing interest in being a good wife and mother because the home environment has become toxic for me …"

"Breathe, Martha, slow down and breathe."

"Whew, that was a ton of shit. Sorry to unload it on you."

"Not a problem."

"I just don't know what to do. Maybe I should find a younger man who will regularly fuck me and make me feel like a young desirable woman again."

"Nonsense. Besides, that only works in cheesy chick books. Then the heroine realizes what a stupid idea it was, repents, and is forgiven by her husband. Based on what few facts you told me, you've done nothing wrong. It's just that you've gotten older and the environment of your life has changed as the girls, too, have gotten older. That's a very normal progression of life and most often healthy. We can't hold on to the past or we'll never progress. You can't be young again. No one can. But, you can, no, must, adjust and adapt to your changing environment. To do this, you must have your own life.

"You must be your own person not simply a reflection of your daughters or husband. You must assert that you have personal needs and that you make meaningful contributions to your family and the society around you beyond being a good Mom and a loving wife. You must stand up for yourself. Not be a tag-along who does what everybody else wants. Make your family see what a good and productive adult woman you are. That's how you can hold it together. Only you can do that. Neither Gabriel nor your daughters can hold you together."

"How do *you* hold it together?"

"Michael and I have to work to make love work. Michael and I have challenging and time-consuming jobs. We both appreciate that fact and each other for being good at our jobs. We respect what each other does. And, here is the important part, we never bring work home or heap any frustration on Micah. Our home life is our special time as a family. We are energized and brought back to reality in this special environment. It was not easy at the beginning, but we wanted to grow strong both individually and as a couple, then as parents. We knew that the pressures of our jobs could destroy us and our relationship. So, we made a pact to separate church and state, as it were. This separation is not always easy. I see dying patients nearly every day. Patients who have lost hope. I must hold their hands while they suffer the crushing emotion of an imminent and painful death. I must answer delicate questions from family members.

"And it's not one and done. The illness-to-death syndrome in my world is never ending, and it could crush me if I let it. When it gets too much, I go for a long run, shower, and then jump Michael's bones with great vigor to reaffirm life, mine, his, and ours. The result of that process is now inside me. A baby created not in anger, but in a feverish celebration of life.

"Michael has a similar routine when the office politics or a difficult client has heaped havoc on him. He doesn't run, though, he swims. Then he romances me with a nice home-cooked meal, wine, and good classical music. After Micah goes to bed, we attack each other as if we were randy teens. This approach culminates in wild passion in our room, mostly. Sometimes in the kitchen or living room. One time in the back seat of the car. Like when we *were* randy teens. That was weird. Fun, but weird. All of this is not easy or necessarily spontaneous. It requires the desire of a higher goal and work: constant work. This work is so constant that it doesn't really seem like work but just part of the cycle of our life together."

"You have a profession. I don't. I think Gabe proposed to me because I won a few beauty pageants. I was arm candy, a supposed value-added trapping for his career. Plus, back then, I've been told, I was dynamite in bed. I have an associate degree from Oakmont Community College. I never had a job that could start a career. And, I certainly don't want to reinvent myself as a beauty queen. There's no future in that. What can I do?"

"You could get involved in the girls' school or be an active volunteer at the Y or a local charity like the Salvation Army. Maybe your church."

"Church. That's almost a bad joke. We haven't been to church since the girls were baptized. And, the girls might freak out if I got involved with their school. They would think I was spying. Although, I would like to see what the sixty thousand a year we pump into their education actually buys other than complaints about homework. I'm not big on charities for people who are down and almost out, because those people are dirty, smelly, and ugly."

"The school might be a good place to start. It would not require much of your time: just enough to make a contribution. And, if your girls complain, tell them that since you are paying for their education, you want to be sure the money is being well spent. I'll bet the school is always looking for parents to run outreach events. First, talk to Gabe. Tell him what you're feeling and ask for his support. Then before you get involved in the school, go away with him. Don't take your daughters. Go away for on four-day weekend. Rekindle your life together and your love life."

"I like that one. We could go to Tahoe or someplace glamorous like that. A place that has all the amenities like tennis, swimming, and, maybe, horseback riding. A place where the beautiful people go. I'll buy outfits featured in the right magazines and some very sexy clothes right from the special fashion magazines."

"You're on the right path."

"I'll tell Gabe that he and I should go away for a retreat. If he hesitates or says he is too busy, I'll tell him the alternative is for me to leave the girls with him while I go for a long retreat. A very expensive mommy makeover. It will be his choice. Thanks for your help. It's been great talking to you."

The nearly hysterical Martha had calmed down and found the path of least resistance to answer her immediate questions but not solve her problems. Martha's problems run too deep to be resolved with a threat to her husband, new tennis shorts or a lacy teddy. Shelia was distracted by the life force within her now clamoring for sustenance. A protein bar, a piece of fruit, and a big glass of milk will have to suffice.

"Dad, we need to talk. I'm concerned and confused at what is going on here. All of it is way too crazy to be real. Help me understand. And, I won't wait until this evening for you to explain it to the other adults. I've seen too much, and I need answers now."

"OK, Michael. Let's go out front."

The two men sat on a bench at the table on the patio.

"When your Hess Grandparents gave your mother and I this land as a wedding present, they told us of the folklore surrounding this area. Reminding us it was just folklore. There is no written proof of what I'm about to tell you. Here goes. It seems that there wasn't always a lake where we see one now. There was a hollow in the terrain about thirty feet below the land on which this cottage was ultimately built. But the lake and house are centuries in the future from the time of the folklore. Grandpa Hess, Neen, wanted us to know the supposed history of the land as it might affect our building on it. The lore or rumors have it that this was a place of execution and burial of those possessed by the devil. It was a dumping ground controlled by those threatened by a malevolent force.

"It all started when the humble farmers, who settled the land centuries ago, periodically suffered the tragedies of failed crops and the death of livestock. These events were most likely the normal cycles of that era. But these were uneducated people. They were deeply religious to the point of being fanatically superstitious. They accepted the words in the Old Testament as literal truths. Their faith was so strong that they took the words, thoughts, and concepts as absolute. They lived life under the threat that there was evil always near them. And that this evil caused the crop failures and livestock deaths. They believed that only the goodness of God could correct these issues and prevent them from recurring. But to secure God's protection, the people had to lead a pure life and occasionally, through sacrifice, rid the land of the minions of the evil force."

"That's not unreasonable, given the fact that they were not well-educated, yet myopically religious. What they could not explain in their limited human terms, they must have thought, was created or sent by either God or Satan. That MO existed for centuries throughout the world. What does that have to do with this property and the events of the past few days?"

"I'm getting to that. The stories tell of a period of troubles, a brief famine and other hardships. During the second year of livestock deaths and crop failures, the local farmers gathered at the meeting house. The community hall was also their church. During the heated discussion of their plight, someone mentioned that a widow, named Grace, did not seem to be suffering as much as the rest of the farmers. The ranting increased, and several farmers, who claimed to be most severely impacted by the maladies, decided to go to Grace's house and confront her. They feared that Grace had something to do with their livestock deaths and crop failures. This fear became belief, which led to a confrontation. The confrontation quickly evolved into a kidnapping of sorts.

"The gang grabbed the old woman and dragged her to the meeting house. There the entire community questioned the woman and hurled insults at her. Ultimately, she was accused of being the mistress of Satan. A witch. The *good people* of the land took her from the village square to the area of land that we now know as Lake Tucquan. The farmers knew the Susquehannock people avoided this area. Some farmers claimed that the natives believed it was possessed by evil. The villagers thought there was no better place to rid themselves of the witch, Grace, than to return her to Satan here on this land, his land. She was stripped of her clothes, beaten and hanged. The farmers returned to their homes, content in the belief that they had done God's work and made the land safe.

"Three days later after a violent storm with lots of lightning and thunder, two of the men returned to the hanging site and were amazed to find that Grace's remains were nowhere to be found. Not an appendage. Not a bone. Nothing. Even the hanging rope was missing. They were convinced that Satan had taken her during the storm. The farmers felt smug. They were sure the farms would begin to prosper due to this sacrifice. And prosperity did return to the land. Within a month, crops began to appear where seeds had been sown, chickens laid eggs, and livestock showed signs of being healthy. In the farmers' eyes, these facts confirmed the rightness and righteousness of the sacrifice. The worst had passed. And they knew God had given them the tools to rectify life. Thus, the legend was born."

"That's it?"

"No. About fifty years later, the area again suffered crop failures and livestock deaths. And again, the farmers and villagers met to decide what to do. In the small village there lived a dirty, stooped man, who many thought to be unclean, maybe even a leper. The man was named Samael. He had come to these parts with his wife and two children, all of whom had died one at a time during a particularly harsh winter. Now he was alone and had little or no contact with the other people. It was this solitude that bothered the folks around him. They thought he was standoffish. Different from them. Again, the unknown was not good. It was evil. The farmers and villagers went to his hovel to confront Samael because they thought that he, like Grace before him, was a spawn of Satan. He was no spawn; he was just a dirty and lonely old widower. Nonetheless, they feared him because he was different.

"They dragged him to the town square so people might question him. Questions were raised that could not be answered to their satisfaction. They took him by cart to the same area where Grace had been dispatched and they stripped him of his clothes, beat him, and hanged him. They made this human sacrifice in hopes that they were appeasing God and ridding evil from the land as had been done years before. And that the next phase in the growing cycle would be abundant crops and healthy livestock. Like it had been previously. When they were convinced Samael was dead, they left him dangling from the rope and returned to the village and their farms.

"A few days later two men returned to the site of the hanging and discovered that Samael and the rope were missing. Just like with Grace, the area showed no signs that Samael had even been there. Within a month, crops began to flourish, chickens and geese produced eggs, and the cows were gaining weight and giving milk. This was a repeat of the earlier phase of the cycle. The farmers were convinced that prosperity was righteous since the sacrifice to God rid the area of evil. They had rid the land of Satan's minion and restored God's order."

"OK, those stories seem a little far-fetched. Two hangings by frightened small-minded religious zealots over the course of fifty years should not be confirmation of good and evil spirits roaming the land."

"I'm not done. About fifty years after Samael's hanging, envy and mistrust among the villagers and farmers bubbled to the surface. The village shopkeepers wanted the farmers to pay a tax, a tithe, on produce and goods sold by the farmers within the town limits. This tax would pay for material necessary to build structures and help the villagers in need. Since the exchange of money was rare, the villagers decided to require that the farmers contribute ten percent of their meat, eggs, or crops as the tax. They felt that because the farmers were enjoying bumper crops, this form of tithing would not adversely affect their food supplies or revenue from sales; and it would improve living conditions of those who were tradespeople and lived within the village. The farmers did not want to donate a portion of their crops or livestock to feed the town's people. They wanted to be able to sell or barter their goods in the open market within the village or any village without having their proceeds diminished by the tithe.

"The farmers felt it was unjust for them to support others who did not work as hard as they did to support themselves. The officials of the town told the folk they were entitled to the tithe because the activities of the village benefitted all: farmers and villagers alike. The farmers threatened to sell their goods in another village and thus force the local villagers to spend more to secure the goods from others. The villagers threatened to close off the roads in and out of the town and charge the farmers a toll for using the roads. The farmers threatened to break the toll barriers. The next village was a full day's trip to the east. So, it would have been a burden for the farmers to sell and trade there. A burden they were willing to undertake. To hear what was rightfully theirs.

"One night while the two sides were arguing the merits if their respective points of view, the shouting became louder and louder. The story says the sound had become louder and more threatening than any wind or storm. It was like banshees screaming for death. Hatred consumed both sides. Foul and blasphemous words were used. No one is sure who said it, but someone on one side accused someone on the other side of being a spawn of Satan. That utterance had a ring of finality and was the spark that ignited the fight.

"Villagers and farmers alike became embroiled in a melee that lasted for several hours. Many were injured. A few were killed. Those left standing when the brawl was over, both villagers and farmers, loaded their dead friends and neighbors onto carts and brought them to this area. The people who were not killed convinced themselves that they were saved by the power of God, and those that died did so because God willed it. The dead somehow were disciples of Satan, while the living were emissaries of God.

"The lore goes on to say that the bodies of the fallen were then hacked to pieces and left as food for the vermin and scavengers in the same area as the hangings. The butchering was done to prevent the evil within them from being used to create new bodies of evil people. A complete and total sacrifice. After three days ... after the vermin and scavengers had their fill, the townsfolk came back to this area, dug a huge hole, threw in all that remained of the bodies and clothing, and set a huge funeral pyre. Later, they covered the ashes that remained with a large mound of dirt. They left this burial pit unmarked. Once again, the people thought the evil that sought to destroy the tranquility and harmony of the land had been vanquished by sacrifice. A massive sacrifice. A week or so later, two of the elder farmers returned to this place and discovered that there was no mound of dirt and no signs of digging. The area that had covered the dead had become flat. Nothing was growing on the land. The ground was smooth and unturned. It looked as if nothing had happened. Anxious, the men dug where they thought they would find bones of the dead but found nothing. The body parts were gone. Clothing was gone. There was no blood mixed with the soil. Somehow, a force greater than theirs had taken the dismembered by-products of the hateful fight and spirited them away.

"One last item. Many years later, when the stream was diverted and the lake formed, the water did not dislodge any bodies, body parts, or bones. No remains of the executions and burials were found. It's as if they never happened."

"OK, I follow. Several bad things happened here hundreds of years ago. Are we to believe that this same evil spirit still stalks the land? Are we to fear that Satan, a chimera at best, is sending messages to us that we are on his land and should not be here? Are we to think that the small half-eaten critters we found when we arrived were driven to the back yard by a force so they could be sacrificed to the birds? Seriously, Dad. Is that what you believe?"

"It's not what I believe, it's the lore of this land. But the physical signs seem to point to an extreme explanation of the inexplicable. There is no logical explanation for the critters, the scavengers, the pebbles, the storm, the nest of vipers in the woodpile, and the yellow jackets. Taken individually, those events could be dismissed as anomalies of nature. But, taken in aggregate, in such proximity, and within a specific time frame, they all could be an indication that something beyond our sphere of knowledge or awareness walks the land and does not want humans to reside here."

"Balderdash!"

"OK. I'm simply telling you what I know and what I think."

They now sat in silence, both pondering what they heard. The silence made both slightly uncomfortable. Joe had never wanted to worry his children about the spirits that walked this land. But he was afraid that the spirits were now in motion.

"Hey, Dad. Mikey. You're not going to believe this."

"Gabby, Dad seems willing to believe anything. What's your great news?"

"I went to the boathouse to retrieve the smoke pots and to sweep away the dead yellow jackets, but there were none. None on the floor. None flying around. None anywhere."

"That's not possible, Gabe."

"You may think it's impossible, Mike, but it's true. When I opened the door, I expected to see a bunch of the little shits on the floor, particularly by the hole in the corner and around the tarp, where you told me you saw possible nests. I saw nada, nichts, nothing, zilch, zero. There was some smoke still floating in the big room, but most of the heavy black smoke had drifted to the floor. It seemed to coat everything. The fires you lit had burned out. The cans were empty and cold. But there were no yellow jackets to be found anywhere. It seems that the smoke approach worked to chase them away. But it's strange that it did not kill any of them. At least, not in the boathouse. And how did they escape through closed and lock doors?"

"This I gotta see. Dad, coming along?"

"No thanks, I need to sit a bit."

"Gabe, is it my imagination, or does Dad seem overly tired all the time?"

"I hadn't paid much attention. But, now that you mention it, his step is a little slower and unsteady. Plus, he rests more than he used to. Hell, he is getting old, so slowing down and resting more are to be expected, they're normal."

"He wasn't this slow last year. Or at Christmas when we saw him. I doubt five months could make that much of a difference. I'm a little concerned. Let's keep an eye on him from now on. OK?"

"OK."

"Now let's see what you could not see."

"Bull. There are no yellow jackets here."

Michael opened the door and they both stepped onto the platform floor.

"See anything, Mike?"

"Not yet."

Michael walked to the corner by which he had placed a smoke pot. There were no dead yellow jackets, nothing except a ring where the smoke can had been. He poked around the small hole. Nothing. He glanced at his next target, the tarp. Cautiously, he slid it away from its resting spot and lifted the top three folds. Again, nothing. It was as if all the flying beasts had vanished.

"Well, big brother, you were not mistaken. There are no yellow jackets, alive or dead, in the boathouse. My question is: How the hell is that possible? They were here when we retrieved the kids. They were here when Dad and I put the cans down. They were here when we closed the doors to stop their escape. Now nothing. Not even a trace that they had ever been here. Very strange. We'll add this to our general discussion tonight."

"What discussion?"

"We have to figure out if all the strange happenings this weekend; the storm, snakes, and the disappearing yellow jackets have any significance or are they unrelated events that all happened during the same time frame."

"Ooooooh! Soooo scary. Like Halloween with goblins, ghosts, witches, and warlocks, good and evil."

"Not scary, just unexplained and thus disconcerting. I've asked dad, and he seems to have a theory that we need to hear and talk about."

"What's the theory?"

Suddenly, Martha appears in the doorway.

"Hi, Martha."

"Hi, Michael."

"Gabriel, we need to talk."

"Can't it wait? We're discussing an important mystery."

"No, it cannot wait! We need to talk. Now! Let's go to the house."

Michael thought his big brother was in trouble and about to be taken to the proverbial woodshed. That was his cue to find Shelia to learn what she knows.

Chapter Nineteen

"Shelia, can I help?"

"This baby has become fussy. I fed him about thirty minutes ago, but now it's way past his nap time ... and mine. I need to lie down. I could use your help prepping dinner. The chicken must be cut into quarters – breast and wing, and leg and thigh. Then the quarters need to be marinated in Joe's special sauce for a few hours in the fridge. The chickens are in the fridge now, bagged and awaiting their surgery. While that's working, it would be great if you would prep the rest of the meal; salad, long-grain rice, and whatever extras you think the family will eat. If you would do that, it would be a big help, Martha."

"Glad to help. I want to help any time you need it. By the way, I spoke to Gabe, and we're going to go away to a resort of my choosing. For ten days. When we get home from here, I'll pour over the internet to find a fancy place I deserve. A real expensive place. I can't thank you enough. Our talk was a huge help."

The two embraced. Shelia headed for her nap. She was concerned that Martha had taken the easy way to gratify her desires without seeking the truth.

"Be sure to wake me about an hour before dinner."

Martha turned toward the back door as she heard the loud voices of her husband and brother-in-law.

"I tell you, that's what she said."

"I simply can't believe it."

"Are you calling me a liar?"

"No, it's just what you said is outside the realm of Shelia's world."

"Shush, you two. There are three family members resting. If you must be loud, please take your squabble outside, far away."

"Sorry, Martha."

"Yeah, sorry sweetheart."

"By the way, we found this jar and envelope on the back porch. It's addressed to you and Shelia."

"What's in the jar?"

"A dark liquid. I have no idea what it's for. Read the note."

> Dear Martha and Shelia,
>
> I brewed some special tea for the children. It will speed their recovery and give them a little energy. It can be served warm, not hot, or at room temperature. One cup for each of the three.
>
> Amon

"How thoughtful, and his handwriting looks like Mary's. See how graceful, yet precise it is. Amon is a gentleman to send the tea for the children. It seems like he cares more for them than two screaming adult male louts I know. Now scoot and get out of my kitchen."

"I'm tellin' you, Mikey, that's what she said."

"I just can't believe that Shelia would tell Martha to demand that you take her to an expensive resort for a week and a half."

"Well, she did. Now, I'm on the hook for a big check, just because your wife stuck her nose where it didn't belong."

"I need to talk to Shelia to get a true perspective on what actually happened."

"So, you're calling me a liar."

"No, I'm not. It's just that the conversation between our wives may have been misinterpreted and slightly twisted by the time it got to you. Like the old game of rumor we used to play at parties when we were kids."

"So, now you're calling my wife a liar. Is that it?"

"No, that's not it. I'm saying that any advice that was given may have been well intended by the giver but misconstrued by the recipient. That can happen when the recipient of the advice is improperly influenced by other factors."

"So, Martha IS a liar!"

"No! What I'm saying is that we don't know if Martha went to Shelia to get advice or if Shelia went to Martha and offered unsolicited advice. The advice could have been construed by Martha to be what she wanted to hear. Not necessarily what was intended or actually said."

"So, Martha and I are BOTH liars. Is that it?"

"No, damn it! You hear what I am saying, but you are not listening to what it is I am telling you. No one is accusing you or Martha of being liars. All I'm saying is that there is confusion as to what was said by whom, why it was said, and the interpretation of what was said. A real-life disconnect. There must have been a severe disconnect."

"Are you trying to confuse me?"

"No. But I need to have a sit-down with my wife to better understand what was said. Hopefully, this will help us thus avoid any further ill feelings over the issues of the conversation. Agreed?"

"Agreed. I need a beer. How about you?"

"No thanks."

"Come back after you've had your talk with Shelia. I need to know both sides of the discussion, so I can understand what the hell happened."

The two teenage explorers were standing in the doorway.

"Hey, you two. How was your excursion?"

"Great, we walked through the big meadow and discovered an old house up on the hill. We explored the old place and saw how the people lived."

"What did you find in the house, Lillie?"

"Nothing really special. It's old and very run down. Just walls and floors. No big deal. But it was fun to go exploring. Micah is a good guide."

Lillie's smile was inscrutable.

"Well, I'll need your help with dinner in a few hours. Then you and Aggie will be transformed into scullery maids. Are you hungry after your hike?"

"I could go for a sandwich. How about you, Micah?"

"A sandwich would be nice."

"Mom, will you make two sandwiches?"

"No, Lillie, you can make your own. It's about time you started pulling your own weight. I am not your maid!"

"Whoa! Where did that come from?"

"Your aunt dumped dinner prep on me and went to bed. I'm busy with that monumental task. So, you will have to fend for yourself. If that's too much for you to deal with, maybe you should skip the sandwich."

"Easy, Mom. Micah and I will make our sandwiches and leave you alone. Micah, can you reach into the fridge and get what we need? I'll make a space on the counter where I can make our sandwiches."

In less than ten minutes, the teens had made their food, eaten it, and left the kitchen.

"Lillie, what's with your mom? She seems to be stressed and in a bad mood."

"Probably her period. She gets really bitchy during that time of the month. She takes her discomfort so personally, as if no other woman suffers like she does. I've learned to avoid conversations with her when she is suffering."

"Wanna go back on the lake?"

"Only if you can guarantee that I will not be attacked by yellow jackets or any other evil insect."

"Can't guarantee anything, but I'll be on the lookout. Should we ask Aggie to go with us?"

"Nah. Just you and me. Do you trust yourself being alone with me?"

"Sure."

He lied.

"Gabe, tell me again what she told you."

"Shelia came to Martha and said she noticed how badly I was treating her. Then Shelia ... *on her own* offered some marital advice. Like she was a professional counselor. She told Martha that she should demand that I take her on a ten-day or two-week trip – a time away from the girls. She told Martha I should take her to a place where she could indulge herself in all the things Martha seemed to be missing. A place that would cost me a pretty penny. Compensation for my bad treatment. She told Martha that she deserved new clothes, and that I should seek counseling about my drinking."

"So, if I understand you right, Shelia was meddling in a place not of her concern. And she told Martha exactly what to do to exact some measure of revenge for your bad behavior. Are you sure that Shelia approached Martha and not the other way around?"

"Now I'm back to being a liar. I told you, Shelia approached Martha. Of that, I am sure. This whole mess is going to cost me a ton of money just to keep peace in my house. Money, I don't have right now. I wish your wife had kept her nose out of our business. So, make damned sure she stays away from Martha for the rest of our time here. OK?"

"I still have a difficult time believing Shelia would go to Martha and say those inciting things. She is not a meddler. She has her work and her family. She never gets involved in the trials and tribulations of anything outside those two worlds. Not even the neighbors. But, OK, I'll keep her away from Martha. Are we done?"

"For now."

"What's that supposed to mean?"

"Hi, Martha. What's for dinner?"

"Bar-b-que chicken, long-grain rice, and salad, Joe."

"Sounds great. Do I have time for some small chores?"

"Oh, sure. We won't even start the grill for about two hours."

"Looks like you have everything under control."

"That's right. I have responsibility for everything. Shelia and Aggie are napping, Lillie and Micah headed out on the lake, and your sons deserted me to go somewhere."

Her accusatory tone and word choice were mildly disturbing. Joe never brooked the shrill whine of self-pity. Not from himself, his sons, or the people he worked with. Self-pity was just a warped expression of misdirected anger. He was uncomfortable around angry people. Mary never whined and was rarely angry.

"OK then. I'll be out in the shed. Have one of my sons come and get me when the fire is started, so I can wash up."

His pace to the shed was quick. He wanted to get away from Martha and whatever was bothering her.

The knock on the back door startled Martha.

"Sorry to bother you, ma'am, but Joe invited me for dinner tonight. Heh, heh, heh."

Amon was standing in the doorway. He had done his best to clean up. He bathed, shaved, and put on cleaner clothes.

"No bother, we have plenty for all members of the family. Joe's not here. He's in the shed doing something."

"Good. I'll find him. Have you had a chance to give the children a second cup of tea? Heh, heh, heh."

"Micah and Lillie came to the house after their excursion. Then, left me all alone while they went out on the lake. I'll give them the tea when they reappear. Aggie is resting. When she gets up, I'll be sure to give her some of your special tea."

"She probably needs it more than the boy and her older sister, because she is younger, and delicate, and therefore more susceptible to the yellow jacket poison. A second cup of tea might be a good idea for her. Now, I want to speak to Joe. See you soon. Heh, heh, heh."

He exited. She reached for one of the fashion magazines that Lillie brought on the trip. A reference for her school clothes shopping. Martha looked for what the beautiful people were wearing at the posh resorts this year. She wanted to develop an extensive and expensive shopping list. She also wanted to know where these glitterati went to relax. She would choose from these places.

Chapter Twenty

"What do you do for fun in Philadelphia, Micah?"

"School and sports take up most of my time. Later this summer, I'll be going to a wrestling camp for two weeks to get ready for the season. Plus, I have a ton of reading and three reports due for school."

"Boring!"

"I don't think it's boring. It's preparation. I want to get into a good college, like my mom and Dad. And, wrestling requires that I be better trained, faster, and stronger than my opponent."

"Don't you ever go on dates with that girlfriend you may or may not have?"

"On the weekends, a group of us usually get together at one of the parks and play softball, then have a cookout."

"That's soooo boring."

"What do you do?"

"Party nearly every night. At someone's house when their parents are away. Or we drive into the country for a special time. Wanna know what we do in this special time?"

"It's none of my business. Besides, it's your time to do with as you please."

"We drink beer and we fool around. We smoke weed. Have you ever smoked weed?"

"No."

"Wanna try some now?"

"No."

"You're beginning to sound like a real pussy. You're forcing me to smoke a doobie by myself."

Lillie removed a joint from her shirt pocket, rolled it over her lips to moisten it, took it to her mouth, and lit it. Immediately after inhaling, she started to cough. Not little coughs, but huge attempts to expel the drug from her lungs. After the hacking spasms subsided, she inhaled a second, deeper drag. This time the coughing was much less violent. She repeated the process. The third time there was no coughing.

"You don't know what you're missing. The effect is wonderful. The world is getting mellow. It is slowing down. There are few, if any, rough edges. I'm almost beginning to like you. I can see the sky is divided into two parts: one part with no clouds and another with a huge dark cloud. I can see shapes and faces in the big cloud. They are constantly changing. I guess the wind does that. I can see into the woods on the other side of the lake. There is nothing worth seeing there. The world has almost stopped so I can inspect all the details."

Suddenly, she was interrupted by a massive lightning bolt and the immediate crash of thunder. Not the big booming kind, but thunder that rolled and sounded as if the sky was being rent asunder ... torn from top to bottom. The noise started at a high pitch, continued down the scale, and ended with a frightening blast. They both looked to the sky over the other side of the lake to see another large, jagged bolt of lightning moving nearly sideways to strike the water about four hundred yards from the boat. Lillie was shocked back to reality.

"Fuck! Get us outta here, Micah."

The sky on the far side of the lake across from their cabin was pitch black and the clouds were aggressively twisting and roiling. Lightning bolts were active within and beneath them. The lightning moved in all directions; left, right, and straight ahead. The bolts didn't come down directly. They moved in unscripted paths to the ground. Every strike was followed immediately by a loud sky-ripping noise. Micah saw no rain. Nonetheless, he turned the boat around and headed for the safety of the shore and the cottage. The storm cloud appeared to be retreating

Had it stopped its trip across the lake? It was as if they were warned to get off the lake by the lightning and thunder.

The thunder had awakened the two nappers.

"Hey, Martha. Thanks for letting me sleep. Is there anything I can do?"

"No, but thanks. I got it. The thunder is nature's alarm clock. I want to make sure Aggie is awake, though I can't imagine how she slept through the racket. Amon said his new special tea should give her energy. She should have some before dinner. By the way, wait until you see Amon. He looks almost human, and his clothes are almost presentable."

"Oh, Amon. I forgot that Joe invited him. Glad we have plenty of food. Where is everybody?"

"Micah and Lillie went out on the lake. Joe and Amon are in the shed. Michael and Gabriel are somewhere out front talking or arguing about something. For the past hour or so the kitchen was like Grand Central; people coming and going, but no one offered to help."

"I'm here now. Are you sure there's nothing I can do to help?"

"Yes, I'm sure. Everything is ready to grill and serve."

"OK, then. I'll be responsible for kitchen clean-up duties. You go wake Aggie and give her some of Amon's tea."

As Martha headed toward the bedroom, Michael entered the kitchen.

"Shelia, how was your nap?"

"Too short, but good, sweetheart."

"Can you leave your post without being shot by the commandant?"

"Sure. Why?"

"I need to talk to you."

"Is it a good talk? Or am I going to regret it?"

"It's a talk to shed light on a confusing scenario. Let's go out front. While we talk, you can lay the charcoal for the fire."

"Joe, whatchya doin'?"

"Just straightening up the shed. We had a fright when we arrived. There were small dead animals all over the back yard and their carcasses were being eaten by birds. We cleaned up the mess. Now I have to be sure all tools we used are cleaned and back in their proper places."

"Scavenger birds are not rare around here, but a back yard filled with their meals is rare. What do you supposed drove the vermin to the killing field? Heh, heh, heh."

"Not a clue."

"How did they die?"

"Not a clue."

"What did you do with the carcasses?"

"Burned then buried them."

"Was there anything besides the carcasses on the ground?"

"One or two pebbles near each kill site."

"That's strange. Anything else strange about the kill sites?"

"Yes, they were hot. Why the third degree?"

"Just curious. Heh, heh, heh."

"Now, Amon, you are more than just curious. You think you know something about the backyard scene. Tell me what you think."

"Nothing for sure, but the dead critters, the scavenger birds, and the hot kill sites you mentioned all could be signs that there is a powerful evil force abiding on the land."

"Balderdash! If you're referring to the folklore about this area being a killing ground for poor souls accused of being Satan's minions, it's all gibberish. We both know that old saw is just a rumor. There is no Satan. There is no land that belongs to Satan. There are just anomalies in nature that man can't understand."

"If you say so, Joe. Heh, heh, heh."

Amon's enigmatic grin intrigued Joe.

"Gabe, we need to talk."

"About?"

"About the confusion arising from Shelia's conversation with Martha."

"What confusion?"

"Well, you told me that Shelia came to Martha and said she noticed how badly you were treating her. Then Shelia … on her own, offered some marital advice. She told Martha that she should demand that you take her on a trip – a time away from the girls. She told Martha you should take her to a place where she could indulge herself in all the things Martha seemed to be missing. The place that you two should go to would cost you a pretty penny … compensation for your bad treatment. She told Martha that she deserved new clothes, and that you should seek counseling about your drinking. Is that about the sum of your conversation with Martha?"

"Yes."

"I want you to hear what Shelia really said to Martha right from the source."

"Another set of lies?"

"No, the unvarnished truth. Honey, tell him."

"Listen to what I say, then comment. Don't interrupt. I remember the conversation very clearly. Martha approached me. She was nearly hysterical and said that her life is a train wreck that happens every day over and over again like a bad movie. She was nearly ranting. Spoke in one continuous sentence with breaks only to catch her breath. She's started to have more than one cocktail before dinner. You at home for family dinner is becoming less and less frequent. You haven't touched her in three months. Her clothes are old and make her look dowdy. Lillie has become sexually active, but mother and daughter don't talk.

Lillie's grades have slipped. You seem to view your home and wife as necessary accoutrements to your climb up the corporate ladder. You were promoted four years ago, then passed over last year. You're bitter about that and stay out late almost every evening. Your wife is confused by her feelings of failure.

"Martha suspects you're having an affair with your admin or maybe a new woman the company hired to run another division. Martha is worried that you're getting fat and soft. You two can pay almost all of your bills almost on time, but the situation is tense, is getting worse, and leads to arguments. You have dipped into your investments and the girls' college funds just to pay for what she claims are the expensive toys you and the girls must have like two new expensive cars every two years, a very expensive school, and all the electronic devices known to mankind. She is losing interest in being a good wife and mother because the home environment has become toxic."

"But…"

"Is that you talking? Please, I'm not finished. When I'm done, please respond. I told her she had done nothing wrong. It's just that she's gotten older and her life has changed. That's very normal and most often can be healthy. She shouldn't try to hold on to the past. But she must adjust and adapt to her changing environment. To do this, she must have her own life.

"She must be her own person not a reflection of her daughters or husband. She must assert that she has needs and that she makes meaningful contributions to her family and the society around her beyond being a good mom and an attractive wife. She must stand up for herself. Not be a tag-along who does what everybody else wants her to do and be. Make her family see what a good and productive woman she is. That's how she can hold it together. Only she can do that. Neither you, Gabriel, nor your daughters can hold Martha together.

"I suggested that she could get involved in the girls' school or the Y or a local charity like the Salvation Army. Maybe even your church. She felt that the girls' school might be a good place to start, because you two spend sixty grand a year there, and the school is always looking for parents to run outreach and charitable events. I further suggested that she talk to you, tell you what she's feeling, and ask for your support. Then, before she gets involved in the school, go away with you alone. Do not take your daughters. Go away for long weekend. Rekindle your life together and your love life.

"She said she liked the long-weekend idea and thought of Tahoe or someplace special like that. A place that has all the amenities like tennis, swimming, maybe horseback riding. A place where the beautiful people go. She wants to buy outfits and some very sexy clothes featured in magazines. She further said that if you hesitate or say you're too busy, she'll tell you the alternative is for her to leave the girls with you while she goes away for a ten-day retreat. A very expensive mommy makeover.

"She approached me hysterical and went away with a small measure of self-confidence and a plan. That's the truth. I did not approach her and tell her what to do. She came to me when she was angry and depressed. Sorry to dump all of this on you at once, but you deserve to know the truth. Your wife feels unloved, unappreciated, and unfulfilled."

Gabe sat in silence. He was bewildered and had no response.

Chapter Twenty-one

With the three generations standing at the table on the patio, Joe, holding Mary's Episcopal Book of Common Prayer, began the Holy Eucharist. The rite was a tradition of hers to begin the summer season at the cottage when all four boys were small children. Joe thus honored her memory. Before each of the family members was a small plate holding a piece of bread beside a wine glass partially filled. Joe's voice was uplifting.

"Almighty God, unto whom all hearts are open, all desires known, and from whom no secrets are hid: Cleanse the thoughts of our hearts by the inspiration of thy Holy Spirit, that we may perfectly love thee, and worthily magnify thy holy Name; through Christ our Lord.

"For in the night in which he was betrayed, he took bread; and when he had given thanks, he broke it, and gave it to his disciples, saying, 'Take, eat, this is my Body, which is given for you. Do this in remembrance of me.'"

Family members took the small piece of bread from their plates and put it in their mouths.

"Likewise, after supper, he took the cup; and when he had given thanks, he gave it to them, saying, 'Drink ye all of this; for this is my Blood of the New Testament, which is shed for you, and for many, for the remission of sins. Do this, as oft as ye shall drink it, in remembrance of me.'"

Nine hands reached for the glass of wine in front of them, brought it to their lips, and sipped the contents.

"And we most humbly beseech thee, O merciful Father, to hear us; and, of thy almighty goodness, vouchsafe to bless and sanctify, with thy Word and Holy Spirit, these thy gifts and creatures of bread and wine; that we, receiving them according to thy Son our Savior Jesus Christ's holy institution, in remembrance of his death and passion, may be partakers of his most blessed Body and Blood.

"And we earnestly desire thy fatherly goodness mercifully to accept this our sacrifice of praise and thanksgiving; most humbly beseeching thee to grant that, by the merits and death of thy Son Jesus Christ, and through faith in his blood, we, and all thy whole Church, may obtain remission of our sins, and all other benefits of his passion.

"And here we offer and present unto thee, O Lord, ourselves, our souls and bodies, to be a reasonable, holy, and living sacrifice unto thee; humbly beseeching thee that we, and all others who shall be partakers of this Holy Communion, may worthily receive the most precious Body and Blood of thy Son Jesus Christ, be filled with thy grace and heavenly benediction, and made one body with him, that he may dwell in us, and we in him.

"And although we are unworthy, through our manifold sins, to offer unto thee any sacrifice, yet we beseech thee to accept this our bounden duty and service, not weighing our merits, but pardoning our offenses, through Jesus Christ our Lord; By whom, and with whom, in the unity of the Holy Ghost, all honor and glory be unto thee, O Father Almighty, world without end. AMEN."

"Amen" from the family members.

Out of the corner of his right eye, Joe thought he saw Amon palming the piece of bread and not sipping the wine. This observation would be their secret.

"It all looks terrific Martha. You did a great job."

"Thanks, Joe."

"Hey, how about the chef?"

"Well, big brother, you didn't turn the chicken into charcoal briquettes, and for that I give you praise."

"What did you contribute to the meal, Mikey?"

"Well…"

"In other words, you contributed nothing. You are a non-contributing critic. Just like always."

"Easy, boys. Let's keep it civil. We're a family, with members young and old. This is a family dinner. If you have something nice to say, do so. If you harbor mean or angry thoughts, please keep them to yourself."

Joe surveyed the seating arrangements; Amon was to his right with Aggie next to him and Lillie and Micah next to her. Martha sat at Joe's left with Shelia, Michael, and Gabriel sitting in that order. There was a place setting at the end of the table, but the chair is empty. Mary will not be joining them.

His eyes passed over the table laden with a traditional family summer dinner – chicken, long-grain rice, and succotash made with cream corn. Pitchers of iced tea for some and beer for others.

"May I pass, Grandpa?"

"Yes, Micah, please start."

Thus, begins the food sharing from large dishes and plates. The passing of the serving dishes was accompanied by brief conversations and a polite "thank you" or "thanks." Plates filled and forks employed, eating silenced any conversation for a few minutes.

"How was everyone's day? Did anybody do anything special?"

"Well Grandpa, Lillie and I went across the main road and into the big meadow. When we went up the hill at the far side of the meadow, we saw an empty old house. I think it had belonged to the farmer who worked the big meadow years ago. We explored the place and saw where the Franklin stove had been and the big room upstairs. Grandpa, do you know who lived there?"

"Well, Micah, the last people we knew of lived in the house a long time ago."

"I wonder whatever happened to them?"

"I know. Heh, heh, heh."

"Tell me, Amon."

Joe's face turns worrisome ... almost stern.

"What I'm about to tell you might be gruesome, but it is true. Many years ago, maybe more, the share-cropper family who lived in the house fell on hard times. Their crops failed, their cows dried up, and the chickens didn't lay any eggs."

"But what about the people, the family?"

"Sometime during the hard times, a tragedy struck. One day, the Sheriff's deputies were called to the house by a traveling salesman who was trying to sell seed and small tools to the farmers in the county. He said there was no one at home, although the table was set for a meal. He said there was a terrible smell coming from the house. He also noted numerous crows, ravens, and vultures circling the house. When the deputies entered the place, they found everything looked OK on the first floor. Then they heard buzzing and the foul smell was much stronger. When they went upstairs, they saw the source of all the buzzing ... flies. Thousands of them. And they found the source of the strong smell ... rotting flesh. It made one deputy puke. On the second floor, the police found three bodies that had been chopped to pieces: the decaying remains of the two small children and their mother. Body parts were stacked in three piles on the floor. Arms and legs on the bottom, torsos in the middle, and the heads on top. The piles were surrounded by pools of dried blood and were covered with flies and maggots. From the rafter, they found the husband hanging. His body was dried out and his clothes hung loosely on his form. Beneath him was a pool of his fluids."

"That's terrible."

"Yes, it is, Lillie. Terrible, but true. I apologize to you and Agnes if you found my description of the facts disturbing."

"We saw three large dark stains on the floor. Those must have been where the body parts were found. Did the Sheriff ever learn what happened?"

"Micah, I believe they said it was a murder-suicide brought on by depression. But after the tragedy, the landowner rented the house to two different tenant farmers. Neither family stayed in the house more than two years. Both families claimed to hear noises at night and feel the presence of an unnatural force. But that was a long time ago. No one has moved into the place since. It just sits there like a castle on the hill overlooking the meadow.

"Amon, you mean that no one has even worked the land since?"

"Gabriel, most people think the land and house are possessed by an evil spirit, and this spirit drove the farmer to slaughter his family then kill himself. But, that's just childish rumors … stories about ghosts and all."

"Amon, besides Lillie and me, do you know of anyone who has walked through the house?"

"I have heard that every once in a while, mostly on Halloween night, teenagers from nearby high schools drive down here and go into the house on a dare. When they get home, they tell ghost stories about the place – the sights, and noises in the house and field. No one believes the kids. It's just teenager hijinks."

"I could believe them."

"Why is that Lillie?"

"Mom, it was scary. I didn't see anything or anybody, but I felt a strange presence in the house that was powerful on the second floor. We only stayed in the house for a few minutes. I wanted to get out of there. So, I ran away. Micah followed."

"Micah, I suggest you not go there again. No good can come of a return trip."

Joe feared Amon's admonishment could have the opposite effect. Not a warning but a statement meant to dare the boy into a return trip. Joe knew the teenage attitude toward warnings. He interrupted.

"That's enough of horrifying folklore. Remember children, it's only folklore. Let's move on to something a bit more pleasant. Aggie, what did you do today?"

"Slept and rested. The yellow jacket stings were too much for me. Plus, I thought I was coming down with something. But I feel better … much better now thanks to Amon's special tea."

"Good. Maybe tomorrow you three can take the boat to the other side of the lake. I understand there's a small piece of sandy beach over there."

"As long as there are no flying stingers, I'll go."

"Thatta girl, Lillie. You're not afraid. Please pass the succotash."

The dinner passed easily with pleasant conversation and discussions as to the school year just completed and the one upcoming. The children cleared the table, and returned with dessert, warm apple pie and vanilla ice cream. A part of the meal no one needed but everyone wanted. After a small helping, Joe felt like a stuffed turkey. Almost uncomfortable. A negative aspect of holiday dining. He must remember to take his pills.

"Grandpa, what are all those for."

"Aggie, these are the magic pellets. I call them my sprinkles. These pills keep me healthy; one for my heart, one to control my cholesterol, a blood thinner so my heart can move my blood easily through my body, one for my allergies, one for my arthritis, and I take this last one to help me be happy and friendly to all those around me, because the pills in concert can make me become sleepy … even grumpy."

"Dad, grumpy? I would have never thought it possible."

"I know, Gabe, it's hard to believe, but I can be out of sorts from time to time, especially when pestered by my sons."

Guffaws from the family.

"When does the last pill begin to work?"

"When you stop asking foolish questions."

Hoots from the two sons.

"That's a lot of pills."

"Only what I need, according to my doctor, Aggie. I plan to live a long time, and these help assure that."

"Joe, I best be going. I've got a lot of chores tomorrow in preparation for the fireworks over the lake. Thank you all for the meal. I will see you tomorrow."

"Fireworks?"

"Yes, Aggie, every Memorial Day and Labor Day, the park has a huge fireworks display. One to announce the opening of the summer season and one to mark its closing. Last fall, I took a job with the company that has the responsibility for the fireworks. I took classes and was certified to manage the display. This year, I'm responsible for setting up the firing platform and discharging the works. Plus, I'm in charge of safety as well as ignition. This year I have something new and very special … Devil's Breath. Never before seen."

"What's Devil's Breath?"

"It's a huge display of different explosives in various colors and lots of colored smoke. It's much more than simple explosions and stars. The display looks like flames in the sky. Orange, red, and yellow flames reaching up to the heavens. The result of special packing and timed explosions resembles fire. The smell of brimstone, or sulfur, is intense. Sounds like an artillery attack and looks really scary. The entire display lasts for two minutes. It will be a great season opener. But I have to leave now so I can get my rest; I have a full day of set up and preparation ahead of me."

"How do you get the flame to rise?"

"An artist never reveals his method, Aggie. But if you would like to help me set up the display tomorrow, maybe you'll learn. Heh, heh, heh."

"Mom. Dad. Can I help Uncle Amon set up the fireworks?"

"Well … I don't know."

"It's perfectly safe, Shelia, because there are no flames near the display."

"Gabe, what do you think?"

"I'm not sure …"

"Oh, come on, you two, let your daughter have some fun and learn what every child wants to know about fireworks."

"OK. If your grandpa says it will be alright, you can help Amon."

"Thanks, Dad."

"Amon, be careful with our little girl."

"She'll be safe with me."

"I'll stop by tomorrow around nine. Wear your work clothes. I'll bring lunch. We have a full day. Again thanks for sharing the great feast and your friendship."

With that, Amon rose and left. The five remaining adults simply sat and enjoyed the early evening air.

"Aggie, better go inside and help your sister and cousin clean."

"Yes, Mom."

"If it weren't so gross, I would loosen my pants. I'm stuffed."

"Yes, Gabe, we all ate too much, but it was very good. Please keep your pants on for the time being. I have something to discuss with all of you."

Joe reached beneath his chair and lifted two manila envelopes. He handed one each to his sons.

"As you know, I am not getting any younger, and the pills I must take are testimony to the fragility of my health. Recognizing this, I recently re-drew my will. I have copies of the document here for you to read. You do not have to initial or sign anything. That was my responsibility."

Four sets of eyes shot glances at each other. Faces that had been relaxed were now tense with the reality of an impending situation.

"Your will! That's morbid. You're not going to die soon, are you?"

"First, Gabe, it's not morbid. It's practical. And second, I don't plan on leaving this earth soon. This is simply good planning. You need to go over the document in the envelope. Please open your folders and follow along with me. I won't recite the dreadfully boring legal mumbo-jumbo. I'll just hit the key points. You'll see that I have left the bulk of my estate, meager though it may be, to you boys on an equal-share basis. I have also bequeathed a small amount of money to the Salvation Army. I have asked that you two maintain this cottage as part of the family legacy. Your children will want to come here with their families.

"The home in town will be sold. The proceeds of the sale will go to you two, equally. I thought neither of you would want to or be able to live there, and I surely didn't want to rent it. Too many headaches for the estate. Beneath the final page, you'll find two sheets of colored stickers. Here's your work. I want you to go to the house and put your stickers on items you would like after I'm dead. Furniture, artwork, dining items, kitchenware. Whatever you want, mark with a sticker. By doing this before I die, there should be little or no rancor as to who gets what after I die."

"Dad!"

"Michael?"

"This is almost too much to process."

"You have time. Look over the will and ask questions."

"What say the four adults go to the house together, so we can go through the house at the same time. Just to be sure that Michael doesn't grab everything."

"Gabe, that's paranoid of you. Clever, but paranoid. If those words were to come from anyone else, I would be offended. But I know how your warped mind works or doesn't."

"It's not that I don't trust you, little brother, it's just that I want my family to have a fair shot at items they like."

"Boys, this is just the type of rancor and bickering I had hoped to avoid with the stickers."

"Sorry, Dad."

"I have a suggestion; before the holiday celebrations tomorrow, why don't the four of you go back to the house, survey all the items, and place your stickers on the items you want? Take all day if need be. Just be home for dinner. In your absence, I'll be responsible my grandchildren. Gabe, you're not flying back until Friday, and Michael, you plan to drive back to Philadelphia on Sunday. So, your trip to the house will not interfere with your plans to return to your respective homes."

Four sets of eyes look at each other.

"Good idea, Dad."

"Thanks, Gabe. Ya know, I didn't get to be old by being stupid."

"Let's head out by nine. Two hours there, three hours to review the household items, and two hours back. Home before five. OK, Gabe?"

"OK, Mikey."

"That's settled. I'm going to retire. You younger adults can inspect the results of your children's chores. Love you all."

Four voices in unison.

"Love you."

"Little brother, we'll take my rental and you can navigate as our trusted native guide."

The wives concurred with the plan. They both wanted to leave after the family has had breakfast, so they could tell their children where they were going, to reassure them that they would return before dinner, and that Grandpa Joe was in charge.

The two sets of adults would review their copy of the document in the light of their bedroom lamps. Now they picked up the remaining plates and glasses and followed Joe into the cottage. He walked haltingly.

Chapter Twenty-two

The crispness of a late-May morning in the woods called for the warmth and energy derived from hot coffee, eggs, bacon, heated rolls, and fresh fruit. The four adults left for the city. Joe was in charge of his grandchildren.

"This is the family's first official day of summer. Now that your parents have gone for the day, do you guys have any special plans? I know that Aggie will be working with Amon in making the fireworks display ready for tonight. What about you two?"

"I'd like to fish the lake one more time. Maybe I can catch dinner."

"That's a great idea, Micah, why don't you take Lillie and show her your piscatorial prowess?"

"My what?"

"Piscatorial prowess … fishing skills."

"Great phrase, Grandpa. Lillie, want to learn how to fish?"

"I'll go if you can promise there won't be any yellow jackets."

"No guarantees. Just my best hope."

The knock on the back door interrupted them.

"Hello, Amon here. Heh, heh, heh. Is Aggie ready to help set up the fireworks?"

"I'm ready."

"Before you two leave, what are your plans for lunch?"

"Joe, I have sandwiches and drinks in my cooler. We'll be fine. We should be able to complete our tasks by early afternoon. I'll make sure

Aggie is back here well before dinner. At dusk, I'll have to return to the launching pad and prepare to set off the works. Sorry you can't go with me, Aggie. But, it's the risky part of my job."

"OK. Aggie, have a great time."

"Thanks, Grandpa."

"Lillie, we should get to the boathouse by ten. I'll make sandwiches for lunch."

"I'm ready for a fishing day with my best buddy."

Micah was puzzled by Lillie's attitude. Her extremely self-interested attitude seemed to have melted, or at least was well-hidden.

Joe cleaned up the kitchen. He took hamburger meat from the freezer and placed it in the refrigerator. Just in case the fisher children were not successful at acquiring dinner. Hamburgers, baked beans, cole slaw, and chips was the alternative meal to lake trout, salad, and wild rice. There were a few small chores he needed to complete before his reading time and nap. He swept the kitchen. Made sure all the beds were made. Mary insisted that the beds be made each and every morning. It was her rule. He would see it was not broken. His duties took over an hour. He didn't move as fast as he used to and bending over to make the beds hurt his back. On the patio, he shifted a chair into the sunlight. His aging eyes have told him that abundant light was critical to reading.

He recently purchased several books for the summer. Historical, spy, and crime fiction were his favorites. He bought two crime novels by a new author recommended by his doctor. No romance novels. Plus, he bought a book of poetry, a form of expression Mary loved. He settled in for a relaxed period of intellectual and emotional stimulation. His brood was out of the house for the day and he could enjoy the silence of the woods, while he had the cottage all to himself. Joe inwardly smiled. He was content. The air was cool. The zephyr off the lake alternated the warmth of the sun with the coolness of the wood's air and created vacillating temperatures. The sun began to wrap her beams around him causing his eyelids to become heavy and his head to nod.

Now arriving on Track Number Two, the Cincinnati Limited. Arriving on Track Two, the Cincinnati Limited. All aboud. The station master's announcement was a call to action. Joe took David by the hand. Mary had control of Joe Jr. The four headed for the stairway down to the tracks. On the platform, they were among a small group of people heading west. The boys peered over the edge of the platform, hoping to see the train before it arrived. Maybe they could make the engine get to the station sooner. There it was. The huge vehicle at the front of the passenger cars gradually came to a halt. Out stepped a uniformed man, who beckoned those on the platform with the words, this is the Cincinnati Limited…all aboud. Joe and Mary guided their sons to the open door and released their grips on two little hands. The boys hesitantly left the security of their parents and headed for the uncertainty of the passenger car. Immediately, they were engulfed by the rush of adults and gone from sight. Joe stood on his toes trying to get a glimpse of his sons. He could not. He turned to Mary and saw tears welling in the mother's eyes.

"We use flies for fishing on the lake, Lillie."

"Flies?"

"See the small feathery things in the top tray? They're called flies because, I guess, years ago, people thought they looked like flies. We attach the fly to the monofilament at the end of the line. See it? It's called a leader. The leader is invisible to fish in the water. The fly stays on top of the water to lure the fish. The fish see the fly as good eating. Lunch or dinner. They attack and gulp down their meal. We tug to set the hook. That means we make sure the hook is dug into the fish's mouth and then slowly reel the fish to the side of the boat where we scoop it up in this net. Don't bring the fish to the surface until it's beside the boat. Those are the basics. We'll tie on the flies after we get to a spot on the lake. Ready?"

"Aye aye, Captain."

They exited the boathouse and proceeded to a spot about halfway to the middle and directly in line with the creek that fed the lake. Micah thought he knew the best spot. It was good enough for him and his father. He paid no attention to Lillie, who was facing the sky to take in the sun and the breeze. The two-pound coffee can filled with concrete, the anchor, was slowly lowered. Micah lifted a rod and began to tie.

"Watch me so you can tie."

"Aren't you going to do that for me?"

Her self-centeredness was back.

"No. You're capable of tying a lure to catch your own fish. Think of how great you'll feel when you can say that you did it all by yourself. You'll be able to brag to all your friends back home. Besides, I'll guide you through it all."

Micah could see how difficult it was for Lillie to do something outside of her comfort zone. Apparently, she had always been able to get people to do the different and difficult tasks for her. Did she play Daddy's girl when she was home, helpless student at school, and flirty cutie to the boys in her circle of friends? All to get someone to do something for her. She was not helpless at the old farmhouse. Maybe that part of her life was different … maybe that's her comfort zone. Lillie was trying to run the leader through the small fly loop, and thus secure it. Micah saw her struggling.

"You must tie the lure in such a way that the fish cannot bite the fly and rip it from the leader. Run the leader through the small loop beneath the feathers and tie it off with a square knot. Make sure the knot is tight. Pull the ends hard. I use my teeth to make sure it is tied tight. There you go. You got it. Now watch me as I cast. The fly and line are lifted off the water in front of me, brought overhead and behind me, and then the rod is abruptly yet smoothly pulled back in front of me so that the line makes a big arc overhead. I've made sure I have a lot of line loose and ready to float out from the boat and over the water. Watch as

I swing the rod behind me. The fly goes behind me in a big soft loop, then in front of me when I bring the rod forward. See the fly land and stay on the surface. Now very slowly I reel in the lure. Slowly, hoping a fish will think the fly is skimming across the water above him ... or her. I repeat this over and over again until I get a hit. Now you try."

Lillie was aft. Her first attempt was awkward. The fly landed about two feet in front of her. She did not have enough loose line.

"That sucked."

"The first time is never as good as you want it to be. But the effort is not a failure if you learn something from it."

"Well, aren't you the old philosopher?"

"That's what Grandpa told me when he taught me how to cast. After several casts, I finally got one right. I can do it so I know you can, too. Remember, you're standing in a small boat. Be careful not to bounce around. Keep your feet steady and use your upper body and arm. Otherwise, you could fall overboard or worse, tip the boat over and we'd both be in the cold water far from shore. Now try again."

The second time was about the same. A little less bouncy and the fly landed about six feet from the boat. Micah was casting from the bow hoping to avoid being snagged by Lillie's efforts. He tried to pay attention to his casts, but periodically he glanced back and saw an attractive girl, whose torso and hair were backlit by the sun's reflection off the water. He wondered if he could teach Pat to fly fish. He wondered if he could invite her to the cottage sometime. His mind found a blissful zone and stayed.

"I gotta bite. Now what do I do?"

"Give the rod a slight, but firm tug to sink the hook into the fish's mouth. If you tug too hard, you'll pull the fly away. If you don't pull hard enough the fish may just spit out the fly."

"That sounds like the three bears: not too hard, not too soft, just right. How do I know what is just right?"

"Experience gained from practice."

"Thanks a lot."

"Just tug."

"Damn, he got away. Now what?"

"Check the fly for damage."

Quickly, Lillie reels in her line.

"Make sure the fly is still attractive to the fish."

"How the hell do I know that?"

"Check to see if it's torn or too loose on the leader. If it's whole and tight, you can cast again. If not, you'll need to retie it or tie on a new fly."

"Then what?"

"Repeat the process. Fly fishing is something that requires repetition and patience. Or as Grandpa says, the power of perseverance."

"Not sure I have the patience for this crap."

"Sure you do. Besides, we're not going back to shore until after lunch. If we aren't successful here, we'll move to another spot."

"You mean, I'm a prisoner like on a slave ship?"

"No. I mean we are on the lake to catch fish for dinner. Fish to feed our families. A noble reason for a noble effort. Now, go at it again."

"Aye aye, Captain Bligh. But, before I do anything more, I need to get rid of my hoodie and take a hit on this doobie."

The Lillie he did not care for had come back with a vengeance.

From a side pocket, Lillie extracted a hand-rolled smoke and a lighter. She held flame to joint and inhaled deeply. The violent coughing began.

"Take a hit."

"No thanks."

"Scared?"

"No. I just don't want to."

"Go ahead. It won't bite or turn you into a junkie. It's just marijuana. Take it, you'll like it."

"I said no thanks and I meant it."

"Suit yourself, wuss."

She took a second hit and coughed some, pinched off the ember, and put the rest of the unsmoked joint in her shirt pocket.

"I'm saving this for later ... when I catch my first fish. It will be a celebration toke."

As she inserted the joint the second button of her shirt came undone. She was not wearing a bra, and her nipples were visible and erect. She knew Micah saw her arousal. Every time she smoked, she got in the mood for male contact. Micah and Lillie returned to the task at hand, getting dinner.

"What should I call you?"

"Amon would be nice."

"OK. Amon, it is then."

"I'll call you Aggie."

"That's my name."

"How old are you?"

"Twelve."

"Twelve!"

"I'll be thirteen in December."

"This truck is older than you. You look older and act more mature than twelve, and you're better looking than this bucket of bolts. Heh, heh, heh."

"Where are we going?"

"To the place where we can set up the fireworks. I cleared an area about halfway to the other side of the lake. I have the fireworks in the back of the truck. We need to complete the platform. Then we can set the items ready for this evening. I'll show you how the professionals do it. There are no roads to this spot. We must drive slowly on this wide path to get to the firing area, it will take us about twenty minutes to get there. Make sure your seat belt is hooked; it's going to be a bumpy ride. And don't put your arm out the window; the branches will be so close they'll scrape the truck. That's no big deal for the truck but I wouldn't want them to hurt you."

The truck bucked and bounced over the rutted path, barely wide enough for the vehicle. Periodically, Amon would glance at Aggie. He watched her upper body seemingly undulate with every dip in the path.

What he saw bouncing pleased him. Tiny mounds beneath a T-shirt and an open sweatshirt. They rode in silence for a short time. Then a clearing appeared as if it is the end of a cul-de-sac.

"This place is really hidden."

"It's my secret place. No one knows it's here. I must launch the fireworks from this place. Can't use the public area, too many people. Can't use the family lots, too many trees. This place is ideal. It's wide open, yet secure. Stay in the truck while I turn it around so it is headed back."

He turned the truck, and they exited. Aggie walked toward the lake, while Amon walked to the back of the truck and removed the tarp.

"Here, Aggie, you'll need to wear these gloves. We will be unloading some planks, and I wouldn't want you to get a splinter. Now, I'll slide the first plank off the rear. Grab the end so it doesn't hit the ground. Then you and I will carry it over to the platform frame I built the other day. Heh, heh, heh. Ready?"

"Ready."

As a team, they unloaded eight ten-foot and several twelve-foot planks and placed them on the frame of the platform. Aggie handled her own end well. They moved to the board closest to the front of the platform.

"First phase complete. Now we must be sure that the platform is level before we nail the planks. Take this level and place it on the middle of the first plank. Do you see the small bubble between the lines of the middle chamber?"

"Yes."

"Is it in the middle of the circle?"

"No. It's to the right of the middle?"

"OK. Then we have to raise the far end until the bubble is in the middle. I brought some shims for this part."

Amon slides the narrowest part of the shim beneath the plank.

"How about now?"

"Not quite in the middle."

"How about now?"

"Gottit."

"OK. Now we nail the plank at the end I just lifted. Have you ever hammered nails before?"

"No. Sorry."

"Don't be sorry. It's really easy. I'll show you. Are you right-handed or left-handed?"

"Right."

"OK. Take the hammer in your right hand. Hold it about halfway from the end of the handle. That will give you more control. Now take one of these nails, hold it tight, and press the point into the middle of the edge. Good. Now hit the head of the nail once to drive it into the frame. Not a baby tap, but a real young woman hit."

Aggie does as she is instructed, but the peen is off target and the nail bounces from the plank to the ground.

"OK. That can happen to anyone. Let me guide you. I'll just get behind you. Heh, heh, heh."

Amon slid onto the plank and settled in behind Aggie. His arms were on her arms as he held her hands. His head rested on her shoulder. She could feel his breathing.

"I'll hold the nail while you strike it. Careful not to hit my hand. Heh, heh, heh. Now strike hard."

Aggie swung the hammer to the head of the nail in a two-foot arc. Perfect hit. The nail sank partially into the plank. During her effort, she became aware that Amon was leaning on her, conforming his body to hers. He seemed to be breathing in her scent. Sniffing like a dog. Aggies was concerned by this, tensed her body, and slid away slightly.

"Good job. Now it's all yours. Hold the nail lightly and hit it until you drive it completely into the frame."

"Good job. Now we have to use the level again. We have to be sure it is not tilting. Waddaya see?"

"I see the bubble a little in front of the two lines in the middle."

"OK. We must lift the plank a little in the front. How is it now?"

"Dead center."

"Go ahead and put a nail at the other end of the plank."

Aggie learned proper hammering quickly and did a good job.

"Now we have to double-check our work to be sure the lead plank is level and straight. Go ahead and check with the level."

"Perfect."

"OK. Let's align the second plank using the level and shims as needed."

Over the next two hours, they repeated the process to gradually complete the platform. The sun had made the still air in the clearing quite warm.

"A level platform is critical to safety and proper trajectory of the fireworks high over the center of lake. You did a great job, Aggie."

"Thanks."

"OK. That's the first phase. The next phase will be to affix the smaller firing platforms to the base platform. It's more complicated than what we just did. So, let's take a lunch break and refresh. I have sandwiches and water in the cooler in the back of the truck. OK?"

"Great job, Michaël. You got us lost twice. It's a good thing Martha had GPS on her phone. Else, we would be wandering around the bowels of both counties."

"Yes, it's a good thing, because you couldn't activate the GPS on the rental. What a flop."

"Boys, settle down. The important thing is that we're here safe and sound."

"Right, Martha. Now who has the key code so we can get into the house without alerting the police."

"I do, Shelia."

The four exited the rental and approached the back door. Martha inserted the key and opened the door. Three enter. Martha stepped quickly to the keypad and entered *1-2-1-7-1-2 OFF*. Michael stayed a few steps behind them ... outside. He spotted his first prize as the car was being parked behind the house. So, he placed a sticker on the water trough. It would be perfect for their new home in the 'burbs once the baby arrives. Maybe in the back yard or on the back deck of their new home. A great reminder of his lineage.

"Come on, slow poke. I don't want to stay here any longer than we must."

"Is Gabby getting crabby?"

"No, I just find the entire event, and Dad's rationale behind it, unnerving. Let's go."

"Martha, is it just me or does this seem weird, like we are picking over the bones of an animal carcass."

"Yes, it feels a little strange, Shelia. It's like we broke the seal on the king's mausoleum and are about to steal the realm's treasure. But it's what Joe wants. So, we have parental permission. How do you want to do this so the results are equitable?"

"I suggest we all enter a room at the same time, survey its contents, and announce where we would like to place stickers. We'll alternate who announces first in each room."

"That makes sense. Let's start in the kitchen. We'll go first. Gabe, I don't want any of the big appliances. How about you?"

"One more thing; this is a team effort. So, there is no I. Gottit?"

"Gottit."

"That was easy."

"To answer your question, we do not want any of the major appliances."

"And we are not interested in the flatware, glasses, and everyday china. But we would like the big cutting board. You know the one that Dad made himself."

"Go for it, Gabe."

"Honey, we could use the carving and serving utensils."

"Good idea, Michael. Ours have another two years or so of life at best. Your Dad's set is much sturdier. We'll need to claim the whetstone to keep the knives sharp."

"OK. We're doing this in an amicable manner; alternating items keeps it fair and civil."

The four poured over the kitchen on this step of the treasure hunt. Inspection completed and stickers affixed, they entered the dining room. The women had assumed control of the process. As homemakers, they knew what would "work" in their homes and what was just an out-of-place memory.

"We have no need for the dining table or the eight chairs. How about you, Michael?"

"I don't know. Shelia?"

"Maybe, let's come back to that. We could use the hutch."

"OK. Sticker it, Shelia."

"What about the contents: the fine china and silverware, Martha?"

"Upon examination, I find that none of it is even close to the patterns I bought about two years ago. In fact, they seem to clash."

"OK. We'll sticker them, too."

"I would like the sideboard."

"Yours, Martha."

"And the serving dishes inside, too."

"Good."

"How about the rug?"

"I never liked Orientals. They seem confusing, with strange patterns and colors, and overused by people with little taste."

"OK. We'll find a good place for it in our new home."

"That's right. I had forgotten. You guys will be buying more expansive and more expensive quarters with your inheritance. You'll need to accommodate your expanded family. These old items would be welcome in your new home."

"Martha, how thoughtful."

A sarcastic chill filled the space between the two women. Shelia still harbored ill will about the lie Martha told when she came for marital advice.

"Done here?"

"Yes."

"Yes."

"To the library."

"Do you guys want this Oriental, too?"

"Yes."

"I would like Joe's three small side tables."

"Great. I'd like the reading lamp."

"Do you want Joe's reading chair?"

"No, Shelia. It would have to be re-built and re-covered. Look at the food and grease stains. Too much time and money. We'd be better off buying a new one … if we want a reading chair. No one reads in my family. But I would like the four granny chairs against the wall."

"Done. Are you running low on stickers?"

"Nope. We have as many left as we need."

The men stared at each other. The chill had spread to the entire room and was becoming frost. It engulfed the foursome and made the males uncomfortable. But they said nothing. Hoping the cold air was momentary and would dissipate. Gabe was the first male voice.

"Done here?"

"Yes."

"Yes."

To the living room.

"I suppose you'll want the big Oriental rug just like the others for your new house."

The tone of her voice was unmistakably acerbic.

"Martha, for crissake, will you give it a break. We'll be in our new house years before Joe dies. We'll have created our own comfort zones by then. And I doubt we will want to do massive renovations when this stuff becomes available. We'll have to fit it in or give it to Micah for his home. It's obvious to me that you are extremely jealous of our choices. If you want what we have selected, say so, and we'll work something out to satisfy all of us. If I'm wrong, say so. One way or the other, stop being bitchy."

Martha was stunned into silence. A blank stare manifested itself as if she was just hit with a pillow case filled with books.

"Now, ladies. Let's be civil. We're doing what Joe wanted. And we shouldn't come to blows over it."

"Wait a minute, Gabe. Shelia is right. Martha has become almost resentful about the choices Shelia and I have made. It's as if she thinks we're stealing something that belongs to her. If that's how she feels, she should say so. If not, she should stop the post-selection barbs."

"What I resent is, that as the elder son, I believe Gabe should have first choice on everything. Shelia and you should get second choice, because Michael is the younger child."

"Martha, that's bullshit! When it comes to Gabe and me, you have little say. Gabe is not the crown prince. We are both Joe's sons. As such, we are equals when it comes to our father's possessions. We agreed that we would look at the items one room at a time. Remember we agreed that we were doing this in an amicable manner; alternating items to keep it civil. But, now you're uncomfortable with that agreement. Damn it, you're acting mean. You're putting into play a twisted emotion ... jealousy, and that is waaaay out of bounds."

The silence was deafening.

Chapter Twenty-three

The rain ... wind-driven sheets. Flashes of lightning and long splitting cracks of thunder seemed to intensify the downpour. This was the last of the rains that the farmers needed to ensure successful growing and harvesting seasons. It's a humdinger. The windshield wipers on the six-year-old station wagon were flapping at full speed to keep a clear portal to the road. The bus, as the boys call it, bounced over the dirt road. The road was alternately illuminated by the lightning then hidden by the gray torrents of rain and darkness of the clouds. The steering was difficult as the driver had to swerve to avoid hitting large, deep holes. Holes that could cause serious damage to the struts, undercarriage, and axles. The winding and twisting road was difficult enough to traverse in dry sunny days. Today, the trip was potentially hazardous.

In many stretches of the dirt road, Joe could not exceed six miles per hour. Thus, the trip will take much longer than usual. The boys were becoming fidgety. They wanted to know how soon before they'll see the cottage. Their mother's gentle, soothing response to the repeated question was always the same, "soon, soon." The big black dog between the boys tried to relax but had to continuously shift its body to avoid being sat on by one of the bouncing boys or falling off the bench seat. Joe felt that even Sarah's patience was wearing thin. The bumps, the questions, and the storm were intrusive distractions to her life. Mary's beatific smile was a constant. Woman and dog had a special bond.

To stay dry, the windows were closed. So, the air conditioning system had to remain on for the entire trip: from highway, to paved road, to dirt trail. The family must wear long-sleeved shirts to stay warm in the car. Last year they kept the windows open to enjoy the air of the outside. The AC and the extra weight in the old car, caused by the people and items they needed for the stay, put an undue strain on the old engine. It was running a little warmer than normal. Joe was only slightly concerned. His greater concern was the trail that has become partially washed out. He couldn't see the deep ruts until he was upon or in them. Each time he came to a fork in the road he had to recall the proper sequence of turns to get to the cottage … left, left, right, left, right, right. There were no signs. That was intentional to keep out strangers. It was a good idea at the time, but today it was a potential problem. Tension was building in his neck and shoulders. Mary put her hand delicately on his arm and whispers, "soon, soon."

Then the bang. The noise he had dreaded since he started on the dirt road. Was it a wheel or an axle? Regardless, Joe must get out of the station wagon and survey the damage. A task he didn't relish. He put the car in park, depressed the emergency brake, and exited the vehicle. The passengers were silent. No whimpering, no complaining. No questions as to source or meaning of the loud noise. When he emerged from the car, he was suddenly immersed in the warmth of haze-filtered sunshine. The air, hot and humid. The storm had miraculously disappeared. At least over the car. Suddenly, gnats…big clouds of black gnats engulfed him and the car. He's assailed. They covered his hands, arms, and face. They were in his nose and ears. They seemed to be attacking his eyes, and two somehow got into his mouth. Their biting painful … like a hundred tiny pin pricks and became almost too much for him to deal with. He wanted to scream and jump back in the car. Not possible; he had no choice but to determine the cause of the noise beneath the car and any damage that may have resulted. He knelt in the mud. There it was. A rock. He must have driven over it causing it to bounce up against the station wagon's undercarriage. He spied a dent, but no break in the metal. The gnats continued their harassment. They had now begun to crawl beneath his shirt collar and down his back. The skin on his hands was totally covered with black insects. He jumped up and re-entered the car. Examining his hands and arms he sees no gnats. Mary smiled and whispered, "soon, soon." He looked in the rearview mirror and saw only the dog. He quickly turned around to see the boys, but they were gone. He turned to say something to Mary, but she was gone. Then back to the dog. Gone.

Joe sat up abruptly. He was sweating. His hands were trembling. He looked at his arms. There were no telltale red bite marks. No gnats. Joe could not rise from the chair. He sat frozen in confusion. What was that all about? The trip. Mary. The boys. The rock incident and those damned gnats. He struggled to pull himself up and head into the cottage for a drink of water. His gait was halting, and he shuffled his feet. Walking was not easy. He tugged on the screen door. Was it stuck or was he weak? He realized his left arm was tingling as if it were asleep. Did he sit on it as he napped? His left shoulder was pulsating, and he felt a sharp pain in his mid-back on the left side. His knees softened, so he sat on a chair just inside the porch doorway. Breathing was labored and sweating profuse. He understood the cause of these manifestations and told himself to relax until the coronary event passed.

Thirty minutes later, he felt better. Not fine, but better. The pain and sweating had stopped. Joe headed for the kitchen for a glass of cool, sweet spring water and some of his sprinkles. He wanted to lie down but would not because he feared a continuation of his dream or a new, more disturbing one. He stood by the sink and took his medicine. Twenty minutes later, his mind was clear and his body was slowly returning to Joe's normal. Now to his tasks. First, he must eat to help the efficacy of the medications … at least that's what the doctor ordered. What was in the fridge? A hard roll and some ham … a sandwich. The hamburger and sides could come out around five. Joe was confident the alternative meal would be ready for a six-thirty cook out. If the teens caught enough fish for dinner, the hamburger would stay in the fridge for the next day.

KP completed, food in his stomach and the meds working, Joe felt much better. What to do now? Make some coffee to ward off sleep, find a good book, and go back outside in the sun. Maybe a book by that new author his doctor recommended. A good crime novel. He smiled at the apparent contradiction in terms. Joe picked up the book about the FBI analyst … conflicted and nearly crushed by diverse evil circumstances thrust upon him. Mug of coffee in one hand and book under his arm, he walked slowly outside and sat back in his chair to await the arrival of his brood's various members.

"How long must I do this very booooring thing you call fishing?"

"As long as it takes for us to catch enough for dinner. I guess that would be four legal-size trout."

"How big is legal-size?"

"No less than eight inches from nose to base of tail fin. Hopefully, over twelve. The bigger, the better. These are lake trout so they will most likely be bigger."

"We've been here for soooo long. We…"

"We've been here for less than two hours. By the way, watch out for the red tailed hawks."

"Red tailed hawks? Why? What do they do?"

"They nest in the woods surrounding the lake … their territory. They love lake trout. And when they see a fisherman begin to pull in a fish, they dive and try to rip the fish from the line. They see us as intruders in their territory. Intruders who are taking their food from them. They will fight hard to protect their food supply. But I think we're safe. The time of day is in our favor. The hawks normally feed in late afternoon."

"What should I do if one of them attacks?"

"When you get a strike, tug to set the hook, then slowly bring the fish to the boat keeping the fish below the surface of the water. Don't rush the process or you'll pull the fish to the surface, and the hawk will see it and try to get it. Just slow and steady. If the hawk doesn't see the fish, he won't dive at it. Does this make sense?"

"I guess. You'll have to help me if I hook a fish."

"OK."

Micah was proud. He was teaching someone to fish like his grandfather taught him. He smiled as he realized she would probably never use this knowledge. Certainly, not in the suburbs of Chicago. The sun was warming the air above the cool lake. The reflection was harsh as it hit his eyes. Time for the sunglasses.

"I got one! I got one! Now what?"

"A firm tug. Not abrupt or hard. Then slowly reel in your catch. Be sure to keep the fish below the surface."

"Come here and do it for me."

"No. It's your catch not mine."

Gradually, Lillie's line was reeled in. She brought the fish boat side. Micah had the net. He scooped the water and brought the fish on board. It fell flopping on the bottom of the boat.

"OK. Now what do we do?"

"We measure the fish to be sure it's legal. Hand me the rule in the tackle box."

"Rule? Do you mean ruler?"

"Ruler is a king. Rule is device for measuring. Congratulations! You landed a fourteen-inch lake trout."

"Take my picture with my trophy. Here's my phone. Do you know how to use it?"

Micah thought ... ever the arrogant one.

"You'll have to hold it near your face for the picture. Grab the line and lift."

He took two snaps and returned the phone

"Now, remove the fish from the line and put it in the bucket."

"You mean I have to touch it."

"Yes, touch it unless you can remove the hook telepathically."

"Smart-ass. It's yucky. Slimy and smelly. I don't want to touch it. You do it for me."

"No."

"Please."

"No. Just do it ... quickly."

"Please."

"No. Damn it! It's your fish. Just grab it and put it in the bucket. Now!"

"Well, aren't you bossy."

Lillie squeezed her face, took hold of the trout, and extracted the hook. Plop! She dropped it in the bucket.

"Good job. I'm proud of you."

"I'm proud of me, too. Now I want to send the pictures to my buds back home. They won't believe that I did this all by myself."

"Don't take too long, we have more to catch."

Micah returned to casting. He saw Lillie relight the joint and take two deep inhales with the usual small coughs. He thought this was no way to fish. But he won't judge. After a few minutes, his bait took a hit. He tugged and slowly retrieved his catch. At boat side, he scooped the fish. On board, he measured it: sixteen inches and placed it in the bucket. A grin crossed his lips; his is bigger than hers. Minutes later, Lillie hooked another. This one was barely legal, and they agreed to return it to the lake. Back to the persistence and patience part of the day.

"Wanna take a break for lunch?"

"What did you bring?"

"Peanut butter and jelly sandwiches and water."

"No beer?"

"No beer."

"Water will have to do."

They sat mid-boat and opened the cooler. They devoured the Spartan meal and relaxed.

"May I ask a personal question?"

"OK with me, Lillie, if I am not obligated to answer something extremely embarrassing."

"Do you think I'm good-looking?"

"Sure. Why?"

"Well, you seem to look away from me. You avoid eye contact. Why do you do that?"

"I didn't realize I was avoiding eye contact. Maybe all the other boys in your life stare at you, and you're used to that. That's not my style."

"Why would you say that?"

"Let me be honest. Lillie, you are an attractive girl, but you flaunt your looks and your sexuality. It may please the boys in your crowd, but it makes me uncomfortable. You seem to throw yourself at me. Like at the old farmhouse. Then you run away as if nothing matters."

"Wait a minute. You didn't object to what we did at the farmhouse. Why complain about it now?"

"I'm not complaining. I'm only saying…"

"Then you liked it."

"Well, sure I liked it."

"Then you would do it again."

"Yes, but not here and not with you."

He lied.

"Why not?"

"It's not right."

"We're not going to have babies. I am on the pill. We're just going to fuck for fun."

"The whole situation makes me uncomfortable."

"If I were that girl you say you have or do not have in Philadelphia, would you be uncomfortable then?"

"That's different."

"How? You're just afraid, because I took the initiative. I have needs that I like addressed. I have the power to make that happen. I can do it myself or with a man. I prefer a man."

He watched in uneasiness as Lillie opened her blouse to expose her breasts. Micah tried not to look and stare, but he could not help himself.

"Wait! Stop right there."

"Would you like to touch these?"

"No."

He lied again.

"Would you like it if I unzipped your pants and put your willie, or should I call it Little Mikey, in my mouth."

"No."

He lied again.

"Stop this nonsense. You are trying to trick me, and I don't like it."

"You don't like that I can take the initiative. You didn't seem to object at the farmhouse. You're like all men. Whether you are fifteen or fifty, you men think you have the power over women when it comes to sex. A man must be the initiator. But you get scared and run away when the woman assumes the initiative. You males are nothing but candy-ass cowards who won't treat women as sexual equals. Why must you dominate?"

"Enough! We'd better get back to fishing."

"Run away, coward. Hide yourself in work or fishing, like now. Don't give in to your desires. All you men are alike. If you can't be in control, you don't want to do anything including fuck."

"That's enough of your crap, Lillie. I want to fish."

Another lie.

"OK. We'll fish. But I bet you I catch a bigger fish than you do. I'll even put money on it. Twenty dollars."

"That's a bet."

Lillie rebuttoned her blouse and they returned to their respective places in the boat. Within two hours, they had caught two more legal-size lake trout. The smallest was fourteen inches and the largest was eighteen. That was Lillie's.

"We certainly have enough for dinner. It's time to head back."

"Last chance to get laid, Micah."

"Shut up!"

"Is that still a touchy subject? You are such a pussy. Meow. Meow. By the way, you owe me twenty dollars."

"I know."

"Or you can work off your debt the way I want."

"That's enough. We still have work to do when we get home. We have to clean the fish."

"I think they are clean after swimming in the lake."

"By clean, I mean gut them and remove the heads."

"Oh, yuck."

"It's part of the joy of catching your own food. Making it ready for cooking and eating."

"What can I do to get out of that gross chore?"

"Nothing."

"I'll let you keep your twenty."

"No. You must learn to clean the fish you caught."

Lillie was nearly crushed. Her seductive guile and harsh teasing had failed her. This would have never happen with the boys back home.

"OK, Aggie, we have ham and cheese on rye bread sandwiches. I thought you would like them, but I didn't put anything on them, 'cause I didn't know if you liked mayo or mustard or both."

"I like a little of both."

"I'll put the cooler on the deck we just built. You can apply the proper amount of whatever you want. There are a couple of plastic knives in the cooler. While we eat, we can look out on the lake like at a fancy restaurant. I think I see someone in a boat. No there are two people. They must be fishing."

"I see them, too. That must be Lillie and Micah. They were going to catch dinner for the entire family. I hope Grandpa Joe has a Plan B for dinner. Lillie has never been fishing. I doubt she'll catch anything."

"At least we'll be ready for tonight with some great fireworks. The next part of getting ready is more complex, so we must be very precise."

"What is it?"

"We have to make sure the individual platforms for the tubes are aimed properly and at the correct angle. We can't be shooting fireballs over the woods or into the lake. They must arc over the water. Some higher than others. Once we get the small platforms in place, we must lock down the firing tubes so that the first explosions don't activate what is in the second, third, and fourth tubes. If they move, we could have a flop of a show at the least, or a fire in the woods at the worst. So, we must be precise and diligent. After the lockdown, we wire the tubes for ignition and run the wires away from the platform, back about twenty yards down the road to a firing box. I'll place it on the side of the road later."

"You really know what you're doing, Amon."

"Thanks."

Lunch was in silence as both stared onto the lake. Occasionally, Aggie caught a glimpse of Amon looking at her. She smiled demurely. She was becoming uncomfortable.

"You're such a pretty girl. I bet you have a ton of boyfriends."

"No. None. I have some friends who are boys, but no boyfriends."

"Well it's their loss. Heh, heh, heh."

"Mom, told me there would be lots of time for boys when I am older."

"You mean in your twenties."

Aggie giggles.

"No. When I'm in high school."

"I'll bet Lillie has a boyfriend. Heh, heh, heh."

"Mom says too many. I think that's why she wants me to wait. She doesn't want me to be like Lillie."

"Maybe she's right to keep you safe from the evil intentions of young men. You know they can be pushy when it comes to affection and the like. As men get older, they mature and become less aggressive. They're kind and gentle. Not like teens."

"I guess you and Mom are right."

Aggie sighed and looked pensive. It was as if she didn't believe what she just said. She was sure she was missing something that Lillie enjoyed. Amon saw the look. Saw the woman who wanted to come out of the little girl.

"Well, it's time to get back to work. If you put the lunch stuff back in the cooler, I'll get the small platforms and other materials from the truck."

"It's a deal."

Small chores over, the pair worked toward finishing the entire apparatus.

"OK. The next step is to place these eight smaller platforms on the large one we built. They must be angled properly to discharge over the lake. The front four must be at 60 degrees, and the back four at 75 degrees. I have a protractor to measure the angles. When they are at the proper angles, I'll brace the back of each firing platform with two small wooden tees. Ready?"

"Ready."

"OK. I'll lift the first firing platform. You hold the protractor at the lever point and tell me the angle."

"Fifty-five."

"Not enough. Now what does it read."

"Between sixty and sixty-five."

"Good. Now you take my spot and hold the platform as steady as you can, while I nail it to the floor. Hold it tight."

As Aggie assumed the holding duties, Amon brushed his hand across the back of hers. He smiled as he looked at the protractor.

"Raise it just a bit. Good. Now hold it steady while I secure it."

Nailing lowered the platform slightly.

"I want to put a shim underneath the front to raise it about five degrees. There we go. Perfect. Another nail to hold it tight."

The two wooden tees are placed at the back to maintain the angle. One firing platform completed. On to number two.

"I want you to lift while I nail, shim and secure. Are you OK with that?"

The first four firing platforms were ready for the tubes. Within an hour, the second set of platforms was ready. All were at the proper alignment and secured.

"Now the tubes. Each one must be secured to a firing platform. After we do that, we must double-check the angle to be sure it has not been altered greatly. A few degrees will not be an issue. Five or more must be corrected. Help me get the tubes from the back of the truck."

When they unloaded the firing tubes, Amon accidentally touched Aggies' hands and arms several times. He did not apologize. He just looked at her and grinned. His look made her uncomfortable.

"These four tubes belong on the first firing platform. Let's start there. We will place the open ends of the tubes over the four circles marked with a cross. We must be sure the bottom of each tube covers the corresponding circle entirely. That way we will know the tube will shoot its contents over the lake in the proper sequence."

"Proper sequence?"

"Yes, each tube has a different display, and they're all visually complementary. The contents of tube one are complementary to the contents of tube two, which leads to tube three and four on firing platform number one. The sequential process is repeated for each platform."

"How long does all this take?"

"Well, each tube shoots it contents which explode in the air in about thirty seconds. There is a sixty-second interval between tubes firing. That's about five minutes for each small platform. There are eight platforms. So, the entire display will take about 40 to 45 minutes. A nice long total display."

"Which one is Devil's Breath?"

"That's a secret."

"You can tell me. I won't tell the others. It will be our secret."

"Well, since you are such a hard worker, and been so kind to me, I'll tell you. Heh, heh, heh. Devil's Breath is not here on the platform. It is loaded on the back of the truck underneath the tarp. Wanna see it?"

"You bet."

As they walked to the back of the truck, Amon gently took hold of Aggie's hand. She didn't pull it away. He grinned. The tarp was removed to reveal a firing platform with four tubes.

"What's so special about that?"

"The fireworks are timed to fire all at once and illuminate the sky from the bottom of the display to the top in thirty seconds. This gives the illusion of flames leaping up into the sky. The colors are orange, yellow, and red. Just like flames. Most fireworks look like they are falling from the sky. This is different. It looks like it is rising. This is the last shot of the evening. It will be spectacular. Heh, heh, heh."

"Cool."

"But we're not done yet. We have to attach the wires to the firing tubes and then run the wire to this box. Then, I'll place it beside the road about twenty yards from the big platform. This last step makes the set-up safe. Ready?"

"Ready. One last question. Isn't the wiring step dangerous?"

"No. Not until it's connected to the battery in the firing box. There's no danger while we get everything ready. When I come back here tonight, I will drop a big battery into the box and hook up the wires. Then there might be some danger, but I have been trained and certified to do this. Now let's get the final step completed so I can get you home to your folks in time for dinner."

To attach the wires in such close quarters meant that their hands occasionally touched. With each touch, Amon smiled or chuckled … heh, heh, heh. Aggie became increasingly nervous. He was beginning to scare her. And, his breath was foul, as if he had eaten rotten meat. She held herself firm so as to not fidget. She worked fast so she could get back to her family.

"If we're done here, let's go upstairs."

"I doubt there's anything up there we want."

"Nothing ventured, nothing gained, Martha."

But what Shelia was really thinking was … *then why don't you stay down here.*

The four slowly walked up the stairs to the second floor past the family gallery from youngest to oldest, from oldest to most recent. Boys with bad haircuts and plastic smiles posed for strangers behind cameras. One boy. Two boys, short-sleeved shirts, and short pants. Three boys. Four. Two in long pants, two in shorts. Four boys with parents behind them, after the admonishment to "be still." Then the real-life pictures. Boys at play. Family on a picnic. Family at the cottage. Joe and Mary at their anniversary party. Joe and Mary working the garden. Mary and Sarah. Michael stared at a picture of Sarah alone. His Dad often referred to her as his only daughter. It was almost as if she is staring back at Michael.

"Wait a second, I want to put a sticker on a few pictures. One of Mom and Dad in the garden. The one of all four boys. And the one of Sarah."

"Well, you got all the good ones, little brother."

"Which of those do you want?"

There was a long ugly silence and all eyes turn to Gabriel.

"Nah, I'm just messin' with you. They're just pictures. I got memories. Let's move on."

"There is nothing in the master bedroom that we want. Right, Gabe?"

"Right."

"Well, I'd like the chest of drawers for Micah. And the small bedside tables."

"Fine. Sticker them and let's move on. I'm getting stressed."

"Martha, if this is stressing you out, you can always go downstairs or to the car until we are done."

"That's just like you, Shelia. Trying to push me out of your way so you can grab all the good stuff."

"Not pushing. Just suggesting that if this is too much for you, you may want to step aside."

"No. I can handle it."

The brothers stared at each other as if to say, 'WTF is going on?'

"Ladies, please be civil. Just a few more rooms to go."

"Gabe, how about the garage?"

"I almost forgot. The garage. We'll go there after we check out mom's upstairs sewing room."

"We'd like the desk."

"I thought we agreed that Gabe and I would choose first?"

"We agreed to alternate selections. You agreed with yourself, Martha, to go first in every room. Michael and I did not agree to that. You went first in the last room."

"Well, I never…"

"Live with it, sweetie, we'll take the desk. Now it's your turn."

The underlying vitriol between the two women was bubbling to the surface. It made their husbands increasingly uncomfortable.

"There's nothing in this hovel that I want."

"Good for you, Martha, you just insulted your father-in-law. A man who has accepted you into his family. Biting the hand that loves you is such a good way to live."

"Shelia, can we step out in the hall and have a word in private?"

"Sure, Michael."

"Honey, you gotta lighten up and stop sticking it to Martha every chance you get. You know she can't handle this and she is becoming more and more irrational."

"What I know is that she is a manipulative bitch. Someone who lied about me. Someone who wants everything because she thinks she is entitled to everything. Someone who thinks she is married to the crown prince. Someone who thinks you are the lesser son; and I, therefore, am the lesser daughter-in-law and a lesser woman. I say fuck her. She wants to rule; she'd better be able to defend. Whew!"

"I don't blame you. In fact, I agree with everything you said, but Gabe is my brother and I don't want to lose his love."

"Then don't choose him over me."

"Let me finish. I will never choose him over you. You are my true and only love … my wife. That's a relationship that is over and above everything and everyone."

"OK."

"I ask you, for the remainder of the time we spend in proximity to this bitch, please be the mature woman and don't let her get under your skin. Is that a fair request?"

"Yes. It will be difficult not to verbally slam her because it's soooo easy. But I'll be the adult for a few more hours."

"Good. May I kiss the victor?"

Their embrace was long and loving. Except for the bump, the embrace was almost passionate.

"Gabe. Martha. Let's move on. We want to get back to the cottage by late afternoon. Who knows what dinner prep there will be."

"Mike, after we go into the den, we'll head into the back forty as Dad used to call it?"

"I dunno. Look. The door is boarded up. I seriously doubt there is anything of personal value behind the door."

"I wanna look."

"OK, Martha. Gabe, how do we remove the boards without destroying them?"

"No idea. We'd need tools to pry them away. Then we might break them and Dad would be pissed. I say we forget about it."

"Fine. Once again, no one pays attention to my wishes."

"Dear, we heard you but the risk of damage far outweighs the rewards behind the doorway. It was a bedroom for the boys. Two bunk beds, a bathroom, and several closets."

"Now, my own husband is against me. Great!"

"I guess we are done on the second floor. Shall we move to the basement?"

"You're in a hurry to pick at Joe's bones, Shelia."

Shelia smiled sardonically and batted her eyelashes.

"No, sweetie, I'm in a hurry to get back to the cottage. Oh, how I look forward to spending two hours in the car with you."

Martha was finally crushed. She had no retort. Her shoulders slumped and tears welled in her eyes.

The four went down the two flights of stairs and stood in the middle of the cold and dirty basement. Neither couple wanted anything except to leave the toxic air that had been created by animosity. After turning on the alarm and locking the back door, they headed to the garage. Lawn and garden tools and machines. Nothing there.

"OK, that ordeal is over."

"Good choice of words, baby brother."

"Wait a minute. Look at the pump and trough. Michael put a sticker on them when we were not looking."

"As a matter of fact, Martha, I put the sticker on them as you guys were entering the house. Would you like the pump and trough?"

"We do not want them, brother."

"Gabe, don't I get a say in this?"

"No. We are being hysterical over historical objects. Besides, where would we put the trough? Nowhere, that's where. We are done. Let's head back to the cottage."

Shelia said nothing, but she had a big internal smile. She squeezed Michael's hand.

"Gabe, on the way back, I'd like to stop at the Stolzfuss market and pick up two Shoofly pies and their homemade vanilla ice cream for dessert tonight. Mom always liked their pies and said she could never quite duplicate them."

The four made the return trip in silence. Icy silence.

Chapter Twenty-four

"Grandpa! Grandpa! Look what I caught. Look at the size of these fish."

Lillie proudly pointed to the bounty in the bucket Micah was holding.

"Good for you. I'm proud of you, Lillie. You learned to fish, and by the looks of it, you were successful at it. You must be a good student."

"I had a great teacher."

She smiled coyly at Micah.

The boy was confused; was she flirting, being respectful, or just putting on an act?

"Good for you, Micah. You passed along a family tradition. Now who's going to clean the harvest?"

Lillie's enthusiasm visibly waned. She glanced at Micah with "please" in her eyes.

"That's the next step in the learning."

Lillie's countenance turned to a pout.

"Can we clean them inside?"

"No, sweetheart, not in the house. That step is done outside the house. You'll need another bucket of water … clean water, two sharp knives, a small garbage bag, and wax paper. Micah, why don't you go to the kitchen, sharpen knives, get the wax paper, and small garbage bag while Lillie fills another bucket. Then you two can go back to the boathouse to clean."

"OK. Where should we dump the guts?"

"Seal them in the plastic bag and place the bag in the big barrel at the mouth of the driveway. Tomorrow is trash day. Make sure the latches on the sides of the barrel are locked. We don't want the forest critters throwing our trash all over the road."

"Yes, sir."

The teens headed to the boathouse. Micah proudly carrying their bounty.

"Lillie, are you ready to assert your female strength and independence?"

"Do I really have to do it? Can't you do it and show me?"

"Sorry, your fishing lesson would not be complete, if you didn't embrace this phase. And I would be a failure as a teacher. Lay some newspaper on the floor. Now, here is what you have to do. Please pay attention."

Micah lays a fish on its side and started the demonstration.

"Grab the fish near the dorsal fin, hold it firmly, and place it on its side on the newspaper. Do not squeeze the fish, because there must be room for the knife to glide easily within the fish without damaging the flesh. Now, insert the knifepoint into the vent and gradually with a slight upward thrust run the blade up the belly toward the head. If the blade meets resistance, you can use a sawing motion. The guts will begin to appear at the incision. See?"

Lillie saw and instantly looked away.

"Damn, that's gross. I'm about to throw up. How can you do that?"

"It's easy if you don't think of the fish as a living creature, because it is no longer living. The fish is just an object permanently altered by man … that's you and me. And by altered, I mean caught, cleaned, and soon to be eaten. You don't need to touch the guts until you're done cutting. Once you're done cutting, splay the sides of the fish to expose the entire cavity. Then, reach inside the fish and grab the guts at the head. Then pull firmly, yet gradually from the gills to where you entered the knife. You will pull the entire inside out of the fish. Once you reach the entry, your hand should be filled with guts. Then you tug firmly to tear the insides out. After that, you cut off the fish's head. With that, you are done."

"Now, I *am* going to throw up."

"Breathe deeply. Take several full breaths. Once you do that, you'll be able to continue cleaning your first fish. Three more steps. Take the knife and cut off the head. Then take the body to the fresh water bucket and wash it, rubbing the insides with your fingers to be sure all the insides are out. Put them and the head in the small trash bag. Last, lay your prize on the wax paper, fold it over and crimp the open sides to keep it fresh. When we're done with all the fish, we'll put the bag in the garbage can."

"Won't you please do it for me? I can't do it. It's going to make me sick."

"No! Damn it! Stop your whining! You're going to do this yourself. Be independent. If you want the power of independence, you must take it for yourself. Show yourself that by doing the things that men do, you are their equal. In this situation, you are not the victim, you are the victor. You have the power."

"That's more bullshit philosophy. I never said I wanted the power that men have in all things … particularly when it comes to gross tasks like gutting fish. I said that men are scaredy-cats if a woman assumes the power in sex. Women can do gross things, like having periods and changing diapers. It's just that I don't want to do this one thing. A thing that you're good at."

She wanted to be independent and equal, but she didn't want to do equal things like fishing and cleaning the fish. Micah was confused, but he wouldn't let her know.

"Tough. You must do it. So, cut the stalling and get to work."

Lillie's defiant glare turned to dejected pout. She knew he was right. She took a knife and started the ordeal. Once she had inserted the knife, she closed her eyes, as if by closing her eyes, the disgusting nature of the event would magically go away. Lillie squinted. She finished the cut with a handful of guts. She tugged, but the guts slip from her grip and dangle from the fish.

"Now what?"

"Pull them until all of them are out."

More squinting.

"I did it!"

"Now the head."

She did not cut the head; she sawed it off. Then she took the body to the freshwater bucket to wash it. After the fish was wrapped in wax paper, she turned to Micah.

"There, smart-ass. I did it. And I don't ever want to do that again."

"Two more fish; one for me and one for you."

"I need some fresh air, Micah. You go first."

He knew she was going for a smoke. He took care of his fish and saved the last one for her. After all the fish were cleaned and ready for cooking, the guts and heads were tightly wrapped in the bag and tossed in the garbage can. The lid was pressed down tight and the latches were snapped as Grandpa had asked. The teens headed to the back door of the cottage where Joe awaited. Micah noticed that Lillie is smiling … almost defiantly.

"Look, Grandpa, I cleaned two fish."

"Good for you, sweetie. Now both of you wash up and maybe change your clothes to make sure the fish smell doesn't follow you to the dinner table. I suggest you squeeze some lemon rind on your hands and arms to kill the fishiness."

"That's that. Heh, heh, heh. Everything's ready for the hook-up tonight. We need to pick up the tools and put them in the toolbox, then make sure we pick up any pieces of wood and nails that we left on the ground. We don't want the critters of the woods injured by them. After I tear down the platform, this area should look as natural as it did before we got here. We honor nature and the spirits by not damaging the land."

Amon and Aggie went about the clean-up phase. Aggie thought that during the cleanup Amon was staring at her. Or, was he noticing her glancing at him? Was he gawking at her when she bent over? She stopped bending over to keep her shorts from riding up. Was he gawking at her chest? She buttoned up her shirt to the top button. The entire clean-up process made her so uncomfortable that she started to turn red. And she wanted to run away. Was all this her imagination?

"Done."

They got into the truck and headed back to the Bickham cottage. Midway down the rutted path, Amon took his right hand from the steering wheel and slid it across the bench seat to touch her left wrist. Aggie was so frightened that she froze. She felt trapped within the truck's cab. Perspiration was now trickling down her neck and back. He slid his hand down to her hand.

"I want to thank you for your help today. I could not have done what was needed in the time available, if you had not been with me. You were great. I hope you learned things that you can use when you get home."

"I learned a lot. Not sure how much of the carpentry I can use at school next year."

The bouncing truck exited the woods and turned toward the cottage. Aggie felt a sense of relief now that she was approaching a safe place. She would be protected by her parents and her grandpa.

"Here we are. After dinner when the fireworks are set off, you can tell your family that you made it happen. Heh, heh, heh."

Aggie tightly gripped the truck's door handle, threw open her escape hatch, and jumped from the truck before it came to a complete stop. She slammed the door and waved good-bye to the driver without turning around and looking at him. Amon stared at the back of her shorts as she disappeared through the back door into the cottage.

"Jesus, Aggie, you look like hell. What happened?"

"Lillie, I spent the afternoon with Amon building the platforms that will be used to launch the fireworks tonight. It was creepy. I mean, he is soooo creepy. Every time I looked up; he was staring at me. And, when we were working next to each other, he would brush up against me. At least, I think so. I don't think I imagined all the creepiness. Maybe I did. Regardless, I'm happy to be safe at home."

"Relax. My guess is that you imagined all the gawking and touching. Look at the facts. Amon is a lonely old man. But he would do nothing to upset the relationship he has with this family. Amon's link to the real world: the world beyond these woods, is Grandpa. Amon is your granduncle. He's family. Plus, he's probably never spent much time, if any, around a young girl. Or around any woman for that matter. So, he doesn't know how to act. He's lonely, no doubt, and craves friendship; the friendship you offered when you volunteered to help. He could have interpreted your volunteering as an offer of friendship. Friendship with a young person. Friendship with a female. A new experience for him. Last, your period has started, so your hormones are raging. Raging hormones can cause women to do dumb things and think dumb thoughts. I know because they hammer me every month. And we both know that mom is a total freaking bitch during her period. The conclusion is that you have made too much about nothing at all."

"But I was scared."

"Scared of something different. Scared of a person different from you. Hormones, Aggie, hormones made you feel something that was not there. But, if you want another opinion, when mom gets here why don't you talk to her?"

"She'll just dismiss my feelings, like she always does. Maybe you're right. It's all in my mind. Thanks."

"Now, wash up so we can get dinner ready. I went fishing and caught some huge lake trout. Wait'll you see them. Plus, I cleaned them. Do you know what that means? That means, I cut them open and ripped their guts out. Then, I lopped off their heads. I was a real fisherman today. The whole family will eat what I caught and prepared for them. I had a glorious day. So, let's get going. Mom and Dad will be her soon."

167

The four adults exited the SUV. While three of them casually walked to the back door, Martha stomped her way past them, angrily pulled the screen door open and headed for her bedroom. The entire family heard that door slam. Joe, not afraid to confront confusion or adversity in his family, turned to Gabriel.

"What's that all about?"

"An emotional dust-up at the house and time to stew about it on the ride home. It's really no big deal. It'll pass. I'll talk to her."

Gabriel looked to the bedroom. He seemed fearful of following his wife into her inner sanctum. His pause told a great deal about their relationship. Joe turned to Michael and Shelia. Michael flicked his head to suggest that he and his father should go outside. Joe followed Michael leaving Gabriel to ponder his next move. Shelia stayed in the kitchen to check on the dinner menu items.

"What do you need to you tell me, son?"

"I think Martha was overcome by the idea that we were, as she said, 'picking over your bones.' She felt very uncomfortable about the process, even though you asked us to look at all that was in your house and select the items we wanted. When we started, the four of us agreed that selection in each room would be done on an alternating basis. That agreement deteriorated quickly, as Martha tried to assert the right of first born. She voiced the strong opinion that Gabe deserved to select first in every room we entered. Her attitude further deteriorated with every selection Shelia and I made. When asked, she admitted she didn't want what we selected, but she felt she should have the right of first refusal. The situation turned ugly. Gabe smacked her down … verbally. And, she stewed the entire ride back. I agree with Gabe; she'll calm down and will be fine by dinner. By the way, what is for dinner? We bought Shoofly pie and homemade ice cream for dessert."

"We will feast on lake trout. Micah and Lillie caught four beauties. And, your son showed his cousin how to fish then clean the catch. Not sure she enjoyed the last part of the process, but she did it."

Enter the teens.

"Dad, look what I caught."

"Good gawd, Lillie. Four huge fish. Did you catch them all by yourself?"

"No. Micah caught two, but I caught the biggest. And best of all, I cleaned them all by myself. Micah showed me how and I did it."

"That's great! Why don't you show your prizes to your mother? She's in her bedroom."

"I'll do that."

"Grandpa, I think Lillie and I would like to prepare dinner since we caught the main course. We'll cook the fish and prep everything else."

"Very grown up. I'm sure your mother and aunt will appreciate that. Will you fry the fish?"

"No. I think we can cook them on the grill. Not sure exactly how we can do that without them falling through the grate."

"Great idea. Just place a couple of sheets of heavy duty aluminum foil folded double over the grate. That'll keep the fish from falling into the coals."

"Thanks. When Lillie comes back after bragging about her trophies, we'll get started."

The girl sulked into the kitchen crestfallen.

"What's the matter, Lillie?"

"My mom just crapped on my catch, Michael She dismissed it like it was no big deal."

"Listen to you. You're feeling sorry for yourself. Catching and cleaning the fish was a big deal. Not only for you, but for the entire family. You are bringing dinner to the table. Tell you what … if your mom doesn't appreciate what you did, maybe she shouldn't partake in the meal."

"As much as I would like to do that, I can't. I just have to suck it up and know what I did was a big deal."

"Good for you. That's settled. I told Grandpa we would prepare and serve dinner."

"That's a huge commitment. I never cooked anything before."

"I've never cooked fish before. But, how difficult can it be. Grandpa put all the sides in the fridge. We'll need a big pot of boiling water for the corn. Everything else will be served cool or at room temperature."

"But how do we cook the fish?"

"On the grill with salt, pepper, and butter. I'll ask mom about which spices we should use. Plus, we'll need to put some milk and sugar in the water to make sure the corn is sweet."

"I'm impressed. You're a regular gourmet chef."

"Not likely. I just think things through. We better get started, it's nearly six."

"What should I do?"

"Make sure the grill has charcoal. Wrap the grate in two layers of aluminum foil and put it aside while you light the charcoal. Once the fire is lit replace the grill so that the foil can get really hot."

"While I'm doing all that, what will you be doing?"

"Getting the water to boil, shucking the corn, prepping the salad. So, you see there is an equal division of labor. Can we draft Aggie to set the table?"

"Sure. OK. Stop jawin'. Let's get hoppin'."

A glimmer of the new Lillie.

"Ladies and gentlemen, dinnah is served."

The family sat at the long table and waited for Joe to say the blessing.

"Bless this food and your humble servants who are faithful stewards of your bounty. Guard, keep, and hold to your bosom those who are not with us."

"Grandpa, may I start to pass?"

"Please do. Micah. Lillie. The meal looks like a feast. The fish smells and looks fantastic. And, let's not forget Aggie who is responsible for the table setting and the wild flowers that grace the table. All in all it's wonderful. Mary would be very pleased."

Tears appeared in the old man's eyes.

Family members voraciously attacked the fish and the side dishes. There was no conversation except requests for more. As the initial attack on the meal subsided, the Q and A started.

"What did you guys use on the fish?"

Lillie was silent.

"Salt, pepper, dill, and tarragon. Mom showed me."

"Well, it tastes fantastic, Micah."

"Thank you, Aunt Martha."

"And the corn. It's so sweet and tender. Another clue from your mom?"

"No. I saw grandma cook corn. Milk and sugar in the boiling water. Cook for eight minutes."

"Well the whole meal was very tasty."

"Thanks, Uncle Gabe. You can thank Lillie. She caught the biggest one … the one you shared with Aunt Martha. Ladies, shall we clear? Grown-ups, stay seated, we'll take care of the cleanup and bring dessert to the table."

The three teens carried the plates and remains of the side dishes to the kitchen. It took two trips. The parents remained seated. Occasionally, they glanced at each other and whispered how grown-up their children were behaving. Then the dessert. Warmed Shoofly pie and handmade ice cream. The teens served. Twenty minutes later, the feast was complete. Once again, the teens cleared the plates and remaining food.

"I'm stuffed."

"Me, too."

"I don't think I can get up. So, I'll just sit here for a while and let the food sink to my socks."

"Does anyone know when the fireworks start? It's already dark."

"I think at nine. No time for a nap. Coffee and scotch anyone?"

"I could go for that, Dad."

"Me, too."

"Martha?"

"Nothing for me and the life force within me."

Joe turned to leave the table.

"We heard you, Grandpa. Please be seated. We'll put the coffee on and bring it to the table when it's ready. Before that, we'll bring the scotch with four glasses."

"I am very proud and impressed with you three."

Chapter Twenty-five

"While we wait for the fireworks, we should acknowledge the work that Aggie put into making the display happen. Tell us all that you did."

Aggie was blushing, although no one could tell in the dark.

"Well, Amon and I built the platform from which the explosives will be fired. Then we attached several individual, smaller platforms to the big platform. Last, we hooked up the wires to the base of the firing tubes on the small platforms. I learned how to use a level. And what a shim is and how it is used. I also learned how to hammer straight. I had a good time."

"Dad … was she alone with Amon or were you there."

"No I was not with them. Remember we discussed this last night after dinner. I felt they would be fine together. Amon may be different, but he is a God-fearing member of this family, and I won't have you hinting that his character is less than honorable. He lives alone because society has shunned him, but he is honest and hardworking. So, lighten up, you two."

Gabe and Martha stared at each other in bewilderment. They felt that Joe had sided with a dirty near-hermit over their daughter's parents. How could he?

"Dad, I … I mean, we would have preferred that you had been with them to monitor their activities."

"It wasn't a play date. Their time together was not cooked up in suburbia. He was a man with an interesting and important task and he wanted to share that with a relative. Besides, I distinctly remember you saying to your daughter and me, 'If Dad says it will be all right, you can help Amon.' Did you forget that?"

"Sorry, you're right. After the super nifty fun time I had today, my mind blocked what happened earlier."

Martha glared at her husband. The icy silence between them morphed into a black cloud that engulfed them.

"And another thing … Aggie is damned proud of what she did and what she learned today. Don't spoil that. Don't crush her spirit because of your misguided and myopic point of view about Amon. OK?"

"Mom. Dad. Have you forgotten that I am right here? And I can hear everything you say. Listen to me. Amon was kind and respectful to me. He taught me a great deal of basic carpentry. I could see how lonely he must be. Nothing bad happened. You act as if I'm a baby, who doesn't know right from wrong. That's disrespectful of me. The fireworks that I helped get ready will be bursting over the lake in a few minutes. I would appreciate it if we could just sit back and enjoy the fruits of my labor. I'm here and I'm safe. So, let's drop it."

Aggie 1: Parents 0

Silence. Joe was proud that his granddaughter had the backbone to stand up for herself. The members of the family had moved their chairs so they could be facing the lake. The bobbing red, green, and blue lights signified the boats on the lake. People brought the boats on trailers to the public beach.

Suddenly, the silence was broken by a three-shot fusillade. Moments later, there were all manner of stars bursting about three hundred yards over the water. Red was followed by white, followed by blue cascading balls of fire. The family oohed and aahed. People at the beach voiced their approval. Silence. Then a four-shot fusillade as the tubes expelled their missiles. This time there were blasts in the sky as showers of colors were created; one on top of another. They appeared at the four corners of the compass. More oohs of appreciation. A third set of blasts. This time the black sky of a moonless night was painted with orange, red, green, and blue. These color fountains were enhanced by white stars spinning like a fire wheel. This time applause.

The three firings were repeated twice, each time with small variations. One fusillade contained yellow stars that exploded in rapid succession like a cannonade. There was a long moment of silence before the grand finale, Devil's Breath. Three explosions, louder than any of the preceding. The sky remained black. Slowly, the red and orange fireworks began burning. Where all the previous fireworks fell to the lake, the colors of the finale seemed to rise like flames. The red and orange were joined by yellow at the top. The three colors held their positions and seemed to flicker. The image was of huge flames licking up to the sky. Then it was gone. The people at the public beach whistled, applauded, and honked their car horns. The Bickhams simply applauded.

"Congratulations, Aggie. Your hard work paid off. The results were beautiful. You and Amon did a fine job."

"Yes, sweetheart, your mom and I are proud of you."

"I'll have a nightcap. Then off to bed. Don't forget the Mary Bickham Memorial Croquet Tournament is scheduled to start at ten am sharp tomorrow. We will have a brief opening ceremony at nine thirty. There will be no reading of the rules. You all should know them by now. And I will have a rule sheet with me just in case you err or forget what is proper. Colored slips of paper are ready to be drawn. Plus, there will be celebratory orange juice and strawberries, with or without vodka. As usual, it will be a double-elimination tournament. The tournament winner gets his or her name etched on the cup. The others must pay homage to him or her for the entire day. Michael and Gabriel will lay out the field. They are required to begin work at seven am sharp."

"Punctuality is critical for both those who set up the field and those who play on it. Tardiness will cost any miscreant a missed turn on each round played. As the official tournament judge, due to my long streak of victories, I will supervise the fieldwork before the game. As usual, there will be hazards to make the game more interesting. Also, they make the progress during the tournament equal for all. After the first two players are eliminated, we'll break for lunch. Bathroom breaks will be at your own discretion. If you are on a bathroom break and miss your turn, that's unfortunate. Or, as Mary used to say, tough noogies. With that I bid you a fond good night."

Joe senses her presence but cannot see her. Mary was with him. He turned on the reading lamp on the bedside table. The room was bare of amenities. White walls bear no art. Joe heard the steady beep-beep-beep of various monitors. There she was. There they were. Mary and the four boys standing at the foot of his bed. They said nothing. They just stared. All four boys appeared to be the same age, between ten and twelve. They were dressed in their fancy dress-up clothes: white shirts, gray slacks, but no neckties. Mary in a simple black dress.

No jewelry. She never wore much jewelry. None of the five was smiling. They appeared not to be sad. They were somberly staring at Joe. Mary stepped forward and pointed to the boys.

"They wanted to come and see you. I told them it wasn't necessary, but they insisted. All of them are doing very well. Joey was promoted to vice president. He hasn't married but has a steady friend. David just received a great job offer from a company in Texas. I will be sad when he leaves the area, but I know he can't pass up this opportunity. I guess it's time for him to leave the nest. Gabriel got all A's on his last report card. He is at or near the top of his class. He's talking about going to an Ivy League college. Maybe Yale or Princeton. We'll have to face that in a year. Michael wants to go to Brown like his father. That's a few more years away. Sarah is healthy and happy to have the boys at home. I miss you, my love. Have the doctors given you any idea when they will let you come home?"

Joe tried, but he was voiceless. This saddened him. From out of thin air, a nurse was standing by the bed and his family has disappeared. The comely young woman was checking all the machines that monitored his health and progress. Progress from where to where? He felt no tenderness in his arms or shoulders. He felt his torso. No bandages. He checked his legs. Both there, clean of any gauze wrap. What did the monitors tell the nurse? She smiled at Joe as if to tell him he was doing fine. He tried to ask her when he would be going home to his family, but he had no voice. In response to his look, he heard her say, "Soon. Soon." She turned and left. He looked around the room. No family. No monitors. Just darkness surrounded the bed.

He sat up and turned on the reading lamp. Just another strange dream.

"What does it taste like? I mean, I've had beer and wine, but never scotch. Is this the good stuff?"

"It is very good and very strong, Lillie. Very intense. At first, the alcohol burns your mouth, then your throat. You can't really taste anything because the burn of the alcohol is so powerful. Then the flavor rises from your tongue to your nose. Then you swallow and the burn is totally gone. Only the flavor remains in your mouth. A strong, sweet, smoky flavor."

"We want to try it, don't we, Aggie?"

The younger sister looked confused. She wanted to be part of this event, so she would do whatever was required. Even if that meant stealing some 25-year-old scotch from Grandpa.

"OK. I'll pour three glasses. Beside each small glass is a glass of water. You may need that after the scotch. Here is the clue to drinking this nectar of the gods, as Grandpa Joe calls it. Take a small sip. Gently draw the whisky into your mouth and across your tongue. Don't swallow it immediately. Let it mingle with your saliva and caress your taste buds. Only then is it truly enjoyed. Only then can it be swallowed…also slowly. Ready? I'll go first to show you."

Micah repeated the process he learned only a few days ago. He struggled hard not to gasp or cough. Within a few seconds, he had swallowed the whisky and was smiling. His eyes were watering, but he showed no discomfort. Any display of the whisky hurting him would diminish his posture as a man.

"Now you, Lillie. A small amount gently sipped."

Lillie took too big a sip … nearly a quarter of a mouthful. The burn was intense. She coughed slightly but swallowed. She did not smile. Seeking relief from the alcohol sting, she drank from her water glass and turned to Micah.

"That was really intense. Whatta rush! Now you, Aggie."

"Aggie, take a small sip, roll it around in your mouth, then swallow."

The younger girl did what she is told. She winced and swallowed, then began to cough spasmodically. Her coughing was so intense that she couldn't take a drink of water. When her coughing stopped the entire glass of water was gulped.

"I warned you guys it would be intense. Not sure why adults think it tastes smooth. There was no smoothness in my sip."

The girls nodded agreement.

"We have to finish what's in the glasses. Can't pour it back into the bottle. We'll do this sip in unison. OK?"

The girls nodded.

"OK, on the count of three. One … two … three."

Three glasses were lifted, three mouths drew in the whisky, three sets of lips closed, and three mouths enjoyed the warmth and rich flavor of 25-year-old scotch, then three throats felt the burn. Water glasses were filled and then emptied. An abbreviated rite of passage was complete.

"I'm go to bed. I'm exhausted, and the scotch has made me woozy. Are you guys coming?"

"Right behind you, Aggie."

The younger teen leaves the kitchen. Lillie turns to Micah and whispers.

"I want another."

"No. One and done. I think Grandpa knows how much scotch is in the bottle when he puts it away. He would, for sure, notice if we had more and the bottle had less."

"Candy-ass. You are such a coward. Besides, I liked the taste, and I want more. What's wrong with that?"

"Still the oh-so-pleasant one. I am beginning to think that you always blame others when you don't get your way. Certainly, nothing wrong could ever be your fault. I'm going to wash, dry and put away the glasses, then go to bed. I suggest you go to bed now."

"Gabe, I'm sorry for the childish way I behaved today. I don't know what came over me. I still think you were entitled to choose first in each room. But, to keep harmony within the family, I'll let that subject drop."

"Thanks, Martha. I can understand how difficult it must be to be put in the situation of making decisions about furniture and the like which you may not even care for, but that which your husband recalls fondly. And I appreciate how you must feel about Shelia's pregnancy. I mean, she is a professional and about to be a new mother. Everyone in this family is very competitive. I always want to do better and to get more than Michael. Your competitive instincts are normal. It was a part of your personality to which I could relate."

"Whoa, there! I feel no competitive instinct with Shelia. I've had my children and you decided years ago not to have any more. So, her pregnancy is of no consequence to me. I do think she is foolish to interrupt her career at her age to have another whelp. But, that's her decision. What annoyed me is that you appeared weak when dealing with your younger brother. You gave in to his every wish. You didn't stand up and claim what should be rightfully yours. I mean that trough and pump. A multigenerational symbol of your family, and you simply gave in to his grabby approach. Hell, he put the sticker on the trough before we even started the in-house process. In effect, he stole it from you and your family."

"Easy, Martha. You are my wife and Michael is my brother. You are painting me into a difficult corner."

"Difficult corner, my ass. As your wife and the mother of your two daughters, I should rank way above your thieving baby brother. If you can't understand that, maybe you should rethink our relationship."

"So, if I understand your words, you're giving me an ultimatum. Either you or Michael, but not both. That is destructively binary. Why can't I love both of you? Why can't I decide that fighting over things is not worth losing anyone's love?"

The verbal sparring had caused Martha to become shrewdly flirtatious. When she wanted to get her way, she reverted to this outward display.

"Speaking of love … you haven't touched me for months. What's wrong with your home cooking? Are you getting enough from that bitch at your office that you have no urges when we are together?"

"First, there is no bitch at my office. I am not now cheating nor have I ever cheated on you and our marriage vows. If I have not been attentive, it's because work is eating me alive. Revenue in my business group is way down. In case you haven't noticed, I have been traveling much more than I did last year. I have had to go to our clients to find out what's going on … what's wrong. Why have they cut back their spending? I must gather information that my team seems incapable of gathering. So, fuck you! There is no other woman. There is only you, the woman I married."

His reactive acrimony dissipated. Martha, in her night gown, was looking pleadingly at her husband. Verbal sparring, her way of flirting, had morphed into aggressive seduction. Tears were in her eyes. Slowly, she unbuttoned the top two buttons.

"Speaking of 'fuck you.' I need to."

Gabriel turned off the lights and moved bedside. Martha rose and removed her nighty. Gabe slid off the bottom half of his pajamas. Their embrace was violent. She dug her nails into his back as she tried to merge their bodies into one form. They fell onto the bed to continue the wild attack. After kissing and rubbing the sensual areas of his wife, he commenced entry, whereupon she gasped and bit his shoulder. Each other's pain enhanced each other's pleasure. The love-fight ran its course.

"Mike, I was really uncomfortable being around Martha today. She can be so greedy and bitchy. But I always like spending time with you."

"You were a trooper in the face of her petty anger. Gabe has mentioned on more than one occasion that Martha can be difficult. Something about privilege. Her family had money and acted as if they had money even after they lost most of it. Martha tried to create a sham life of luxury after her father lost her inheritance in a series of very bad real estate deals. She was embarrassed that her marriage did not resemble a coronation. She felt cheated. I guess that's carried over to today. She felt that she deserved everything and became unglued at not getting it all. It is apparent to me that she will not take responsibility for her own actions. I mean, look how she tried to blame you for that mommy makeover issue. If Gabe had believed her, he would have never spoken to you or me again. Thank gawd, you deflected that mess back onto her."

"She needs help. They could benefit from couples counseling."

"How about us?"

"How about us what?"

"Could we benefit from couple counseling?"

"Nearly every couple, and particularly professional couples, could benefit from counseling. But, as I see it, we are not in need of extramarital guidance."

"If that's what the doctor orders than who am I to disobey."

"Speaking of doctor's orders, I order you to come here and kiss me."

Shelia's playful grin filled Michael's heart with love.

"That's easy."

"But wait, there's more."

"I remember the more, but your belly's protuberance concerns me."

"Not to worry, oh noble knight, where there's a will there's a way. If you have the will, I have the way."

"Believe me, I have the will and am ready to exercise it."

They embraced gently, running their hands over the other's body. He bent down to kiss and caress Shelia's distended stomach. It held the treasure of their lives. Tender excitement was easy for a loving couple. The kissing, embracing, and touching slowly came to a logical next step as they slid onto their bed. Shelia, naked, rolled onto her right side and raised her knees to her stomach with her back to her husband and lover. He took over. Insertion was delicate and slow. But he was only doing what the doctor ordered. A grin appeared on his lips. He locked his arm over her pendulous breasts. Shelia emitted a low moan. Her body began to tremble, then throb actively. They were both still but remained in the lovers' embrace.

Chapter Twenty-six

Two alarms rang. Two adult males awakened. It was time to make the field ready for the big game. They could smell the aroma of fresh coffee. As usual, the eldest male in the house had been up for a while.

"Better have something to eat with the coffee. The lunch break will be a while."

The two sons each slathered big gobs of peanut butter on toasted English muffins, grabbed their mugs of coffee, and followed their dad to the front of the cottage.

"I brought out all the wickets, stakes, mallets, and balls. Now you two can lay out the field of play."

The ground in front of the cottage was almost in tournament-playing condition. The grass was trim, and the sod had been rolled so it was firm and level. Amon did all the lawn work the day before the arrival of the Bickham clan. Years ago, Mary had asked Amon for this special favor. He had done it because he was family. On the morning of the tournament, the brothers were responsible for removing any storm debris and set the course ... precisely.

Precise measurements were just the beginning. The full-size croquet lawn measured 35 yards by 28 yards. The boundary was marked by corner pegs and flags. The field was laid out on an east-west axis. East near the house and west near the lake. Mary insisted there never be a north-south layout of the playing field. No one knew why this was mandatory. A string line, one yard inside the boundary, extended around the perimeter. The four outer wickets were positioned seven yards in from the side and end lines. A peg was placed in the center of the lawn, with the remaining two wickets seven yards from it on either side along the center line. Imaginary *baulk* lines extended along the yard lines from corner one and corner three to the center.

Tournament play could start from only one baulk line, east. The course and direction of play were depicted on a paper diagram, enlarged, laminated, and placed at the starting wickets. After laying out the course, a few hazards would be added to the paths from wicket to wicket to make for an interesting and challenging family game. This also helped make it a level playing field for adults and children.

Mary insisted that the history of the game be read before the start of play. Joe had this bit of pageantry printed so players could read it and not be required to suffer through his *basso profundo* reading. It read …

Croquet: A game in which balls were knocked around a course of hoops or wickets was played in medieval France. A variation of the game known as "Paille Maille" was played in a field near St James's Palace in the sixteenth century, which later became known as Pall Mall. The modern game appears to have started in England in the 1850s and quickly became popular. The Wimbledon All England Croquet Club was founded in 1868 and the National Championships were held there for a number of years until the croquet lawns were transformed into the tennis courts of today. This probably accounts for the fact that the size of a tennis court is exactly half that of a croquet lawn. Croquet was, and still is, one of a few outdoor sports in which ladies can compete on an equal footing with men. Today, croquet is played all over the world with international tournaments being held annually in several countries. Variants of the game are also played in Egypt and Japan. It is encouraging that an increasing number of young players are participating in the game at all levels.

On the reverse side of the history was a listing of the rules. Mary Bickham croquet was played using the rules as guidelines. Not stringent laws. Mary's chief deviation from the official rules dealt with a player being hit out of bounds. The official rules dictated that the person who was hit out of bounds or whose ball accidently rolled out of bounds forfeited a turn. Mary thought that was too harsh, particularly for children, so she changed that rule to state that the person hitting from out of bounds to the playing field must hit the ball laterally or in a backward direction. Never forward. There would be no forfeiture of a turn. Joe was the final arbiter in any dispute. Anyone could appeal an issue to this judge, but his decisions were final.

The object of the game was to hit a ball through the course of wickets, in the proper sequence. The player's course could be in either a clockwise or counterclockwise path. Regardless of direction, the circuit had to be completed. The player completed the round by hitting the ball against the last peg, which was the starting peg. The individual who completed the course first won that round. All players must finish every round they start, thus establishing order for the next round. In the preliminary two rounds, if a player finished in the bottom two places twice, he or she would be eliminated from play. This first elimination stage could take several rounds of play. After the first cut, the reduced field moved to the next stage. Again, if a player finished in the bottom two places twice in the second phase, that player would be eliminated from play. This stage may also take several rounds of play.

In the semi-final rounds with four players, if a player failed to finish in the top two places twice, that player would be eliminated from play, until there were only two players remaining. The final play would commence with these two players. Like the others, this was a double-elimination stage and could take a few rounds. Hitting from out of bounds during any of the rounds could be an advantage, because it allowed the player to strike opponents who were on a return path. Cheering sections for the semi-finals and finals were supposed to be raucous. The noise from adults was often fueled by alcohol.

After the course was laid out, the two sons had to decide what kind of obstructions or hazards would make the game more interesting and where they should be placed.

"Dad, remember a few years ago, Mom had us place coffee cans in the homeward path? They create a challenge for players starting and ending. Let's do that again. I'll make sure that a ball can go between the cans ... but just barely. If they don't like the obstacle, players can always hit around and not through it."

"OK, Gabe, go get three cans and fill them with stones so striking them won't knock them over."

"I think a small bush would be a great hazard."

"We can't dig into the playing field to place a transplanted bush. The field must remain solid and level, Michael."

"How about I retrieve a couple of small pine branches, and stick them in the ground? To create a Lilliputian Forest. A seductive hazard that says hit through me. But a hazard that will capture and hold any ball that becomes entangled in the branches."

"Good idea. What about a water hazard? You could soak one area and re-soak it before each round. It will be a real quagmire. Now we need a fourth hazard."

"I got it. Dad, what did you do with the white stones you found in the back yard?"

"They're in the shed, Gabe. Why?"

"Let's spread them out two inches apart across one of the paths. If struck by a ball, they will cause any ball to bounce wildly in any direction."

"Good. While you boys are altering the course, I'll get us some more coffee."

As Gabe placed the stones in a line, he thought nothing of their warmth. At nine forty-five in the morning, the three men had completed their tasks. Other family members were waiting anxiously in the kitchen. They were not allowed to approach the field of play until Joe announced that it was ready for play.

The order of play had to be established. Each participant drew a colored slip of paper from a bag that Joe held. The color of the slips corresponded to the colored stripes on the poles. The person who drew the color of the top stripe hit first and so on until all players had hit. After each round, the players begin the next round in reverse order of their respective finish.

"Hear, ye! Hear, ye! Gather around. The annual Mary Hess Bickham Memorial Croquet Tournament is about to commence. You all have the rules, selected the appropriately colored ball, and surveyed the course. So, I pronounce the game officially open."

Shelia hit first, then Aggie, Gabriel, Micah, Joe, Lillie, Michael, and finally, Martha. The area before the center wicket was crowded, as players jockey to get ahead of the crowd or hit an opponent out of the way … preferably out of bounds. It was their competitive nature. The family love and comradery was manifested in the civilized trash talking.

"You can't hit the broad side of a barn. If you hit me out of bounds, I'll stalk you and stuff your ugly colored ball in your ear. Open your eyes before you hit and maybe the ball will go where you want: nice hit, girlie … exactly four inches. Nice hit King Kong … out of bounds is exactly where you belong. Blue suits you, 'cause you're play is so sad. Are you shooting for early elimination?"

The first round was completed in under forty-five minutes. The players seemed to pick on Shelia and Joe, knocking them out of bounds on the return path. No one could avoid the stones, which made each shot bounce wildly out of its intended path. The water hazard also got all of them, but it didn't slow the round. Shelia finished seventh and Joe finished eighth. The second round started with Joe hitting first and Shelia second. Again, there was a traffic jam in front of the center wicket. Again, Shelia and Joe were knocked out of bounds. Again, Shelia finished seventh with Joe eighth. They were relegated to the sidelines. Shelia sought condolences.

"I simply couldn't get out of my own way. But I have a natural handicap. No one else has a large lump in front of them. I'll be back with a lawn chair, so I can sit in comfort and watch you flail in futility. Ha! Ha! Ha!"

As she left the field, the remaining family members whistled and whooped.

Joe, too, did not make the cut and had retire. He shuffled away and retrieved a lawn chair. Micah finished sixth. With the two longest games in hand, lunch break was called. Sandwiches and iced tea were in the kitchen. The food and bathroom break was brief.

"I pronounce the tournament reopened."

The coffee cans, stones and forest hazards had been moved to different locations on the green just to keep the game interesting. Joe rested on the sidelines. Slowly, his head bobbed in pre-nap rhythm. Gabe, went to Michael and whispered.

"Mike, does Dad look inordinately tired or is it just my imagination?"

"I think you're right. His skin is pale and there are sweat marks on his underarms and around his neck. It's not hot enough to sweat, and he has not exercised enough to warrant the moisture. Do you think there's something wrong?"

"I dunno for sure. I think his health is as stable as he wants us to believe."

"Let's keep a close eye on him."

"Good idea. It's your turn. I wish nothing but bad luck."

"Guck you, Fabby."

Six players clogged the middle of the field. They all avoided the small forest. Martha hit a breakout shot and the chase was on. Micah was right behind her as the others struggled. They fought to be the next through the center wicket. On their way back down the field to the finish, Micah's ball was hit and driven back toward the top of the field. He couldn't easily get past the cans. Micah finished out of the pack. One loss. Lillie also finished near the bottom of the cast ... her first loss. Her father knocked her ball out of bounds twice.

Round Four started at once. No rest for the weary, but no one was tired. Joe lifted his head from his chest and watched intently with a smile that was internally driven, his expression of love of family. Michael and Aggie finish out of the pack. One strike each. Gabriel had no strikes against him.

Round Five. Michael and Micah finish behind the others and were out. Joe struggled to rise from his chair for his duty as the official announcer.

"The semi-finals are about to begin. Gabe is unscathed. Aggie, Lillie, and Martha each have one loss. Before we start, I will give you another bathroom break."

There was a mad dash to the cottage, and a loping return.

"On your mark, get set, go."

There were now four cheering sections. Each chanted their hero's name to encourage aggressive play. The players and their play were intense. Family friendly aggression was on full display. Gabe attacked his family members to eliminate them rather than hit his own ball into the lead. Lillie was knocked out of bounds … twenty feet out of bounds. She ran to the spot to hit the ball onto the playing field.

"Eeek!"

Michael ran to Lillie.

"What's the matter, Lillie?"

"My ball. It landed on something. A pile of bones."

The ball had indeed come to rest on a pile of small animal bones. The bones seemed to have been burned and stacked. Was an entire carcass burned and the chard skeleton was all that remained?

"Not to worry, Lillie. They won't hurt you. They're just dried bones. Here. I'll lift your ball off the pile, and you can hit back into play."

As Lillie returned to the field of play, Michael was struck by the smell of Sulphur rising from the stack of bones. As he moved the bones with his foot, he saw a second animal skeleton. Then a third. Then a fourth. Each was slightly larger than the one on top. This collection was not an accident. The spot appeared to be a place of multiple small animal deaths. A sacrificial altar. But, by whom? Why? He said nothing as he kicked over the pile of bones and destroyed the altar. Slowly he returned to the game. He decided not to tell anyone what he had found. Explaining would only cause unnecessary concern among the family and raise more unanswerable questions. He would talk to his father later. It was always better to say nothing until all the facts are known. Three players remained in the tournament.

Lillie went first, Aggie second, then Gabe. Lillie stubbed her second shot and the ball dribbled feebly near the out-of-bounds line to the left. Aggie's shot hit one of the cans and bounced in front of the second wicket.

"Lucky break, sweetie."

"Thanks for nothing, Dad. You're going down. No mercy for the old guy."

Her cheering section hooted and hollered.

"Stomp your dad! Stomp your dad! Stomp your dad!"

Gabe scowled. Lillie pouted. Father and older daughter chased younger daughter. She skillfully avoided them on the return path by staying as close to the out-of-bounds line as possible. They would be fools to hit at her. If they missed, they would go out-of-bounds and lose any advantage. She had seen her grandpa use this ploy. Aggie finished first. Gabe second and Lillie was eliminated. Gabe had hit her out of bounds. She pouted.

The championship round remained. Because both Aggie and Gabriel have one mark against them, the winner would be the champion. Joe was asleep in his chair. Shelia had wrapped a blanket around his shoulders and torso to keep him warm. Gabe started. His shot was true to midfield. He planned to hit behind the cans and through the first side wicket. Aggie would have none of that. She hit her ball hard and it caromed off Gabe's ball to rest at a good angle to the first wicket. Gabe was on the far-left side of the center wicket. He had to waste a shot just to get back to the center of the field, while Aggie went through the wicket and stayed wide. Gabe shot to go through the wicket, but the ball nicked it and bounced far to the right. Aggie avoided the stones and wound up front and center to the midfield wicket. In an effort to get beside Aggie, Gabe risked a shot over the stones. There was no reward. His ball bounced wildly out of its intended path. Aggie was through and headed for the double wickets and the win. Gabe appeared confused. Michael yells.

"Oooh, big brother is going to lose to his younger daughter. How pitiful!"

Gabe shot him a withering stare.

Aggie was heading down the side away from her dad. Her path hugged the out-of-bounds line. Gabe made a great recovery shot from the stone miscue and was through one of the double wickets. Tapped in and he turned around heading for home. He was not out of the game yet. Aggie had to hit toward the middle to get through the center wicket. That's when Gabe struck. He hit her ball and it bounced to the left, far from the center wicket, but not out of bounds as was his intent.

She was still in play. Gabe's ball rested nicely in front of the center wicket. She hit back to the middle of the field and her ball came to rest between Gabe's ball and the center wicket. He couldn't go around her or through her. He had to waste a shot to clear a path through the wicket. Gabe stepped up and tapped his ball. It struck Aggie's ball and landed directly in front of the wicket. Her ball slid to the right. She has no single shot through the wicket. Gabe was through and heading for victory.

Aggie decided to gamble. She would not shoot to the wicket. She would go after Gabe's ball and drive it into the water hazard, which was now a four-inch-deep mud bog. Her shot is perfect. The ricochet sent her ball toward the center wicket. To get through it, would require two shots. Only half of Gabe's ball was visible in the quagmire. His first shot moved the ball ... just not out of the swamp. Her first shot lined her up for a clear through-and-through on the second. Gabe hammered his ball on the second shot. Splat! It begrudgingly exits the mud. He called for a ruling. Could he clean his ball of the mud and grass that cling to it? The audience huddled and answered with a resounding NO! They all flashed two thumbs down. Joe stirred and looked dazed and confused. Not sure where he was and what he was supposed to do. Quickly, he gathered his wits and smiles.

"Please repeat the question."

Gabriel presented his case. Joe gave him two thumbs down. The family howled with laughter. Gabe looked angry. He hated to lose. And he really hated to lose to a teenage girl. But the game must go on. Aggie's second shot placed her beside Gabe heading for the home double wicket. He hit toward the opening. With the mud and grass from the water hazard on the ball and in his anger, he had not hit the ball squarely. It came to rest against the outer wicket. Aggie seized on this opportunity and hit her ball toward Gabe's knocking it past the double wickets and the stake. He was nearly out of the field of play. She had a clear shot to victory. Desperate, Gabe tried to come through the wickets in reverse order from the stake and smack Aggie's ball away. Gabe's ball bounced off the back wicket and kicked to the left. Aggie slowly stroked her ball through both wickets and against the stake for the win. Gabe smiled, rushed to his daughter, congratulated her with a kiss on her cheek, and hoisted her jubilantly so that her head is above his. The family erupts in cheers and laughter.

Chapter Twenty-seven

"Yesterday, I pulled the last of the hamburger from the freezer. And, we still have enough sides to make a complete evening meal. But we're almost out of luncheon food. So, there must be shopping tomorrow. My questions are: Who is staying beyond tomorrow and for how long?"

"Dad, my appointment in Harrisburg is scheduled for 11 on Friday. So, we will be staying until very early Friday morning."

"Shelia, Micah, and I will be here until Sunday morning."

"OK, let's take those plans into consideration for the food shopping. I've put a list on the fridge. Write down what you want for main meals through Saturday night. I'll be here after that and I can eat leftovers for a day or two, then shop for myself."

"Joe, we'll make sure we buy enough to carry you through Wednesday."

"Thanks, Shelia."

"When's dinner?"

"How about six-thirty, Micah? I'll put you in charge of prepping and lighting the grill for the burgers. I put Aggie and Lillie in charge of getting the sides ready. It's now four-thirty. I'm going to take a brief nap before dinner. Thanks to all of you for the glorious day. Ooops, I almost forgot. Aggie, as this year's champion, your name will be etched on the trophy over the winter and will be on display on the mantel over the fireplace here at the cottage next Memorial Day. Would someone take a picture of Aggie and me holding the trophy. I want to frame it and look at it all year. Should we say that Aggie or Agnes won this year's tournament?"

"Aggie."

"Aggie, it will be, Aggie."

Gabe gathered the remaining members of the family in the kitchen and whispered.

"I have a question: Does Dad look OK to everyone?"

"Grandpa looks fine to me."

"Thanks, Lillie."

She felt that her father's dismissive reaction was typical, but it still hurt.

"He looks a little tired, Gabe."

"That's what I think, Mike … only I think he is more than a little tired."

"Of course, he's tired. He's been up for hours. He probably got out of bed before five. He made the coffee for us. He got all the proper equipment out to the field. That must have taken several trips. Then he supervised the layout of the playing field. Finally, he sat through the five-hour game."

"Shelia, didn't you see. He slept in his chair for most of the second half. Why the long nap? I noticed his skin is pale, and there are dark circles appearing around his eyes. I think he is not well."

"Well, of course, he slept, and yes he's not well, Michael. Have you noticed how many pills he takes and how often he takes them during the day? I've patients who don't require that much medication."

"Do we know the purpose of the meds?"

"I've seen some of those pills in my practice. His heart and circulatory system seem to be the at-risk factors in the body of this 84-year old man. They may be wearing out, which is normal for a man that age."

"What can we do?"

"Not much. First, he is under a doctor's care, and anything the two of them want to do is protected from our intrusion by doctor-patient confidentiality. Second, as you boys know better than the rest of us do, he is independent and stubborn. I fear if we start digging into his health, he will get pissed. And, I don't want to spend three minutes with a pissed Joe Bickham. So, I suggest we check on him during the last few days of our vacation together. When Michael and I get back to Philadelphia, I will call Joe's doctor and express the family's concerns."

"That sounds great, Shelia."

"Where have Micah and my girls gone?"

"They went to the kitchen to lay out plans for dinner. The next step will be getting the grill ready, Martha. I need a shower."

"Welcome to Bickham's Burgers. Home of a unique culinary delight, a hamburger made by yours truly and served by the best servers in the county. These burgers are lovingly handcrafted and gently molded into the perfect patty. Special, secret herbs and spices have been folded into each patty. There is no special sauce to hide the full rich flavor of the burger. Each one weighs one-half pound before cooking. Please be seated. As you can see, Aggie and Lillie will be your servers tonight. First question: Who wants medium rare and who wants medium? There will be no well-done Bickham Burgers. Please give your order to one of our lovely and accomplished servers. They will also take your order for the sides and the beverage you wish to go with your scrumptious Bickham Burger."

The three teens had taken control of dinner. Each was dressed in jeans and a white T-shirt. They had aprons at their waists and the girls carried a piece of paper and pen for the orders. Their demeanor was one of self-confidence.

"Aggie. Lillie. This is magnificent."

"Thanks, Dad."

"You look so cute yet grown up."

"Gee, thanks, Mom."

"Where did you find Grandma Mary's aprons?"

"Micah found them in the kitchen buried in the back of the pantry."

"What's with the paper hats? I would die an early and agonizing death if my daughters wound up working in a place that required paper hats."

"Not to worry, Dad. We both want to go to college first ... for the parties and the boys. After five or six years, we'll leave college to become part of the fast food industry."

"Great. Now to the important question: Did someone remember to bring beer?"

"Uncle Gabriel, beer is in the cooler at the head of the table. There is also water in the cooler for those who want that. Do not serve yourself. Give your beverage order to one of the servers."

Joe stood.

"I propose a toast to Micah, Lillie, and Aggie, three wonderful members of this family. Hip, hip, hooray!"

Everyone echoed Joe's sentiment.

"Thanks, Grandpa. It was Lillie's idea for Bickham's Burgers, and Aggie's idea for her and Lillie to be the servers. Aggie also designed our uniforms. I'm just the cook."

"The three of you make a great team. Please pass the chips."

The post-game meal passed calmly and casually.

"We'll clear the table, bring the scotch and coffee, and clean the dishes."

The adults settled in for a well-deserved adult beverage. No ice and sipped slowly.

"I had a great time today. I hope all of you did also. Mary would be happy that we still play her game."

"I remember one game when she knocked me out of bounds at least four times. She was five wickets ahead of me when she finished."

"Dad, do you recall the year she had a sore shoulder and arm from the fall. She held the mallet with one hand and still beat everybody."

And thus it went; the retelling of favorite memories ... sometimes enhanced to improve the story. A second round was poured to empty the bottle.

"Hey, I'm surprised Amon didn't drop by today. It almost seems like it was not a complete day without him now that I know he is my uncle."

"I'll bet he was occupied breaking down the fireworks platforms and cleaning up the firing zone. He is conscientious about keeping the woods clean. He provided a nice display. We should thank him for his contribution."

"Mikey, you can do that when you see him."

"I moved the shopping list to the kitchen table and put a few items on it. Please add to it based on two factors: who and how long. Well, ladies and gentlemen, I am off to bed. I think all of you should think about coming inside soon. There is a big storm brewing to the west. The lightning is all over the far horizon. That's a big storm. And the wind has picked up in the last half hour."

Gabe leaned into Mike's ear.

"Mike, did you just hear Dad go over the days and meals' questions for the second time today? Did he forget he asked us before? Is his memory slipping?"

"Gabe, the information is important to him, so he repeated his request. No big deal. I think you're reading too much into his innocent reminder."

"I must leave for my meeting early Friday morning. So, we will be here through Thursday night. How about you guys? Still planning to stay until Sunday morning?"

"Yes, we'll be here through Saturday."

"I'd like bar-b-qued chicken for one main meal. Or a pork loin."

"Nice, if we get both, there will be enough left over for Dad to enjoy two more meals. We'll take him shopping again on Saturday morning so we can be sure the larder is fully stocked before we leave."

"Settled. Time to move the outdoors indoors. Gabe and I will grab the chairs, if you ladies can scoop up anything else that could be blown away by the storm."

Four adults made the outside eating area safe from the oncoming storm. Chairs were moved indoors. The table and grill were secured so they took places on the front porch as they watched the storm's path. Now the thunder sounded as if it started in the next county and rolled to the other side of the lake.

"It's mesmerizing to watch the full power of nature come out of nowhere and approach us."

"The thunderhead appears to be stalled. In the past few minutes it hasn't moved to this side of the lake. It's remained on the other side of the lake. And I don't see any rain."

"I think you're right it is hovering on the far side. The absence of rain is not uncommon from summer storms. They just crackle and boom but wet nothing. Mom referred to this type as heat lightning."

"I'm … I mean, the two of us are going to bed. This bundle of joy is becoming fidgety. He or she needs me to lie down. I need me to lie down. So, goodnight to you guys."

"I'll be right there, Shelia."

Gabriel and Martha were alone on the porch. They sat in silence. Gabe felt the emotional chill emanating from his wife.

"Sweetie, is there anything wrong?"

"Nothing new. I'm still upset at the way Shelia and your baby brother got everything they wanted, and we got the scraps."

"I apologize for being so blunt, but why are you still stewing over yesterday?"

"Yes, I am stewing, because it was not right."

"Why don't you do this? Write down a list of items of theirs that you want so the four of us can discuss the items. See if we can work out a trade, or something."

"What do we have to trade that they would want? They have everything they want."

"OK. What do you suggest we do to wipe away your sour mood and make you happy?"

"I don't have any concrete ideas. Somehow, I feel cheated, and I'm angry. I don't like being angry, so I blame my sour attitude on them. It's confusing. I think I need time to think it through again and again until the mood goes away. Shit! I hate being in this situation. I'm going to bed. Coming?"

"Right with you."

As the last of the adults walked through the cottage toward their bedrooms, they saw the teens sitting by the fireplace. A small blaze warmed the room.

"Hey, you guys, the grown-ups are going to bed. We brought all the chairs and other items from the table onto the porch. There's a storm out there. You're the last ones awake."

About five minutes after Martha closed her bedroom door, Lillie casually walked to the liquor shelf and lifted an unopened bottle of scotch. She held her finger to her lips and makes the sign for silence or whispering.

"Care for a nightcap, Aggie? Micah?"

"I'll have a small one. I really don't like the taste. It burns my tongue and throat."

"Sip it slowly, let it mix with your saliva, then swallow it, Aggie. Just like I told you before."

"I tried that last night and it still burned my throat."

"Try it again. Very slowly."

"Let's enjoy our nightcap outside … on the porch."

The three walked out the front door. The wind was more than brisk. It was howling, bending the trees, and pushing the bushes around.

"I'd better make sure the grill top is secure. If it opens it would act like a sail and carry the grill to who knows where."

Grill secured; Micah re-entered the front porch. Lillie handed him his drink. He sipped and held the nectar on his tongue. Aggie sipped, coughed, and swallowed. Her face is scrunched in discomfort.

"That's enough. I'm going to bed."

"We'll be there shortly. We're going to have a second."

Lillie poured two hefty drams and walked the bottle back to the proper shelf. Micah stared at the fire.

"I have been meaning to thank you for showing me how to fish and how to clean the catch. It was considerate of you. You didn't laugh at me. I appreciate that. Here's to you."

"Thanks. Here's to you for overcoming your fears of something new and different."

The two sat in silence as they gazed at the fire inside the cottage and the lightning and the roiling black clouds outside backlit by the flashes. Drinks finished, they arose and headed inside. At the door, Lillie turned and wrapped her arms around Micah's chest. For the first time, her physical contact with Micah expressed appreciation and friendship … not sexual temptation. No rubbing. No kissing. Just hugging. It felt good.

Joe, standing in the front doorway, lovingly watched his family playing soccer on the front yard. The goals were marked by large trash cans. There were no lines on the field. Everyone was laughing and yelling as the ball was kicked among all participants. Sometimes a kick was on target. Sometimes wildly inaccurate. The mix of adult voices and the shrill of small children was filled with love. There were no team jerseys or colors, but they knew who was on their team and who was on the other team. The smaller players ran faster than the larger ones. Both teams kept one player between midfield and their goal to prevent any breakaway attempt to score.

Joe was puzzled. All the players seem to be much younger than he knew them to be. Gabriel and Michael looked like they did when they were teens. Lean and limber. Martha and Shelia did not look like women in their forties who have had children. The three others looked like very young children. Small limbs and bodies. Their faces and the volume of their voices reflected the fun they were having. Everyone was smiling. Everyone except the smallest girl. When she turned toward Joe, he saw she has no face. Just a blank stare and a black hole where her mouth should have been. No mouth. No lips, but a black oval stretching from chin to where her nose would have been. The hole was wide open as if in great fear or pain. She had no eyes. But he saw tears. Many tears flowed down her cheeks. What was troubling this little girl? Then he heard Mary's soft motherly voice telling him to protect the girl. Take care of her. Keep her safe.

One clap of thunder followed another about twenty seconds later. Joe peered out the bedroom window and saw the bolts of lightning dancing around the sky. Never straight to the ground but splintering across the horizon. More thunder. The small trees nearby were bending almost to the ground. Twigs and leaves were blowing every which way. Between two thunder rolls, Joe heard something banging … wood on wood. Most likely a screen door. He grabbed his special bedside flashlight and walked into the living room. The banging noise was coming from the back of the cottage. The latch on the screen door from the kitchen had never been tight. He saw the door opening and closing against the frame. He moved to close it and latch it tightly. Odd, that this was not done before bed. Castle secured; Joe walked to the bunkroom door to check on the children. He saw Micah on an upper bunk and Lillie on a lower but he could not see Aggie. He entered the room and saw a lower bunk bed with rumpled bed linen, but no one in bed. Joe panicked. Hurriedly he dressed.

Chapter Twenty-eight

He didn't want to awaken the family. So, concern drove him quietly to the kitchen and the back door. He stepped outside and peered toward the road. He thought he heard the roar of an engine. He exited the cottage and walked hurriedly to the road. Nothing to the left. To the right, he spied tail lights slowly bouncing along the road. Now he was suspiciously curious. There was nothing at that end of the road except Amon's home. What was he doing awake at this hour? Did Amon see something? Joe rushed back to his room, grabbed a rain jacket, and scooped up a big flashlight and his car keys. He needed answers.

The Land Rover was engineered to deal with the rutty road. Still, Joe could go no more than six miles per hour. The simple trip seemed to last forever. What he knew to be about a three-quarters of a mile between the two properties felt like a greater distance. He turned off his lights about fifty yards from Amon's place, let the car roll to a stop in the dark, and parked it. His legs feel a little wobbly. No time for discomfort. He walked the rest of the way to Amon's house over rough and rock-strewn terrain. Joe took each step with caution with the flashes of lightning and his flashlight illuminate his path. The brightness of the bolts made him squint. Twice he nearly fell. Maintaining his balance took a lot of strength. He felt the hood of Amon's truck and it was warm.

He spied flickering light emanating from between the slats in the shutters that covered the front windows. The window to the right of the door was Joe's target. Carefully he leaned against the shutter and peered into the large room. The glass behind the shutter was filthy. Smoke and soot limited his vision. He saw a roaring fire in the large fireplace. Looking to the right, he saw a table covered with a red cloth. Looking to the left, there was a male figure leaning over a sink. Amon looked like he's dressed in a black robe. Was he cleaning something? Was he making something? Joe couldn't tell. How could he learn anything about Aggie's disappearance without confronting Amon? What did Amon know? Should Joe knock or just walk in? It would be an invasion of privacy to simply walk in. But Aggie was Joe's youngest grandchild. He needed any information Amon has.

"Mom? Dad? Is Aggie with you?"

"What? No. She's not in here. She's with you and Micah in the bunkroom."

"Micah's asleep, but I can't find Aggie."

"OK, honey, I'll be there in a second."

The door opened and a sleepy-eyed Martha stood backlit by the bedside lamp.

"Now, tell me slowly, what's going on."

"I got out of bed to go to the bathroom, and when I came back, I looked over at the bed Aggie was sleeping in ... or supposed to be sleeping in. The bed covers were pulled back and she was not there. I looked in the kitchen and all over the house. But, no Aggie."

"Did you look on the porch or out in the boathouse."

"No."

The conversation between the two females had awakened all the family.

"I'll go to the boathouse, Aunt Martha."

"Thank you, Micah."

The boy dressed and scurried out the back door.

Gabriel went to the front porch.

"She's not on the front porch."

"How about down by the lake?"

"I don't think she would go near the lake, but I'll look anyway."

"She's not in the boathouse. And here is something strange; Grandpa Joe's car is missing."

"She's not down by the lake."

"I'll bet Joe's with her. But where would they go at this hour of the night and why would they go anywhere? If she is with Joe, she is safe. Gabe, what do you think?"

"Put a hold on the theory of travels with Dad, Martha. I think she's alone out there somewhere. Dad may have gone looking for her. We should turn on all the lights in the cottage to give both of them a return beacon. We should start a sweep around the cottage. She's probably been missing for less than half an hour. Dad probably less. Given that time frame and being on her own, she couldn't have gotten far. She doesn't know these woods. My guess is that she walked a little, couldn't find her way back, and then sat down. She may even be asleep under a bush."

"Gabe, find my baby before anything bad happens to her. I'm worried for her."

The tone of Martha's voice was one of deep and tumultuous anxiety. Gabe knew he must act before the anxiety turned to flat out panic. At that point, he'd lose control of his wife and family.

"I'll help, too."

"Thanks, Micah."

"How about me?"

"And me?"

"OK, both of you. Shelia, would you mind staying here in case Aggie and Dad return before our sweep is completed? Is that OK?"

"That's fine with me. Not sure me and my bump would last very long in the dark anyway."

"Do we have enough flashlights? One for each."

"I found the supply. I'm checking the batteries."

"Michael and Lillie will search the woods on the south side of the house. Martha and Micah will take the north side of the house. I'll start in the back toward the road, then over to the other side. After that, I'll walk along the road. Remember to call her name every thirty seconds then wait for any type of response. Be sure to listen carefully. I'd love to know where the hell Dad went and if Aggie is with him. Aggie is our priority. She's vulnerable. Dad can manage for himself for a while, at least. Go slowly. Look under all bushes and fallen trees. She may have given up walking and simply lay down to sleep. Examine everything. OK, everybody check their watches. The first search will take about thirty minutes. At which point we'll come back here and exchange information. Is that clear?"

"Yes."

As one, the searchers left the house. The lightning and thunder seemed to intensify, but there was no rain. The world around everyone alternated between brilliance and darkness on this moonless night.

Chapter Twenty-nine

Joe, tightly gripping his flashlight, slowly approached the door to Amon's house. Before knocking, he noticed a disc the size of a serving platter on the door. He shone a beam to illuminate the disc and saw a goat's head in the center of a pentagon. The goat's head was frighteningly lifelike. The pentagon was red, on a black the background. This was not like any hex sign Joe had ever seen on a farmer's barn door. A bright lightning flash and Joe thought he saw the goat leering with moist red lips. The animal's stare was almost hypnotic. The thunder brought Joe back to the moment. Raising his flashlight to knock, Joe sensed something or someone behind him. He turned. Nothing was visible despite the flashlight beam. But the sense of a force behind him, almost looking through him, would not go away. With the next lightning flash, what he saw disturbs him.

A massive black wolf was about thirty yards behind him. He was sure it's the same black beast he had seen a few days ago. Its hackles were up and ears laid back, but the beast was silent. The wolf appeared ready to strike. Behind the leader was a pack. Joe saw twelve. They formed a triangle fanning out from the leader. They stood stock-still. The canine panoply startled Joe but did not frighten him. The brief sky illumination of the wolves was followed by blackness. The world around the house is plunged into darkness. No moon nor stars. The light from inside the house did not carry more than three yards from the building. Then another flash and the wolves were gone. No leader. No pack. They were gone. But where? How? Behind Joe was only the vague outline of his car.

"Aggie. Aggie. Where are you?"

"Aggie, it's Lillie. Are you out here?"

"Uncle Michael, what happens if we don't find her?"

"We will find her and she'll be OK. Frightened, but OK."

"But what happens…"

"Don't go there. Just keep looking. Make sure you search everywhere. Be sure to look under thickets and logs. Thoroughness is key. Speed is not."

"Micah, I'm worried."

"Aunt Martha, I know she's out here. She's cold and scared. She's probably disoriented in a dark and strange environment. Hopefully, she's asleep beside a big tree waiting for us."

"Crap."

Gabriel stumbled and almost fell into a rut in the road. He was shining his flashlight ten yards ahead, forgetting that his paces would cover a shorter distance.

"Aggie, sweetie, it's Daddy. Holler if you can hear me."

Different voices repeated the plaintive cry. No one had gone far from the cottage. No one had found any trace of Aggie. There was no panic in the voices yet, although dread was creeping into their minds.

Joe turned to face the door. He knocked. No answer. He knocked again. No answer.

"Amon, I know you're in there. I can see you through the window. Aggie has disappeared. We are all looking for her. Have you seen her? Do you know where she is?"

The door opened a crack. Joe could see half of Amon's face peering around the door's edge. Amon looked strange. Excitedly happy. His countenance was maniacal. The firelight was reflected in his glazed eyes and there was spittle on his lips.

"Joe, what brings you to my house?"

"I'm looking for Aggie. It seems she got up in the middle of the night and wandered off. Have you seen her?"

"No."

"Do you mind if I come in? I could use a drink of water."

"Now is not a good time for you to come in. Stay here and I'll bring you a glass of water."

Amon pushed the door closed and headed for his kitchen. Fortunately for Joe, the door did not latch. He pushed on the door and it swung open to reveal Amon's large living and dining area. The hot light and smoke came from the fire and the many candles that surrounded the big space. To the right, Joe spied a few chairs around the fireplace, as if they had been placed there for an audience. To the left, he saw a table covered by the red cloth. At one end of the table was an object. A small statue. The light from the flames reflected off it. Brass. A small brass figure on a pedestal. The figure was holding up a pentagram. There were five tall black candles at the other end of the table. Joe noted the color, because all the other candles in the room were red. He stepped into the house to get a better view of all that was in there. Amon approached from the kitchen sink. His robe was open revealing his hairy, totally naked body.

"Whoa, Joe. Where are you going? I told you this is not a good time for visitors … and right now you are an unwelcome visitor. You must leave me alone. Leave me to my world."

Joe's inquisitiveness was piqued.

"What in God's name is going on here?"

"Your feeble God has nothing to do with what I'm doing."

"OK, then, what are you doing?"

"None of your business. It's my business. Now turn around and leave. Get out of here."

As he turned, his eyes gazed upon the table. Now he saw a few small black cloths and a large silver knife. The table was laid out to look like an altar. A sacrificial altar! Was Aggie the sacrificial lamb? But where was she?

"Amon, I'm not leaving until I am convinced that Aggie is not here."

"She's not here. Why don't you believe me?"

"I just want to be able to tell her parents that she is not in your house with you."

"Tell them. Now leave!"

As Amon screamed, he lunged at Joe. The two hit the floor … Amon on top. The fall and the extra weight knocked the wind out of Joe. He had a hard time catching his breath. Amon slid off Joe and turned as if he were heading for the knife on the altar. He paused. He turned and extended his hand to help Joe up from the floor. An unexpected hint of humanity. Joe was grateful and accepted the help. Once standing, his eyes searched the big room.

"Where is she, Amon?"

"Not here, but she is safe."

"What do you mean safe?"

"Nothing has befallen her. She is in no pain."

"I know she is in this house somewhere. Let me see her."

Intently walking through the room and scanning the dark corners, Joe did not notice that Amon had slid surreptitiously to the door, closed it, and turned the bolt.

"Well, my friend, since you insist on seeing your beloved granddaughter, I will bring her to you. Stay where you are."

Amon left the large room through a door in the rear. Due to the fire in the fireplace, the many candles, and limited ventilation, the room was hot and very stuffy. Breathable air was at a premium. In a few moments, Amon returned carrying Aggie in his arms. She was dressed in a white nightgown that bore several strange symbols. Her hair was pulled back. She was shoeless and appeared to be asleep or in a coma. Her head bobbed with each step Amon took. Joe was sure Aggie has been drugged.

"Here she is in all her innocent splendor. You can see she has not been hurt. She is fine. Just resting."

"Let me talk to her."

"No. You have seen your granddaughter and know she is not harmed. Now leave."

"Not until I talk to her."

"You must leave now."

Amon lovingly laid Aggie on the table with her head next to the figure on the pedestal. Suddenly he spun, grabbed Joe by his upper arms, and pushed him toward the door. At the exit, Amon had to let go of one arm to unlock the door. At that moment, Joe swung wildly and hit Amon on his nose. The crack of the cartilage was fore-noise to bleeding, dripping then streaming over Amon's upper lip and down his chin. Amon raised both hands to his nose and backed away from Joe. The unlocked door was ajar.

"You stupid little man. You have no idea what's going to happen. Your life and your world are insignificant compared to the power and majesty that exists here … now. Joe, you are meddling in things you can't possibly understand. Now leave, before …"

"Before what? You've taken Aggie from her bed. Why? It's safe to say you've drugged her, because that's the only way she would go with you. And now it looks like you are about to sacrifice her. To whom? For what reason do you want to kill an innocent child? I will leave this place of evil, but only after I have Aggie."

"This is not a place of evil, my home is the house of my Lord, Heylel. My Lord has kept me safe for many years. Despite all the harm that was thrown at me by this world, my Lord has kept me safe. He has asked for nothing except my obedience. He is always with me. He is here now … this weekend. He is putting my faith to a test. Your God demanded Abraham sacrifice his son Isaac, who was completely innocent. I have no son. I have no heir. My Lord has demanded I sacrifice a pure and innocent child. If I truly have faith in the power and majesty of my Lord, I will prove it by doing exactly what he asks. Heylel is kind and gracious to those who obey his wishes. He strikes down those who blaspheme him and those who belittle his servants. I obey him, while you are a blasphemer."

"I'm leaving now and I'm taking Aggie with me."

Joe turned toward the table. Amon placed his hand on Joe's shoulder to stop him. At that moment, the door burst open and the massive black wolf hurtled into the room. The entire pack was close behind. They wedged between Joe and Amon and forced Amon back to the wall near the fireplace. Joe snatched up Aggie and hurried out the open door. He placed the little girl on the front passenger seat, strapped her in, turned on the emergency flashers and honked the horn five times so anyone could find where he and his granddaughter were. He turned on his heels to see the source of the ferocious noise inside the house. He cautiously headed back to the house and stepped through the front door.

Inside, there was a melee. The pack of wolves was attacking the evil man, who feverishly tried to protect himself. Joe saw Amon wildly swinging a chair at his attackers. When he hit one, others leapt at his leg or outstretched arm. He fell to the floor. The pack leader sank his teeth into Amon's right thigh. Small blood pools, pieces of Amon's robe, now removed, and animal fur, littered the floor around the battle. Amon's hairy body is splattered with blood. His own.

"Heylel, protect me. I have served you all my life. I beg for your strength now. Protect me from the forces of the other, your nemesis. There is only one God, and that God is Heylel. All others are false Gods who send false prophets. I implore you, Great Lord, keep me safe from this attack on my flesh. Heylel, save me."

Amon was looking at the ceiling as if he were looking for a sign. But his chimera would never appear, because it didn't exist ... on earth or in the heavens. Amon screamed and pled for relief. His entreaties went unanswered. The only noises other than human crying were the deep-throated growling and barking of the feral canines and an occasional yelp as they were struck. Their attack was relentless. After Amon had fallen, the pack continued its biting, clawing, and ripping. The human desperately punched and kicked in his defense. To no avail. Now, the leader of the pack had Amon's throat in a death grip. The massive jaws closed viciously, and blood sprayed everywhere ... on the floor and wall. In fewer than ten seconds, Amon's death spasms had stopped and the life was gone from his body. Silence.

The pack leader turned and looked at Joe. The animal approached the human and stopped in front of him. The beast bowed his head, then raised it. Their eyes met and locked on. Joe recognized the blue-gray eyes. He had seen them several times before. The wolf's muzzle and chest were soaked in blood. Some dripped to the floor. Nonetheless, the black beast leaned his face against Joe and directed him ... pushed him to and through the door. The pack followed in silence. Their battle was over. The house was quiet. The wretchedly destroyed nude body of its owner, the altar, candles, and the dying flames in the fireplace remained in the silence. When Joe tried to walk toward the Land Rover, the large wolf stepped in front of him and guided him away. Joe tried resistance but was no match for the determination of the animal. There was no growling, only nudging. The human was being herded.

Chapter Thirty

Gabriel looked down the road toward Amon's house because he heard the horn honks and thought he heard dogs fighting and growling. He saw the blinking hazard lights of a vehicle. A lightning flash revealed the outline of Joe's Land Rover. Gabe's heartbeat quickened. He had found his father. He would surely find his daughter. As fast as he could over the bumpy road, Gabe ran to the car. As he neared the vehicle, he saw the door to the house was wide open. Inside, he could only glimpse the carnage. He wanted to move closer to the sight, but first he must find Aggie. Opening the driver's door, he saw his daughter on the passenger side with the seat belt fastened. Her eyes were closed. Her head was bowed. Was she alive? He felt her wrist. Yes! Her chest was moving slowly and rhythmically. She was asleep. Gabe gently closed the car door and headed for Amon's house. Entering, he saw the aftermath of the butchery. Pieces of Amon were strewn over a small area in the large room. A piece of an arm here and a hand somewhere else. There was a large pool of blood in the middle of the room. He would have to deal to that later. He must find his dad.

Back at the Land Rover, he searched for the car keys. The visor pocket. He started the car and turned it around. Driving home was not much faster than running to Amon's house. He turned into the driveway and feverishly honked the car horn. Then, he exited and lifted his daughter from the passenger side. Gently, he carried her into the cottage and put her on her bed. Martha was the first to arrive.

"You found my baby. Where was she? Is she hurt? Is she all right?"

"I found her in Joe's Land Rover parked by Amon's house."

"What the hell was Joe doing there?"

"When we find him, we'll ask him."

Michael, Micah and Lillie entered. The family gathered around the sleeping child. She did not stir. They left the bedroom and went to the front porch. Aggie's health and well-being were the most important subjects.

"Is my baby safe? Shelia, will you examine Aggie to make sure she's OK?"

"Sure."

The conversation turned to the last family duty.

"We now have to find Dad."

"The first place we should look is where Gabe found Dad's car … Amon's house."

"OK, Michael and I will go to the house. You three can stay here. When we return, we'll have some answers. Then, we can discuss our plan of action. This night is crazy. Mike, you ready?"

"Ready."

Responding to the animal's nudges, Joe walked beside the black wolf. He was unaware of his path or destination, yet he had no fear. Then the saw their destination. A clearing was just beyond the next stand of trees. In the clearing the pack awaited the arrival of the two honorees. Stepping through the bushes, Joe entered the open area. Now what? The pack leader stared tenderly at the human. A form of communication. In the stillness of the woods, Joe listened to his heart and the small voice all humans have. The pack leader put its bloody muzzle on Joe's right foot. The human was not sure exactly what he was to do, but he felt compelled to sit. Man and wolves sat together on the clearing floor.

The leader moved its big head on to Joe's lap and looked up into Joe's eyes as if probing his soul to communicate. This massive black beast, so vicious in battle, was so loving to Joe. The leader let out a whimper and a deep breath as if they were its last. Those small actions spoke volumes about love and death. The two of them sat together on the cold wet ground, waiting for something. Joe had no idea what will happen next, but he was not afraid. He was at peace.

Suddenly all was white. Then nothingness. The flash of lightning had been bigger and brighter than all those before it. It struck the center of the clearing. Then the clearing was empty. A huge hole remained. Everyone and everything had disappeared. No wolves. No Joe.

The sons drove toward Amon's house.

"Mike, when I was here before, what I saw was unnerving. It looked like Amon had been attacked by a pack of dogs, or wolves. Body parts, blood, fur, and clothing all over. Attacked and partially eaten. But we both know that's not possible. There are no wolves or big dogs in these parts."

At that moment, the brothers saw a huge lightning bolt piercing the sky and hitting the ground about two hundred yards behind Amon's house. Sparks and a great deal of smoke rose from the ground where the bolt hit. But there was no fire. Then a second larger strike. This one hit the house which splintered and disappeared in a huge roar of explosives that produce a display of various colors. The colored flames rose above the house, but the house was not burning. It was simply shattered and totally destroyed. A few hundred yards above the house, the flames seemed to come together. Orange, red, and yellow tongues now reaching up to the heavens. The flames appeared to be hundreds of yards high and very active. Finally, a third bolt hit the multicolored flames and caused them to completely dissolve and disappear. The sky was instantly empty and black. The area around Amon's house was strangely silent. There were no fires. A few sparks continued to crackle. Smoke wisps remained.

"What the hell was that all about?"

"Not sure, but Amon and his house are gone."

"How the hell did that happen? And where is Dad?"

"I don't know. And I don't know. We can't go to Amon's place and ask him. I think we should wait until the smoke clears, and sparks stop popping before we enter. Besides, Amon and the contents of the house are not going anywhere. Our first duty was to get Aggie back home. We have done that. We should go back to the house and get everyone involved in the search for Dad in this part of the woods."

"Gabe, no! We can't go back to the cottage and tell our families we stopped looking for Dad. We haven't finished looking. We can't wait. He can't wait. We must find him now. Aggie is safe. Let's make sure Dad is safe, too. I say we press on. He's probably out in the woods lost and exhausted."

"We could check where the first lightning bolts hit. Behind the house."

"Yeah, behind the house. Let's start there. We'll come back to what's left of the house after that."

They skirted the house and wound their way through the forest. Gabe was the first to see the clearing and spy how the once idyllic open space had been drastically altered by the bolt of lightning. The glade now resembled a bomb crater. All the ground from the small area was chewed up, charred, and spewed around the strike point. The mounds that surrounded the hot, smoldering hole made it appear deep. The bushes that surrounded the clearing were completely burned and the leaves on the trees back from and above the bushes were seriously singed. The men cautiously approached the hole. The smoke that rose from the pit had a human waste odor.

"It stinks. Wait, I smelled that stench recently near the house. What the hell is it?"

"Sulfur."

"Never knew lightning contained sulfur."

"All fire does. Some more than others. Most don't stink as much as this air does. Lightning is a type of fire … a natural, electrical fire."

"Mike, shine your light over there! What's that? Is it a shoe?"

Michael climbed a nearby mound and cautiously slid down into the ten-foot-deep pit. There, with a stick, he picked up what looked to be the remains of a shoe. A smoldering man's shoe. His father's right shoe.

"I'm afraid this is or was Dad's."

Tears welled up. His body trembled.

"Is that all that's left of Dad ... a torched right shoe? That can't be. We must find him. I know he must be around here somewhere. It makes no sense that he would simply disappear without his shoe. Did the lightning get him, but not the shoe? How is that possible?"

Tears ran down Gabriel's cheeks as both sons stare blankly at the burned shoe.

"How can we make sense of something that makes no sense? How can we comprehend the incomprehensible?"

"There's got to be a logical explanation."

"The explanation is that he was in this clearing when the lightning struck, and the force of the strike incinerated him and caused him to vanish. All of him is gone except for his shoe. I mean, look what the strike did to the ground."

"Why was he here in the first place? Was he looking for something? He must have known that Aggie was safe, because he put her in his car and left the hazard lights on. Why didn't he stay with Aggie and the car? Did he go back into Amon's house, then leave, and wind up here? Why did he enter the house to begin with, and then leave? What was in the house that was so important that he had to go back? What made him leave the house? What drove him here? Trying to retrace his actions leads me nowhere."

"Let's go home and quietly talk over the situation with Martha and Shelia. Maybe they can help us make sense of this. We must make no mention of Dad's disappearance to the kids until we have a plausible explanation or can contrive a lie they'll believe. Let them be happy that Aggie is safe. OK?"

The sons silently trudged from the clearing, got into their father's car, and returned to their families. Jaws clenched and shoulders slumped, glassy-eyed, they stared straight ahead in near catatonia. Their world had been turned upside down. Plans would have to be changed. Life would change.

Printed in the United States
by Baker & Taylor Publisher Services